Dream Catcher
by Tricia L. Currier

Synopsis

Featuring 19 year-old dream sleuth and ingénue Tara Mason, *Dream Catcher* is set in upper Manhattan. Plagued by premonitions Tara Mason, new to New York City, found it difficult to ignore her murderous dreams. Nightmare after nightmare she slips into the body of a killing machine. When the descriptions of recent murder victim's match those in her dreams she knows it's more than a coincidence.

After her roommate Melissa has gone missing, Tara begins to piece the scenes in her dreams together to find her and invokes the local authorities for help. Knowing full well that if she doesn't hurry Melissa will soon be the next victim, Tara uses the power in her dreams to track down the illusive monster only to end up behind bars herself as the number one murder suspect.

"Dream Catcher" is a thrilling mystery and touches on the occult and the paranormal. It has a love triangle and side story between Tara, her boyfriend Jake and Devin. The story travels to upstate New York onto the Mohawk reservation where Tara learns from what the Native American people call "Dream Guessers" on how to control her dreams and to use that power to fight the evil that haunts her dreams. I am a Mohawk Indian and used my reservation as a description for the setting in my book.

Dream Catcher by Tricia Currier

Chapter 1: Movin' Out

It was time to move out. I'd been planning on a way to tell my parents for some time now; I've just been waiting for the right time. I knew they wouldn't have a problem with it, but they might have a problem with where I wanted to move to which was far away from my small town where everyone knew everyone, where they greeted you by name wherever you went and if you were out too late neighbors from 10 blocks away would call to give your parents the 411. You see I lived in a small town called Huachuca City, Arizona.

They have many nicknames for the little city I grew up in because no one new to town or visiting could ever pronounce Huachuca City. Hoochie-coochie city was one of my favorites. They say my town's so small that if you sneezed you would pass it by. But this has been my home town since I was two years-old and since 7th grade I have been conspiring on ways to find my way out. I hatched one idea while sitting in my 8th grade math class with my two best buds. We were all into acting and following the Hollywood scene. We actually gave each other our autographs so that when we became famous we would already have the coveted signature. I remember the day as if it were yesterday.

I was first to announce my grand plan. "As soon as I have enough money I'm heading to New York."

"Tara, do you know how far away New York is from here, it's gonna take forever and cost you a fortune. You'll never make it. You should go to Hollywood, its closer." Marie whispered as Mr. Thatcher explained in detail long, very long, division.

"Well it's not like I'm taking off on my bike and going tomorrow. Plus, I want to be up on the stage, under the bright lights, not on some television set. I'll make it there and my autograph will be the first one everyone wants."

"Let's bet on it!" Matt seemed interested now and stuck out his hand. We shook on the deal and from that moment forward all my thoughts were on moving to the "Big Apple."

My mom always told me I'd get over my desire to live in New York, that it was just a phase I was going through. But I never have. I wanted to live in the total opposite of where I was living. Agreed, there were big cities a lot closer to home. Even Phoenix was huge. But I wanted to live in the city that never sleeps, I wanted to act and sing and just be creative and I felt that the only place for me was New York City.

"Mom," I said apprehensively biting my lip a little too hard.

She looked up from the sink full of morning dishes, "Yes?"

I wasn't sure how to ask her this and her plump cheeks smiled when I didn't speak right away. I leaned up against the cabinets, fingers crossed behind me.

"Well I've been thinking that since I'm almost finished with my second year of college at Cochise that maybe after this quarter I should move out."

The smile crept into her eyes. "Why, did you get accepted to U of A?"

I could hear the excitement in her voice and I hated to dash her hopes.

"Well...no." Her face was confused. "I was thinking of taking a small break from college, but of course I will finish, I promise. But" I paused, this was harder than I thought, and then blurted out "I want to move to New York City."

She rolled her eyes. "I thought you were over Leonardo what's his face?" she said trying to be funny and continued to wash her dishes not taking me serious.

She was referring to the huge crush I had on Leonardo DeCaprio when I was 11 and according to the teen magazines he supposedly hung out in New York. In all honesty, that had really started my obsession with New York and my acting bug but my feelings for Leo have changed and I no longer wished to be Mrs. Tara DeCaprio as I had written over and over a thousand times on my school notebooks.

I have to admit I still have my Leo folder which consists of numerous clipped photos of him from magazines I bought with every last bit of allowance money I had at the time. He would probably be impressed or scared. The latter was more like it.

"I know mom. I just want to experience something more and I'm ready to get away from here." I huffed and pulled myself up on the counter trying to think of my next tactic. "It's not a permanent move. I just want to try out acting and singing and see how I measure up before I get too wrapped up in other things." I waited for her response.

I think she knew this day would come but was hoping it would be after I earned my degree. But that was the thing. I didn't know what I wanted to be. I knew what I liked doing but I wasn't sure if I was really good enough to make a living out of it just yet and it's hard to pick a major when I don't really know what I want to do.

She continued to wash dishes, not looking at me. "Well you know what your dad is going to say?"

I dropped my head and mumbled. "I was hoping you could help explain it to him."

She shot a look over to me and shook her wet hands. "Ugh." And she marched out leaving me alone in the kitchen.

The next few months drug on at a snails pace. I continued with school trying hard to concentrate but all I could think about was my upcoming move. I tried to work as many hours as I could at Bernie's, a local 99 cent DVD rental place, so I could save up every last penny. My friends were pressuring me to go out but my nights were filled with recommending movies, putting away empty movie boxes, and reorganizing misplaced titles. Plus I was stressed over dad. Since my mom broke the news to him about my moving out in May he stopped speaking to me. School was very important to him and that fact was grilled into me as I grew up and he couldn't stress to me enough the importance of getting my education. Both my parents failed to graduate High School and my attending college was a pretty big deal. I mean it's a big deal to me too, however so is following my dream. I don't think I could ever explain this to him in a way that would reassure him I was doing the right thing.

The tension in the house was causing me to lose sleep and when I did sleep I was having vivid dreams that wore me out like I hadn't slept at all. Ever since I was a kid I have been a vivid dreamer. Often times I would dream the same dream for a week as if someone were trying to tell me something but hey I was only seven and at that age what would I need to know? Other times I would sleep walk. Once I remember or I was told the story so much it seemed like a memory, I got up in the night thinking I was playing with my pop a lot toy I loved so much when actually I had a wine bottle and an onion. It totally freaked my mom out when she found me in the kitchen trying to pop it in the air.

I didn't mind the dreams so much until I started seeing some of the events in my dreams play out before me the next day or a week later. I never told my mom about these occurrences because I didn't want to worry her more.

When I was 14 I dreamt of a terrible car crash on interstate 10. In the dream it was night time and there were cows wandering all over the road. It seemed so unusual and out of place that I thought nothing of it until the night we were driving home from Tucson and a Semi jackknifed on the freeway in front of us. We had no idea what caused the accident but my dad had to swerve to keep from hitting the truck and our van ended up off the road in the dirt. I was thrown to the floor of the van because I was lying across the back seat not wearing a seatbelt. Once dad made sure we were okay he got out to check on the others involved. I peaked out the side window and the semi was lying on its side blocking the whole highway. The sides of the trailer were bulging out in places and cows were running out from behind, it was a livestock semi trailer. The poor cows were running everywhere they were so scared. Once the ambulance arrived Dad got back in the van and drove around the crash. That's when I saw a gaping hole in the trailer where the crash forced a few of the cows out onto the road. There were more cows lying on the sides of the road, steam rising from their bodies. We came close to one and I could see into her eyes, she was still alive but her breathing was labored, she was dying and I began to cry.

From that day forward I began to pay more attention to my dreams but it was pretty exhausting trying to figure out what meant something and what was just a dream. Now I was a walking zombie, just as I was back then, as I examined every dream to see how successful my trip was going to be. My college friends were giving me grief and couldn't believe I was going to skip out on the next few years of college to head to New York and only my best friend knew that I was actually giving up my acceptance to the University of Arizona.

"If your parents knew you were giving up the U of A they would never let you go. You owe me big!" She said in her commanding voice.

"Well when I'm famous I'll pay you back" I said sheepishly.

Her eyebrows raised, she flipped her nose up in the air, "Well I already have your autograph." She smiled slyly.

Surprised she would keep those silly pieces of paper all this time, "You still have our autographs?"

"Of course I do. Of all of us I knew that you would be the most likely to get the hell out of this small town and make us all proud."

Marie came by my job and forced me to take a break since I wasn't spending much time with her. We sat on the hood of her car and soaked up the warm, dry air. I looked up to the sky. Oh how I did love the crystal blue skies of Arizona.

"You're not getting cold feet are you?" She touched my shoulder.

"No. I'm just tired and a little nervous." I looked at her now with pleading eyes hoping she didn't pry further.

Nervous wasn't the word, scared was more like it. My dad still wasn't talking to me, instead he resorted to communicating with news articles on New York taped to my bathroom mirror. Only these articles weren't about tips to eat cheap, best deals in the city, or 10 clubs with no cover charge, these were articles about homicides, muggings, robberies, rats found in kitchens. He was trying to scare me into staying in my small town and I had to admit it was almost working.

And the haunting dreams invading my nights hadn't made things any easier. My vivid dreams that were once wearing me out with nonsense were now filled with flashes of dead bodies and blood stained sidewalks. I was truly beginning to worry. Last night I had a horrible vision of a young woman who was stabbed and beaten with blood dripping down her face, eyes open, lying dead as though just dumped, on a dirty sidewalk. A small girl stood above her looking down. I couldn't see her face. Was it her sister, her daughter? I woke sticky with sweat and trembling. Was this the city I was longing to leave my quaint little town for?

Chapter 2: the little girl

The image of the dead women on the sidewalk put a huge damper on my excitement over leaving. I just couldn't get her out of my mind. I was planning on an early start this morning but after the horrible night I guess I was so tired I slept through my alarm. It was close to 9 a.m. when I sauntered into the kitchen for my cereal.

"I was beginning to think you had changed your mind." I heard a hopeful ring in my mom's voice which flipped my mean girl switch.

I snapped, "No, I just didn't sleep well, besides there's more than one bus that leaves today."

Mom offered to pay for a flight but I wanted to bus it so I could see the countryside. I had never gone any farther East then Kansas and I flew there when I was ten for a softball tournament. I wanted to be sure to take in every experience this trip had to offer.

I finished eating and woke up enough that the agitation left my voice. "Where's dad?"

"He's in the back yard watering that stupid grass."

Mom never understood why he tried so hard to grow grass in Arizona. She wished he would just let it go and fill the yard with gravel and cactus like most people did. I took my shower and finished packing. Mom was taking me to the bus and I didn't expect dad would be coming so I thought I better try and say my good-byes now.

I strolled outside in my Arizona garb of T-shirt, shorts and no shoes. My hair was just long enough to put up, where it stayed most of the time, either in a pony tail or in a hair clip. It was just too hot for long hair but I couldn't bring myself to cut my hair short. I did it once and cried cause I hated it.

The patio was cool; a huge contrast to the 80 degrees under the beaming sun and it was still mid-morning. It was going to be a hot one today. I won't miss this that's for sure. They say you can see the seasons change in the dessert when you've lived here long enough but I want to experience real seasons and I want to play in the snow. It snowed here once, we actually got a foot, everything was at a standstill, at least that's what I was told. I barely remember because I was only six years-old.

As I came around the shed my dad was working hard on his garden. He worked hard at everything he did. He was always moving, never settled down. His brown skin glistened under the sun, roasting a shade darker every minute he was out here. Everyone thought my dad was Mexican but in all actuality he was full Mohawk Indian. My mom was half Mohawk Indian and part French Canadian; their families were from the same reservation in upstate New York. My mom looked more white than Native American. So I look white too but I tan even though I try to stay out of the sun. My skin is a light copper and my dark brown eyes are almond shaped. I always wished I had bigger eyes. When I was in elementary school the kids used to think I was Asian but I think that was because when the arthritis in my mom's hands was too painful for her to handle my dad would fix my hair and pull my hair so tight into a ponytail that it made my eyes stretch back making my eyes look even smaller. I really hated it when he gave me piggy tails, they were always crooked.

With hesitation I took a deep breath and began.

"We're getting ready to leave." I dug my foot into the ground, forcing a puff a dust into the air.

No comment.

"I just thought I would come say good-bye."

No comment but he stopped picking weeds.

"I know you are disappointed but I promise I will make you proud Dad."

No comment.

"Will you at least look at me?" My throat began to tighten and I could feel the tears start to fill my eyes.

He stood and turned to me. He had tears in his eyes. I'd never seen my dad cry before. Am I doing the right thing?

"Promise me you will be safe?" he said.

I lunged toward him and gave him a huge hug. It had been nearly two months since he'd spoken to me, I thought I had I broken his heart.

"I promise." The tears flowed and I was able to release the stress of the last few months.

The ride to Benson was uneventful. When will I see the mountain ranges again, the dry dessert, hopefully not too soon? We arrived at the bus station in about 20 minutes. The next bus was leaving at 11:50 a.m. I barely had enough time to say good-bye to my mom and get on the bus, which was good because I hated long good-byes and my mom was already crying.

Thank goodness the bus wasn't crowded. I had a row to myself for a little while but of course I had 2,700 miles and three bus transfers to go. I'd never ridden on a bus besides my school bus. These seats were a lot more comfortable. Of course I probably wouldn't think this after the next 24 hours.

My eyes were heavy with exhaustion from my sleepless night. I propped my head up on my hand and leaned my elbow against the warm window. I stared out at the brown, hot dessert landscape and blowing dust, the rumbling of the bus in the background.

I found myself drifting in and out only waking slightly during the quick stops to pick up more passengers. Once the ride was continuous the bus rocked me into a deep sleep. I saw the little girl again, a bit clearer now. She was staring downward; dirty blonde, stringy thin hair lay flat against her head. She was wearing a dress a couple sizes too big for her making her look even more of a waif then she was. She was about 7 years old. All I could see was her. Was the dead body still there? I was afraid to look down.

Not raising her head, the girl turned her head toward me, hair draped across her face. "They killed her. Now you must kill for her."

My throat tightened. She said this so matter of fact. Who was this girl? I thought she had been a sister or daughter, I thought she had been grieving. Now it appeared as though she was just checking to see if the lady was dead. And why was she asking this of me, no, telling me!

She stood still hunched slightly over with her head turned toward me as if waiting for my reply. The little girl's right hand came out from beside her; a glimmer of steel caught my eye. She gripped a blood stained knife. Was this the murder weapon?

Before I could tell her to put down the dangerous weapon she turned and started walking towards me, gliding was more like it. Immediately I tried to step back but I was frozen. My legs were paralyzed. "They killed her. Now you must kill for her." She repeated.

What in the hell is wrong with this girl?

"I don't know what you are talking about, I can't kill anyone, and, and, you shouldn't be holding such a sharp knife, you'll hurt yourself!"

As she got closer her knife wielding arm rose above her head.

"If you don't kill for her then you will be next. They will make sure of it." The girl grinned and slashed the knife towards my heart.

"Miss...Miss...You okay?"

My arms were across my face and a screeching sound trembled above the rumble of the bus engine. I took a breath and the screeching stopped. I pulled my arms away and opened my eyes to a round concerning face peering at me. My face sweltered and I was glad the darkness hid the blush that must cover my whole body. I quickly looked around. No girl. No knife. No blood. I felt my chest, I felt no wound. It felt so real like I was there.

"I'm fine. Sorry." I said embarrassed.

"You were screaming and it was dark, I couldn't tell what was wrong. I'm glad you're okay," he said, sweat running down his temple.

"Umm, where are we, do you know?"

"We just left out of Arlington. We should be in Dallas soon."

Wow, I slept through half of Texas. I glanced at my watch; Pooh's hands were on the 6 and 8. 6:40 p.m.? No wonder I'm hungry. I checked my bus schedule and saw that I had a transfer in Dallas at 7 a.m.

"Excuse me sir, did you say we would be in Dallas soon?"

"Yes ma'am," He looked at me like maybe something really was wrong with me.

Holy molly, it was 6:40 a.m. not p.m., I slept the whole night. If I kept this up I'd be in New York before I knew it.

Within 20 minutes we were in Dallas and at the bus transfer station. I was switching busses but had over an hour to wait. I immediately headed to the public restroom. I thought I was going to burst. I figured I could just wait until I got off the bus to use the restroom since we were so close. I shouldn't have waited; I barely made it to the stall. Afterward I washed my hands and looked into the mirror. My hair was disheveled and my eyes were glassy. I looked exactly like I'd been sleeping on a bus for 10 hours. My t-shirt had a rust colored stain on the front. I wet a paper towel and dabbed at it.

"OW!" The pain was immediate. I pulled the neckline of my t-shirt down and saw a 1 inch long cut with dried blood. How could I cut myself with these flimsy things I wondered looking at my fingernails? I must have scratched myself when I threw my hands up to protect myself…in my dream. This is crazy.

I heard the door to the bathroom swing open and I turned to see a women and child come in. I finished fixing my hair and gathered up my stuff. I checked myself out in the mirror one last time and there she was, the girl, standing behind me in my reflection. I gasped and turned around but it was just the little girl that had come in with her mother. I was losing it. This was supposed to be the best trip of my life and I was having hallucinations. I'm not even doing drugs and I'm seeing things.

It wasn't long after I raided the vending machine and grabbed a USA Today that I was back on the bus headed for Mesquite, Texas. By nightfall we would be in Tennessee. Let's hope the rest of my trip would be more relaxing and dreamless.

The warm sun rose over the landscape as I sipped on my diet soda. I glanced through the paper and skipped to the state section and found New York. City finds murdered teen outside nightclub. 5th victim in past month, cops have no clues. Wow, was my dad right, was the city too dangerous? I don't think we've ever even had a murder in my town. Within 24 hours I would be living my dream so now was not the time to doubt myself.

The bus came to a final stop at the George Washington Bridge Bus Station, New York. I can't believe I'm finally here! With my legs wobbling underneath me I shuffled off the bus and the warm humid air enveloped me causing me to gasp for air. The air was so thick and moist and it smelled funny, maybe it was coming from the water. Tiny beads of sweat were already forming on my neck. I grabbed by duffle and walked towards the edge of the guard rail to peer over into the river so I could stretch my legs. I was in no hurry.

I had a few numbers of realtors that I pulled off the internet while searching at home but I knew I couldn't afford much. It would probably be better to find someone in need of a roommate then trying to find a place of my own. I had a couple thousand saved up that was supposed to go towards tuition in the fall that I could use until I found a job. But I knew that this wouldn't last long if I didn't find something right away so I had planned to start auditioning right away too.

I grabbed the local paper and scanned the classifieds as I propped myself up against the ledge. I dug my cell out of my purse and started making phone calls. Right away I dialed the number of a fast talking, city girl who was desperate for a roommate. Her former roommate fell head over heels for her professor and was now being wined and dined at his summer cottage in the Hamptons. Now she was a month behind on rent with the landlord knocking on her door every day telling her he was going to kick her out. The only down fall was the apartment was about a 100 years old and was in upper, upper Manhattan if there was such a thing. It was always under repair but it had an elevator, which I was told was installed to make it ADA compliant.

I had really wanted to live in the city but knew in my heart that I would never be able to afford it and now I would be spending most of my extra cash taking the subway to auditions, that's if I was lucky enough to audition for a show in the city. At this point I would be happy to just have auditions to go to.

I took a cab to the address I scribbled down on the back of my bus ticket. I was pleasantly surprised when it stopped in front of a red brick high rise with gated windows. There were quite a few trees that added little comfort and contrast from the iron protectors bulging from the brick walls. Once inside I was directed to take the elevator to the 5th floor and head to apartment 541. I entered the elevator and slid the metal gate in place. This

15 Dream Catcher by Tricia Currier

was all so new to me and I was so tired. The elevator slowly chugged upward, convincing me that I would take the stairs next time.

The elevator stopped on 5. I could hear Latin music blaring down the long hallway, the light was buzzing on and off. I took a deep breath and pulled the iron gate to the side and stepped through. I could hear a baby screaming, people arguing. "Home sweet home" I thought out loud. I knocked on 541 and waited. A quick patter of feet grew louder.

Through the door I heard "Are you here to look at the apartment?"

"Yes, I'm Tara Mason." Chains clanking, locks clicking, and the door was open. Before me stood a little waif of a girl, big eyes, messy bottle blonde hair.

"Hi! I'm Melissa. Come in. You got here quick." She glanced at my suitcase "Did you already make up your mind about the apartment?"

"Well I just got here today from Arizona."

"No shit! Wow! Excellent." She grabbed my arm and led me inside.

"There really isn't much in my price range so I'm actually pretty excited that this place looks so nice and you look…"

"Normal? It's okay. I know what you mean. Come take a look around. Actually there really isn't much to look at. It's only 600 square feet, one bedroom, so we'll be sharing a bed. We're close to the train and there is a park nearby, so that's cool."

She took me around the small place. The kitchen was like a hallway but I wasn't much of cook anyway. The bedroom was a big square and the living room was a big square. There were lovely hardwood floors that looked as old as the building.

"Rent is $950 so your half would be $475 which is due as soon as that landlord catches us at home. He's been coming by a couple times a day now. I could really kill Sam for leaving me hangin' like this."

We were back in the sparse living room and I took a seat on the coach.

"It's no problem. I will be looking for a job right away and I have some money saved that I was going to use until I found a place to stay so this works out great for me if you'll have me?"

With a sigh of relief, her face held a huge smile. She sat next to me and gave me a huge hug, "You bet, welcome roomy."

I untangled myself from her overt kindness, "I think I'll put my stuff away, freshen up and actually start looking for a job."

She patted me on the shoulder. "That's the spirit. Here's your key, now since it's before noon I'm going back to bed." She lithely rose up, turned and walked towards our only bedroom. She was like a little pixie.

I attached the brass key to my ring of keys that really I didn't have a use for anymore and followed her. I unpacked my clothes and placed them into the empty dresser Melissa pointed out to me. Our bedroom had a small window with bars on the outside. I grabbed a change of clothes and my toiletries and headed to the bathroom.

The bathroom was like the old fashion washrooms. It had a tub, shower, toilet, and sink stuffed into the smallest room possible but it was clean and now it was part mine. I decided I didn't need to run off in such a hurry and drew myself a nice a hot bath. I stuck my pointed toe into the water and sucked in my breath "Hot!" Slowly I immersed myself into the steaming water and once I was all the way in and leaning back I thought I was in heaven. I loved baths. The heat of the water released my muscles as good as any muscle relaxer. Sleep hung over me like a drug, the water like a warm blanket. The steam filled the tiny bathroom blocking out the light. Drip, drip, drip the water dripped into the tub like a melody lulling me to sleep.

"Sam" I heard someone yell. I looked around and I was in our hallway outside our apartment door.

"Just leave me alone." She was walking quickly trying to get away from the figure behind her.

"Wait Sam!"

I could see her walking away but not who was coming after her. She reached the elevator but the door was stuck.

"Stay away from me!" She was scared.

"I won't hurt you if you just come back and do what I say." The voice was powerful.

"Never!" She spat in his face.

"You Bitch!" I heard a click of a knife opening and then she screamed. I couldn't move to get closer, I was frozen. Then all I could see was her body slumped next to the iron gate in the elevator, a blood stain growing across her white blouse. When I looked up the little girl was standing there next to her. She reached out her arm to me and stumbled towards me. She was mouthing something but I couldn't make it out. Her face was gray and ashen. She was so young but so frightening, what did she want from me? I tried to back up but there was a door behind me. It was my door, 541. I opened the door, turned quick to close it and lock it. I turned around and the girl was standing right in front of me, her hand grabbing at me. I jumped back.

"Tara!" I heard over the splashes of water.

I tried to push further away but ended up under water, I gasped and sputtered "No! No! No! Don't touch me!"

"Tara, please you'll drown." I opened my eyes and saw Melissa kneeling over me trying to keep my head above the water. I immediately sat up. "Oh my God! I'm so sorry!"

"It's okay, it's okay. Are you alright?!" She looked crazy concerned, probably wondering if she had made the right decision accepting me for a roommate.

"I think so. I guess I fell asleep."

"Well I thought you were drowning what with all the screaming."

"Screaming?" Did I do that out loud?

"Yeah, you kept yelling Sam's name." She stood up and walked towards the door. "Well now that you are saved I'll let you be." She turned to look at me, her head tilted slightly. "You are okay, right?"

"Yes, just a bit over tired. I'm going to get dressed and go look for that job. Thank you and sorry again."

"Don't be." She smiled and was gone.

I dried my hair, wiped the mirror with my towel and peered at myself. The trip had taken its toll on my looks. My face looked pale except for the dark purple circles under my eyes. I got dressed and brushed my hair up into a ponytail. *I'll get all the sleep I need when I'm dead* I could hear my dad say. So I decided to push it further and go and hunt for a job.

Chapter 3: The Job

I got off the bus after about 20 minutes where I walked the sidewalks looking for a job, any job.

Dunkin Donuts, "Sorry Miss, nothin'"

Baskin Robbins "Nope"

Pizza Haven "I have to check with the manager."

I wait and fidget. Pizza aroma fills my nose, my stomach is rumbling. In all my nervous excitement I'd forgotten to eat. Since I'd gotten here it had been such a whirlwind, I found a place to stay, found a new friend, and now I needed to find a job.

I should buy a slice but I didn't want to meet a potential employer with pizza sauce on my face. I licked my lips, imagining the taste of the pepperoni. Just then the employed teenager came back interrupting my vision of me eating a slice of hot, cheesy, greasy, pepperoni pizza. "Sorry, he says he's got all the help he needs but you might want to check next door."

"Thanks." I hung my head, turned and walked out. Dejected, pizza-less, jobless, and starving, I headed next door. It didn't look like much from the outside. I could hear music coming from inside, a guitar. I walked past the wooden door to read the white sign "Best hamburger in town." I was so hungry it could be raw and I would think it was the best hamburger in town. My mouth was watering and I felt dizzy. A soulful voice rose above the guitar and as I looked to the door I saw the help wanted sign in the window.

"No freakin' way!"

I pulled on the brass handle and opened the door. The voice, soulful, smooth as silk, it sounded angelic, I was overly curious to see who it belonged to but my stomach interrupted my thoughts with a loud grumble. Once again my mouth began to water and I could think of nothing but the satiating aromas filling the air. I willed my legs forward, toward the bar but instead of walking in a straight line I wobbled to the left and then the right and then it went black.

"Hey, Hey, Miss, Wake up." Someone was shaking me.

I furrowed my brow, my head was dizzy, and I slowly opened my eyes. Brilliant blue eyes were staring down at me, what a magnificent face, tousled hair swept across his forehead; he was holding my head and shoulders up off the floor. It felt like a scene from a romance novel but I wasn't much of a heroine.

"Where am I? Who are you?" It smelled so good in here, my stomach was rumbling.

"You just fainted. But by the sound of your stomach I think you're in the right place, I think you need to eat." True concern lingered on his words but I was lost in those eyes. I wanted to lie here awhile longer and enjoy the feel of his arms holding me but I was embarrassed as to how I ended up in this predicament. I slowly started to stand. My blue eyed rescuer held me as I got my footing. I realized just then where I was and looking around I noticed everyone staring at me and the heat spread across my face, my throat tightened, and my voice squeaked as I spoke "I came in about the help wanted sign."

"Oh, well I'm just the entertainer." He smiled a lovely smile and gestured to a booth. "Sit. I'll get Patrick."

Was he the one? The angelic, soulful voice, that played guitar? He was beautiful and was an accomplished musician. *Keep your thoughts focused Tara, you need this job.* Another young, lanky guy with black eyes, dark hair and white skin walked over to the booth where I was sitting and handed me a glass of water. He wore a black t-shirt, jeans and black motorcycle boots.

"You look like you can use this." It looked like he tried to smile. Didn't this guy ever wash his hair? Guess he didn't have to spend any money on hair gel.

"Thanks." I smiled, remembering my manners.

"Here's a menu, you should probably eat something." He averted his eyes and walked back behind the bar but kept stealing glances my way. I knew he was just looking for a sign that I was ready to order but the way he looked at me gave me the creeps. It was like he was measuring me up or trying to figure something out.

After a few minutes he walked back over even though I still didn't know what I wanted. I was so hungry the whole menu looked good. "You from around here?" he said trying to make conversation. No smile.

"No, well yes, well I just moved here." I stumbled over myself sounding confused. His presence unnerved me.

This seemed to pique his interest, "Oh yeah, where from?"

"From Arizona." I took a sip of the water to settle my rattled nerves.

"Wow! That's a long way away. What brings you here?" He leaned over the back of the booth in front of me waiting for my answer. I guess I should get used to the probing when you tell people you just moved somewhere then obviously they want to know why. No harm done.

"Well..." Just before I could get into my life story my guitar guy was back with whom I could only assume was Patrick. I stood up quickly and just as quickly fell back into my seat from lightheadedness. The middle-aged man quickened his pace "Whoa, careful there."

I gazed up and caught the concerned looks of all three of them. Not knowing how to react from all the worry and my sudden woozy condition all I could do was blurt out "Hello I'm Tara Mason," with the biggest grin I could muster.

"Yes, well Jake here tells me you're looking for a job; do you have any waitressing experience?"

"Uh, not exactly but I'm a quick learner. I work hard, I don't live far from here so I can work whatever hours you need. I can do anything you want." Did I sound as desperate as I felt?

"Well I do need someone right away. The last girl just disappeared, no notice or anything. So why don't we give this a go on a trial basis and see how you do?" He said questioningly.

"Great! Thank you! I promise you won't be disappointed."

"Can you start tomorrow afternoon?"

"Sure."

"As an employee you get 50% off meals so why don't you sit and enjoy something. I don't want you passing out on my floor again. People might get the wrong impression." He winked and then turned and walked away. My blue-eyed guitar player stood there smiling and seemed as genuinely happy for me as I was. Thankfully the creepy guy sauntered back behind the bar.

"Well I have to get back to work. I'm Jake by the way." He smiled and my stomach tingled or maybe it growled again I wasn't sure. He peeked at the menu, "I recommend the burger," he said with a wink and walked away.

Creepy guy came around again, replaced my water with a soda, took my order and I quietly waited for my food. You wouldn't guess the place was this big from the outside. It had a fun Irish look to it but also a bit of sports bar mixed in. It had a nice long bar with a mirrored background. Every type of liquor you could possibly want was displayed. Since I didn't drink I was amazed at the many types of alcohol there actually was. I mean really, could there be that many taste variances in all those bottles? Booths surrounded the edges of the room and tables filled the middle area. The tables were a mix mash, some were square and some were round. It was almost like an obstacle course. I could already see my agility being tested. The room was sort of sectioned off with booths down the middle with a wooden privacy wall covered with stained glass adorned with 4 leaf clovers. On the other side was a small make shift stage where Jake played his mesmerizing music. Smaller round tables filled this side allowing for more tables. All things Irish and sports related covered the walls. It looked like a really fun place but right now it wasn't very crowded. If it stayed like this I could probably handle being a waitress here. With that thought my confidence was slightly boosted and my fears eased.

It wasn't long and my food arrived. I took the advice of my guitar player and ordered the burger. I savored every bite of it and fell in love with the music that flowed from my soulful singer. His repertoire didn't exactly match the surroundings but I got the feeling he was hired more for his looks then his talent. I knew him for all of one hour and already I was smitten. Could he tell? Just thinking of my new crush gave me another blush. I looked down and when I looked up I saw the bartender's cold, black eyes boring into me. He stood, stiffly behind the bar, just staring at me. Why was he staring at me?

It was a long day, I was tired and so I quickly finished eating, left money for my meal, and picked up my purse to leave. I really wanted to hang out and listen to the music but it was getting dark outside and the guy at the bar was creeping me out. I waived quickly to my blue-eyed crooner, he tilted his head and brought up the right corner of his mouth crinkling his eyes. My heart skipped a beat. My God Tara you act like no boy has every smiled at you. The swing of emotions was causing me to feel so unsteady. I needed to get home.

The air outside was warm and sticky but the breeze made it tolerable. I waited at the bus stop, which wasn't far up the block. So far Innwood seemed like a nice little town and I couldn't wait to explore it more. I was so happy I was quickly able to find a place to live and with such a nice person. I didn't have to wait long and my bus pulled up. I stood up and realized that I wasn't alone; I could feel the presence of someone behind me and the reflection in the bus door window proved my intuition correct. I could see the black haired man from the bar behind me. I sucked in a breath and let out a slight gasp. Did he hear me? I didn't want him to know that I feared him. The doors slowly screeched open and I dug in my pocket for change and quickly found a seat.

He walked passed me not saying a word and took a seat about four rows back. The 20 minute ride seemed to take forever. I was trembling but didn't know why, he meant me no harm I'm sure of it. My stop was coming. Should I get off? He would know where my stop was, would he get off too? It was dark now and I was afraid to keep riding the bus because I didn't know where it would take me or if I would be able to get back to my stop. It slowly pulled up and stopped. I didn't move. A few other people got off. I didn't see him get off. At the last minute before the doors closed I flew off the bus. The bus drove off and I saw him sitting there staring straight ahead. I only now realized that my heart was pounding and sweat was dripping down my neck and back. I hurried to my apartment building. I pulled the gate shut on the elevator, it started up and stopped, the light flickered. "Damn Elevator!" It started again and soon it was on the 5th floor.

I put my key in the door to no avail. The bolt and chains were on and the door wouldn't budge. Hearing my struggle with the door Melissa unlocked it and let me in. She resumed her spot on the couch where she was watching T.V., waiting for me to get home.

"How come you didn't call me? What took you so long? Did you find anything?" She fired her questions at me at an enormous rate of speed. I could hardly comprehend them I still hadn't calmed down from my ride home. Why was I freaking out like this? He was probably just leaving at the same time I was and taking the same bus. Melissa's eyes squinted, "Are you okay?"

"Yeah… I found a job" I said trying to move the attention off my obvious anxiety.

She jumped up from the couch, "Oh my God! That's great! When do you start?"

"Tomorrow afternoon," She hugged me and we both plopped back down.

"Where, doing what?" Her obvious excitement wasn't contagious; I was just too tired and nervous about my new job.

"The Piper's Kilt, it's an Irish Pub." With uncertainty in my voice I continued "They need a waitress,"

"No way! That's where Sam was working before she up and left me high and dry." She arched her eyebrows "This is really freaky, first you take over her apartment and now her old job, it's like invasion of the body snatchers. Doo doo doo doo, doo doo doo doo," she wiggled her fingers at me as she hummed the Twilight music.

"Stop it, it's not funny. How was I supposed to know she used to work there?" I was sulking.

"Hey I'm just teasing you. It's great you have a job and so quickly."

With my eyebrows raised, "Yeah, I'm pretty happy but a little nervous. I've never waitressed before and he said it's on a trial basis."

"I'm sure you'll do fine. Well now that you are home safe, I'm going to bed, I'm tired." She got up and headed toward the bedroom.

My thoughts drifted to my blue-eyed Jake, "Oh and guess what?" She stopped and turned towards me.

"There was a very cute guy there and man could he play guitar and what a voice. It will make working there that much more fun." I said looking off lost in my memories of our first meeting.

"Yeah, well unless he's paying for the rent I'm too tired to hear about it now," she said shuffling off to bed.

I brushed my teeth, washed my face and changed into my pj's. I was pretty exhausted now that I thought about it. I still couldn't get that other man's piercing black eyes out of my mind. Geez, why did he have to be so freaky?

Sharing a bed with Melissa was going to take some getting used to. She was already snoring by the time I tucked myself in. I closed my eyes but not even her guttural noises could keep the wave of sleep from enveloping me. I could feel a force pulling me down, it was paralyzing, I couldn't speak, and it was pitch black. I was scared and tried not to panic as the weight over me held me down against my will. Instead of trying to push against it I let it pull me down, down, down into the blackness and then just as quick as it started the grip released me and the darkness disappeared. I saw bright lights, people walking by. I was in the city, it was Manhattan. The cabs were sounding their horns and people were brushing by me clipping my shoulders. A young lady turned in front of me and I felt the intense desire to follow her.

She was wearing a cocktail dress, red, with high heels. She had ivory skin, red hair and bright red lipstick and a black shall or scarf. She was waiting for someone. I stood back so as not to be seen. Why was I hiding? I looked down at my feet but they weren't my feet. I saw black leather work boots with jeans. I held out my hands and they were mans hands with a jean jacket to the wrist. I raised my hands to feel my hair and it was short and greasy. I quickly tried to find my reflection, who was I, but the lady began walking and I had to follow her. My heart was racing; my steps grew quicker as she took a less populated path. My hand instinctively swept to my back pocket and touched something cold and hard. I pulled out the long object and when I glanced down I saw my manly thumb click the switch and the blade popped out making me gasp. This was a horrible dream and I want to wake up. *Wake up Tara! Wake up!*

Now the young lady was standing in an alley yelling into her cell phone oblivious to anything around her. She had no idea that I was standing here, no, not me but the body of a man that I was in. It sounded like she was stood up and she was letting them know she wasn't happy about it. I was right behind her. I could smell her cherry blossom perfume and feel the heat from her body. I was excited and I wanted her but more then anything I wanted her dead.

I wanted to warn her to run but my hand came around from behind her covering her mouth and she struggled more out of surprise then worry for her life. My other hand rose with the steel blade and within seconds it was over. The blade sliced through her throat as smooth as butter. The crimson stain against her ivory skin was the only indication that anything happened. She didn't scream, she didn't struggle, she hardly made a sound. My arms let go of her and she slumped to the ground. No, his arms.

And there she lay. I stood there staring at her, the blood pooling around her, she was beautiful and now she was dead. I looked up and the little girl was staring at me. "They killed her and now you must kill for her."

"No! No! No! I can't! Who are you? What do you want?"

"Tara! Tara! Wake up!"

I opened my eyes. No city lights just the soft dim glow of the bedside lamp. I looked around the square room and saw the moon through the barred window.

"Tara, you awake?"

"Yes. Yes." I felt such a relief and intense remorse at the same time.

"What were you dreaming about?"

"I don't know, some girl." But I screamed inside that I had just slit a woman's neck!

27 Dream Catcher by Tricia Currier

"Well it sounded like more than that. You were twitching and yelling. I was afraid you would wake the neighbors."

"I'm sorry." Thank God it was just a dream. I've never harmed anything in my life and right now I felt like I just committed a murder.

"Well I need to get ready and get to class. Are you going to be okay?"

Was it already morning?

"Yeah, I'm fine. Thanks."

Chapter 4: First Day on the job

It was 7am. I didn't have to be to work until the afternoon but I was too scared to go back to sleep. I got up and made some coffee. If I didn't sleep I couldn't dream. The hot coffee was just what I needed. I switched on the T.V. and settled into the couch. The local news was reporting on traffic, weather and then breaking news chimed in with news of another murder. My interest perked up as they reported on a young lady stabbed outside a nightclub. I couldn't breath but surely it was a coincidence. The report continued:

"Apparently she had been lying there for most of the night but clubgoers assumed she was just passed out on the sidewalk when actually she was dying from a stab wound to the heart. What a tragedy."

See there. In my dream her throat was slit and this girl was stabbed. It's just my nerves and I'm over-tired. I tried to rationalize my fears but apparently this was one of several murders in the past month that have all gone unsolved and with no apparent similarities authorities did not believe it was the work of a serial killer.

They continued to describe the victim as she had no identification on her and my mouth dropped open. The young lady was approximately 25, 5'7, with long red hair. She was wearing a red dress with a black scarf. My hands began to tremble as the description was repeated and I used both hands to set my coffee down on the table. Was it a coincidence, how was it possible, could it be, the same girl from my dream? Why was I having these horrible dreams?

Bang! Bang! Bang!

I jumped 10 feet off the couch. The pounding at the door interrupted my thoughts. I ran to the door and peeked through the peep hole. It was the Landlord Mr. Lee, Melissa told me to expect him this morning. I unlocked the door and opened it. "You're up bright and early, good morning Mr. Lee."

With his hand outstretched palm up he demanded "Melissa said she have money for me today."

"Yes, of course. One second. Would you like to come in?"

"No. I wait here for money."

"Okay. Just a minute, I'll be right back." I closed the door and ran to the kitchen to get my purse. I dug through it and found my wallet and counted out $475. I turned and Mr. Lee was standing right there and I jumped. "Oh my goodness, I thought you were waiting in the hall?"

"You said come in, so I come in," he looked confused, as was I. Our wires must have crossed.

"Well no matter. Here you go. There's $475 and we'll get you another $475 in 2 weeks, okay?"

"Thank you." And he quickly left. I followed him to the door, shut it and locked it. What a strange man.

When I got back to the couch the news was finished reporting on the murder and was on to robberies and traffic accidents. The interruption had calmed my nerves enough that I decided to scan the paper for auditions, casting calls, singing gigs etc. I found a couple plays looking for actors and one band looking for a singer. I wasn't sure I wanted to invest that much time singing for one band unless the money was really good. I called the number on the auditions and got the address. I decided to go try out before work this afternoon.

The result of the audition was a "don't call us we'll call you" so I headed to work a bit dejected. I'm not sure what I was expecting though. I was early so I decided to get a bite to eat before my shift. I casually scanned the place but my blue eyed guitar player wasn't there; I was really hoping he would be. The freaky black haired guy was there behind the bar. Today he seemed to be in a serious conversation with another man sitting at the bar. In the reflection of the mirror, this guy looked pretty handsome but there was something dangerous about him. Just as I was sizing him up he turned to look in my direction. I blushed and looked down at my plate of food. I remember the look on his face, his green eyes, and eyebrows arching upward, hair slicked back as though he ran his hands through it a lot, staring as if he just found what he was looking for. Were they talking about me? I was just finishing up when Patrick walked over and gave me the run down of the job. My nerves were on fire since I had never waitressed before and I was sure I was going to end up owing him money after all the dishes I was sure to break. Maybe I should suggest plastic baskets. That would be a smart investment and save my job.

He handed me my apron and I got right to work taking drink and food orders. Drink orders I gave to the bar and food orders went back to the kitchen. Patrick helped in the kitchen as did another young kid named Jim. I soon found out that creepy black haired guy was named Ed after he introduced himself with the first drink order I placed.

"I forgot to introduce myself yesterday, my name is Ed, well Edward but everyone calls me Ed," he said smiling, his black eyes like pools of ink.

"Hi. I'm Tara. Can I get two Miller Genuine Drafts and a Heineken?" I said trying to stay calm in his presence. I could feel the other gentlemen staring at me as I waited and I fought the compulsion to turn in his direction but willpower alone was not strong enough. When I looked at him his green eyes were searing into me and he was smirking as if he knew some secret that he wasn't going to share with me.

"Here ya go." Ed set the beers down on my round, brown tray. I forced my eyes off the stranger and delivered my order. What was up with these two?

The bar was pretty quiet; it was only 3 p.m. so the dinner and happy hour crowd hadn't arrived yet. I took advantage of the lull in business and headed for the bathroom to give it the hourly once over cleaning. While in there I checked myself out in the mirror. I was average looking I thought. My brown hair was up in its usual ponytail; my dark eyes looked like almonds. I looked better then most days because today I took the time to put on a little makeup for my audition earlier. I always felt like I attracted more attention when I wore makeup and when I wore my hair down. Most girls appreciated the attention but ogling eyes made me ill at ease. I never knew how to handle it so I would go out of my way to just look plain.

I walked out of the bathroom straight into the chest of the green eyed man spilling cleaning solution all over. "Oh! I'm sorry!" It was like hitting a brick wall. He held my elbows to steady me which kept me from falling.

"That's okay, it was my fault. I wasn't watching where I was going. Are you okay?" His voice was smooth as honey, his hair wavy, golden brown, he was probably 25.

"Yeah, I'm fine. Did I get any on you?" I looked down to check but really it was to conceal my blush. Why was I bushing, sure he was attractive, but geez Tara, can't a gorgeous guy look at you without blushing, apparently not.

"Nope." He dropped my elbows.

"Sorry again for almost running you over."

"You can run me over anytime." He smiled coolly.

I bowed my head again as I walked by, my face burning red. Ed was washing glasses when I headed to the bar; he glanced up. "Everything Okay?"

I shook my head up and down and headed to the group of college guys that just sat down. The big, athletic jock spoke up first. "What's the special besides you?"

Smiling as nice as I could and ignoring the flippant remark, I went through the specials. They were celebrating the fact that it was Friday and they were finished with finals. "A round of shots for all of us with beer chasers." He grabbed my hand before I could turn towards the bar to fill his order. I whipped my head around to glare at him. "You're new here, what happened to the red-head?"

I knew he meant no harm so I let my guard down, "Yep, I'm new. I'm not sure where she went. Do you want your drinks?" I raised my eyebrows and he let my hand go.

I could do this I thought. I tried to stuff my shyness into a dark corner and hide it away, along with the naïve little girl that didn't drink or smoke or frequent sports bars such as this. I walked to the bar quickly to place my order with Ed. The bar was really beginning to fill up now. I checked the clock and it was close to 5 p.m. More 20 some-things flowed in. I must have been wearing my nerves on my face because Ed chimed in,

"Don't worry kitten you'll do fine. Just keep the drinks flowing." He set my round down on my tray.

I held my breath, slid my tray off the bar with two hands and held it securely in front of me as I slowly walked to the table of really cute guys. I kept my eyes on the tray, careful not to spill anything. It wasn't that I couldn't be graceful if I tried hard at it, I was just accident prone. Walls jump out at me, ledges rise up and trip me, I turn corners too sharp and take out my shoulder, I run into things that people don't see, stumble over my own feet, basically I could fall standing in place. So now with every bit of concentration focused on my walk across the room the door opened and my beautiful blue eyed guitar player walked in, my eyes lifted from my tray of drinks to take him in and at that moment one of those invisible stumbling blocks flew in my way. The drinks reached the table rather quickly then but not in the manner I had hoped. The tray flew out of my hands as I fell to the ground. The drinks splattered across the table and all over the unsuspecting group of hot college guys.

I hit the ground pretty hard and all I could hear was "What the HELL!" "Son of a Bitch!" "Hey the next round better be FREE!!" I wasn't hurt just afraid to look up. The second day in a row I was laying on this floor, how could this be happening to me? Out of the corner of my eye I saw a hand reaching out to me. "Are you okay?" But the voice was smooth as silk and not my Jake. I turned to look up and it was the green eyed golden haired man from the restroom. He was smiling and when he did that I could feel my heart thump harder. I grabbed his hand and he pulled me up. "Thank you for your help."

I quickly grabbed a bar towel and wiped up the table and profusely apologized to the table of five. Patrick came out as I was carrying the empty glasses to the bar.

"What happened here?" his face hard as stone.

Please don't fire me. Please don't fire me. I kept repeating in my head. I couldn't look him in the eye.

Ed chimed in, "There was a small accident but it's cleaned up now. No harm done."

Was he sticking up for me? Patrick seemed satisfied with the answer he received and walked back into kitchen. I took another tray of drinks over to the table but this time looked straight ahead to my destination instead of at my tray. I made it a lot quicker, smoother, and I was less nervous. The guys were pretty gracious after their initial outburst. They would smell like alcohol after a few hours anyway. Plus it didn't hurt matters much that this next round was on the house that would come out of my paycheck. I knew I would end up owing Patrick before the night was out.

I stopped and took another order and headed up to the bar. "Thanks again." I said to the green-eyed stranger.

"My name's Devin. And you are quite welcome. You're not the first one to spill a drink in this place," he said smiling.

I smiled and took my next order. I glanced over to the makeshift stage and saw Jake setting up for his set. I wonder if he knew he was the cause of my sudden exploitation of clumsiness. He was sitting, hunched over, tuning his guitar, wearing a white t-shirt with blue jeans tennis shoes and a black knit hat that covered his long tousled hair. I liked how his hair hung over his forehead yesterday all out of control and wild but now his hat held his hair out of his face so I could see his beautiful eyes and the perfect angles of his face. I wasn't sure which I liked best. After I delivered my drinks I decided to approach him.

"Would you like anything to drink?" I stood there holding my tray flat against the front of me, biting my lip-a terrible habit-nervously waiting for his answer.

He looked up and smiled. "I saw your first act over there, what are you doing for an encore?"

Although I knew he was joking, it hurt my feelings; I was still getting over my mortification of falling flat on my face. I could feel the heat rise up over my chest and throat and burn my cheeks. His comment caught me off guard in such a way that I didn't know what to say so I just turned and walked away.

"Hey! Wait. Where are you going?" He jumped up and grabbed my arm.

I turned, my eyes were wet, a lump in my throat. I was trying so hard to hide my humiliation from earlier that I think I was expecting some sort of compassionate remark from him, the guy who just yesterday held me so tenderly when I fainted. Why was I being so damn sensitive?

"I'm sorry Tara. I didn't mean to tease. Please forgive me?" The corner of his mouth turned up, his eyes smiling.

"Fine. I'm sorry; I didn't mean to be so sensitive." I turned and walked towards the bar. Why was I apologizing? He was apologizing to me; I had no reason to apologize for my feelings. I hated when I did that. I grabbed a bottle of water and brought it back to him.

"Here you go."

"Thanks. Hey how long you working tonight?" He continued to tune his guitar, his nimble fingers plucking at the strings.

"Um, you know I don't know. Patrick never said. I guess until closing. What time does the place close?"

"Well it is Friday night so we don't close until 2 a.m." He sat his guitar down and opened his water.

"Wow! That's a long shift. I guess I'll work until he tells me to go home. I need the money."

"Well maybe when we close up we can get a drink together." He smiled his lovely smile at me and he could have asked me to do anything and I would have said yes.

"Sure, I'm not sure how much company I'll be by then but I'd like that." My heart was pounding and I was deathly afraid he could hear it. Just then my moment was interrupted by Patrick's booming voice across the room.

"Tara! We've got thirsty customers over here! Quit flirting with the help!"

I wanted to crawl under a table from embarrassment but I turned quickly and got back to the job at hand. Jake began playing and I was floating on a cloud the whole evening. His music lifted me to new heights. Nothing bothered me, not the creepy bartender, the drunken frat boys, my nightmares, or the ogles from sloppy drunken men. Anytime I needed a push of adrenaline I would look over to him sitting on his stool, guitar under his arm, black and white checkered jacket over his white t-shirt, occasionally his eyes closed as he sang and I could tell he really felt his music and I admired that most. I wished I could just sit and listen. Music was always a way into my heart but this was different, he had a gift and it was like he reached out and held my heart in his hands with his songs.

I could see that I wasn't the only one he did this to either. Groups of girls at various tables were also gazing up into his blue eyes, whispering to each other, smiling, giggling. My insecurities were edging out my pleasant thoughts and I began to wonder how I even thought I stood a chance with this guy after seeing my competition, sexy blonde college girls with their perfect skin and perfect 10 bodies. It was at this point in my daydream that the natives were getting restless. The frat boys were hootin' and hollerin' trying to get the attention of the Barbie girls.

I walked over to their table and casually asked, "Can I get you guys anything else?"

One guy from their group, who was returning from the restroom, walked up behind me, grabbed my hips and pulled me against his groin. "Yeah you can get me something else."

Shocked by his sudden intrusion of my personal space I froze. No one had ever acted like this towards me. When I didn't resist he took this as a sign that I approved of his advances, so he took it a step further and moved his hand up to my breast and squeezed. The other guys sat their ogling his performance and just egged him on.

I bent forward trying to move his hand away from my breast but his other hand gripped me tighter and pushed me forward against the table. The glasses on the table went flying and because I had leaned forward I was now laying across the table. I tried to straighten up but he put his hand on my back and pressed his groin against me harder. I could feel his hardness as he pressed up against me. The other guys at the table just sat and watched. My eyes widened and panic began to flood my body. What if he didn't stop?

I finally found my voice and screamed "LET ME GO!" The music stopped, everyone in the place turned to look in our direction. The guys kept hollering and chanting,

"Go Ted! Go Ted! Go Ted!"

I was like a ragdoll in his strong arms. The harder I pushed against him the tighter his vice-like grip became. He moved his hand from my back and forced me up against his chest and he leaned in and started kissing my neck. I tried to wiggle out of his grasp and he groaned. "Oh yeah baby, that's the way I like it, fight me."

Panic set in again as the guys at the table continued to be of no help. Self-preservation took over and I grabbed the tray from the table and slammed it against his head just as two other guys grabbed him. I was free from him and turned to look behind me as I ran towards the front door. I saw Jake and Ed slam him up against the wall.

I hadn't realized that I was crying but now I could feel the tears burning down my cheeks. I was mortified. I ran outside. Once outside the fear came gurgling up to the surface and I started to hyperventilate. I slumped down against the wall and tucked my knees up against my chest and curled my arms around my head. I rocked myself against the wall. It wasn't long before I heard footsteps.

"Tara! Oh my God! Tara, are you okay?" I could hear the fear and concern in Jake's voice. I couldn't speak. I couldn't tell him I was fine because I wasn't. "Please Tara, look at me." He held my shoulders and gently shook me trying to pry my head out of my hands. I was trying to find a safe place but I didn't feel safe. I looked up into his eyes. I must have looked bad because I think I heard a small gasp. I always did get puffy and red when I cried.

He held my hands as he stood, pulling me up with him and took me in his arms. He was so warm and strong and comforting and safe. It was then that I really began to cry, sobbing was more like it. I wasn't crying only for what just happened inside for that surely scared me to death but it was for all the stress of the past few days. I just let it all out, wetting his shirt as he held me tighter and the sobs grew louder. Not caring about the people passing by he kissed my head and told me it was going to be okay and I knew then I was falling in love with Jake. Was this even possible after only a few days? What I needed to do least on this adventure was happening but I just couldn't help it. He pulled away slightly and held my face in his hands looking down at me with those blue eyes.

"Are you okay?" He wasn't smiling his usual crooked smile, he was really concerned. Had I scared him with my near breakdown?

"I think so. I'm sorry I got your shirt all wet." I said half smiling.

"Don't worry I have others and a few tears won't do any harm."

At that moment Patrick came out. We both turned to look at him. Patrick walked forward shaking his head looking down at the pavement.

"Tara I just want to say how sorry I am about what happened. It does get rowdy from time to time in my place but we've never had an episode like that. I threw those guys out and told them they were banned for life. Please will you come back to work?"

I really didn't feel like it but I needed the job. "Sure."

Jake squeezed my hand which I didn't even realize that he was holding. "Are you sure?" I shook my head up and down and we walked inside.

The atmosphere of the bar had changed drastically once I reentered the bar. My table of five was gone. I could feel sympathetic eyes staring me down and of course I was being overly self-conscious. Jake gave my hand another squeeze and he headed back to his stage and admiring fans. I wish he'd given me a kiss in front of all of them but I knew that was asking too much seeing that we've only just met.

I ran to the bathroom to give myself a once over. I looked exactly like I had been crying. My eyes were puffy and red like I'd just had an allergic reaction, my makeup like melted wax had dripped off my face, with some still smudged on my cheeks. I rubbed at my red nose and sniffed but I was too stuffed up. I looked horrible. I washed my face and took a paper towel to dry it. I glanced in the mirror a final time to straighten my hair and saw the little girl standing behind me with a smile. I jumped and turned at the same time. No one was there. I turned back to the mirror but she wasn't there either. I took a deep ragged breath. Keep it together Tara, she's not real. As I pulled the door open I heard a soft voice reach out from behind me "they deserve to be punished" it was the little girl and I knew exactly who she was referring to at least in my mind I knew who I thought deserved to be punished. I decided not to acknowledge the voice and continued out the door.

Just as if the disturbing event had never happened, I quickly fell into the motion of checking on my tables and collecting mostly drink orders. I headed to the bar and Ed met me with concern in his eyes. "You okay?"

I began loading my tray with drinks. I have to admit his concern for my wellbeing caught me off guard. I really didn't know what to make of him. "I think so. Hey, thanks for your help."

"No problem." He smiled. Something I rarely saw him do.

It seemed an unusual place to be; in a position to be thanking Ed but I couldn't leave a good deed go unnoticed. Devin was still standing there at the bar looking quite confused at our exchange. "Thank you for your help?" he repeated aloud as he turned to look at Ed "What happened?"

"We had an incident with a group of frat boys." He continued to explain as I took off with my drinks. I really didn't want to stick around for the play-by-play. When I returned Devin looked at me. But it wasn't just any look- it was the look of shock, torment, like someone had just killed your dog kind of look. I wanted to ask him if he was okay and then realized that the alarm in his face was directed at me and I blushed from his overt concern.

He was the first to break the trance like gaze he held over me.

"Tara, are you okay, did he hurt you?"

Through all the chaos I hadn't noticed that he wasn't there, just that Ed and Jake pulled the guy off of me. Why was he acting like this, I'd only met the guy tonight and he acted as if he he'd die if he lost me.

"I'm fine, just a little shook up." I quickly left. I realized that his presence was un-nerving causing me to stumble over my words and he was making me a bit uncomfortable or was it that I wanted to try and console him, run my fingers through his messy hair and peer into his green eyes and whisper everything was going to be alright. What the hell was I thinking? I was the one that was groped and attacked tonight. Plus how could he make me feel like that after I had already silently pledged my love to Jake? Where the hell was Devin anyway while this was all happening? I was already headed back to the bar after making my rounds while going through this banter in my head and caught the tail end of the conversation between Ed and Devin.

"Yeah, it was a good thing you were occupied because you would have probably killed that guy, man. I mean it, he was all over her." How could they still be talking about this, give it a rest.

"Ahem." I cleared my throat. "I need a round of 6 tequila shots for the ladies in front of the stage. Hey what time is last call?"

"1:30."

"1:30?" I wish it were earlier, I mumbled under my breath as I glanced at all my customers. I felt like my feet were going to fall off. Plus all these people had more than enough to drink, I felt guilty giving them more.

"Nope, last call 1:30, doors close at 2 a.m."

I hoisted my tray up on my shoulder and carefully started towards the fake Barbie girls stealing a glance at Jake on my way. My heart beat faster when I saw that his eyes were already on me. He smiled and my face flushed. Don't drop the drinks on the Barbie girls... as fun as that might be. The thought made me smile slightly and all the girls at the table looked to see who he was smiling at and their eyes landed on me walking towards them. I could feel the heat beaming from their staring eyes as if they were waiting for me to burst into flames. "Here you go ladies. Flag me down if you need anything else."

One of the girls touched my arm. "We were wondering if the entertainment was single?"

I raised my eyebrows the jealousy accelerating. I swallowed hard to keep the green-eyed monster at bay. "Oh, well you'll have to ask him that." I actually didn't know. I really didn't know much about him except that I had a total crush on him and that I wanted him to be mine and mine only.

"Well do you think you could have him meet us after he's done?" Her words were mockingly sweet and I wanted to kick her out.

I glanced over to the stage. "I can let him know but it might be better if you just asked him yourself." I was not in the mood to play matchmaker with my Jake and blondie here.

"Well, what's his name?" she urged.

Would she ever give up? However this is one I could answer- blue eyes, guitar guy, angel voice, soulful singer- but instead I said "Jake."

At that moment she stood up, pushed me aside like the hired help i was, and flipped up her top to reveal bare, huge perfect breasts, and yelled "Hey Jake!" Jake snapped his head up. "Why don't you sit with us when you're done?"

I thought Jake's eyes were going to pop out of their sockets. His jaw dropped open and I wished I was standing next to him so I could close it for him. So he was a big boob guy, it figures, as I looked down at my size b's on a good day. That's it those girls are cut off! I walked away feeling quite small, literally. Jealously didn't allow me to see the blush on Jake's face.

It was getting late and the place was really thinning out now. My feet were numb from standing and walking all day. Jake was playing his final song of the night. I knew this because he said this is my final song of the night. The Barbie's at the table were getting very inpatient waiting for him. Well mainly it was the four Barbie's that were ready to go who were annoyed waiting for Barbie number one to get her music man.

I was cleaning up, wiping up tables. Jake's song ended. Here it goes I thought. I risked a glance over to see him heading to their table but he wasn't. He was heading to the bar. Must need a drink before going to their table? Yep, I was right. He was walking with a beer in his hand except he was heading towards me, I sucked in my breath and held it. "You ready to have that drink with me?" His blue eyes glistened as he flashed his crooked smile at me.

I was in shock. I couldn't talk. I had forgotten the request he made of me earlier. All the excitement of the evening had caused temporary memory loss. I glanced around him and saw the girls grab their purses looking a little pissed off. Having forgotten I was still holding my breath I let it out like a tire exploding "Um, in just a minute I need to finish cleaning up these tables and I'll join you." Smooth Tara. His smile crept up into his eyes and made my heart flutter. Just then the Barbie girls arrived.

The big boobed Barbie spoke first. "What the fuck? I was waiting for you; you were supposed to sit with us."

Jake looked very uncomfortable. "I'm sorry ladies but I already had other arrangements before your request." He turned and winked at me. Oh my god how could he be so daring?

BBB looked over at me green with envy. "Her? The mousey bar girl? You pick her over me?" condescendence dripping from her voice, I wanted to disappear. "Well let me show you something." Right then she reached her arm up around his neck, pulled him down to her and kissed him full on the lips, her other hand traveled down the front of him and cupped him between the legs. I could hear Jake suck in his breath. What the hell was wrong with these people in this city, they were so bold. She rubbed him and pulled him closer to her, rubbing those big boobs against his chest and then flicked her tongue across his face to the sensitive skin of his neck until she ended her foreplay with a kiss on his ear. I thought I heard Jake groan but that may have been my jealousy unleashing itself. I hadn't even kissed him yet! His one arm was still at his side and the other was holding his beer. I turned; the flush on my face was something I couldn't hide and my envy was about to get the best of me.

"Now that ought to change your mind." I could hear the smugness in her voice.

"Have a good night ladies. You'll excuse me." Then I heard Jake's footsteps fading away.

I couldn't believe what I just heard. Had he really denied her? Just then I heard quick steps coming from the bar and I turned and saw Devin quickly walking towards the door.

"Here ladies, let me assist you. How did you arrive here tonight, do you need help finding your way home?"

Oh he was smooth. The Barbie's quickly forgot they had been dissed by the musician when the green-eyed dark horse came running to save them.

"Well we could use a little help getting back to our dorm unless you have another place in mind?" BBB said coyly.

What a slut I thought to myself. I shook my head and finished my work. All the dishes were done, tables wiped down, floors swept and mopped. I thought I was going to die. I was hungry, thirsty, and tired. Jake was sitting in the booth with his back against the partition and legs stretched out across the booth. His black knit hat was firmly in place, holding back that tousled hair, that one day I will run my fingers through, allowing me to see those heart pounding blue eyes up close and personal. I grabbed a soda from the bar and slid into the other side of the booth and let out a big huff.

"Tired?"

"So not the word for it."

"So what's your story Tara? Where are you from?" Those blue eyes peered into my soul waiting for an answer and as soon as I caught my breath I would give it to him. Why did he have to be so damn handsome?

"I just moved here from Huachuca City, Arizona." I took a long draw on my straw and the diet pepsi tasted so good.

Jake's eyebrows arched up "Wachuca what?"

"Huachuca City." I leaned back in the booth. I could probably go to sleep right here if it weren't for the company I was keeping.

"Never heard of it."

"It's about an hour south of Tucson. Ever heard of Tombstone, the town too tough to die?"

"Oh yeah. Doc Holiday, Wyatt Earp…"

I interrupted, "Yeah, and the O.K. Corral, Crystal Palace, Big Nose Kates…Well that's where I went to High School."

"You went to High School at the O.K. Corral?" His eyes got huge.

I giggled "Not exactly, the school is down the street."

"So you left Arizona to work at the Pipers Kilt?" He took a swig of his beer.

"Yep. You got it. That was my dream." I tilted my head sideways. "I came here for the same reason every other young girl comes to New York City to see if I can make it in the Big Apple. I want to act and sing." I hung my head. I already felt dejected and I had only been on one audition.

He looked up at me through his long eyelashes, "You look like you've already given up."

"Is it that obvious?" I took a drink of my soda and decided to give him some details. "My first audition was a lot harder then I thought and the competition was really, really tough. The girls looked like tonight's Barbie girls. How can I compare to that?" The tears were already welling up in my eyes. Why do my tears always have to give me away? Damn it!

Jake reached across the table and lifted my chin with this hand and a little traitor tear spilled over. "Not all roles are looking for, what did you call them, Barbie girls?" He chuckled. "Please don't ever compare yourself because there is no comparison, you're better than that. There is a role out there just for you and if you give up now you won't find it." His smile soaked up my tears and made me feel better.

"I know. I'm just tired and not giving myself enough time to prove myself. I haven't called my parents yet and I didn't want to until I could tell them something great but I really miss home."

"You found a job; I think that's pretty great. Your not sleeping on the street are you?"

"No, you're right. It's just my dad didn't want me to come and I was hoping for a little more to tell him so that he would be proud of me."

"Worry about making yourself proud." He finished up his beer just as I slurped up the last of my soda.

"Do you want me to walk you home?"

"That's okay, I'll take the bus."

"Well I'm afraid we stayed too long and the bus isn't running anymore."

"Oh, well maybe I better call a cab. I don't know how far of a walk it is to my house and plus I don't want you having to go out of your way."

Patrick came out from the back. "It was a good night kids. Come on I'll give you each a ride home."

We both smiled at that offer. Free! We locked up the bar and went out the back way to Patrick's car. I sat in front and Jake sat in the back along with his guitar. The ride to my apartment was silent. I directed Patrick to my apartment along the same route as the bus takes me but he showed me a quicker more direct way that I could possibly walk if I needed too just not at night. We were at my place in no time. I couldn't help but wonder where Jake lived but I didn't want to be so forward and ask him in front of Patrick. I stepped out and Patrick was the first to speak.

"I hope the events of the evening won't keep you from coming back Tara? I think you did a fine job for having no waitressing experience and trial or no trial you're hired if you want the job."

His oratory took me by surprise. "Yes, of course. I would love the job. Thank you." With that I glanced at Jake who was already smiling and I smiled. I closed the door and headed inside. The car drove off and I ran back to the front door just to peek at where the car would turn but it was already gone. Damn! I'll have to get up the courage and just ask him where he lived.

I stepped into the elevator and slid the iron gate shut. It slid with ease tonight as though it had just been oiled. I pushed five and it chugged along. It was so quiet except for the squeaking of the elevator and the buzzing of the flashing light above. It jolted to a stop and I pulled open the gate and stepped out onto our floor. No noise like before. No screaming, baby crying, music. Just silence. I rummaged through my purse as I walked to 541 looking for my keys. My tennis shoes patted and squeaked on the linoleum but then I heard click, click, click, of hard soled shoes walking. I stopped, quickly turning to look behind me but there was nothing there. I tried to stay calm. It's only in my head. I turned and started walking and again click, click, click. I walked faster and click, click, click. I found my key and reached the door. Fumbling with my keys I tried to stick it in the keyhole but it slipped to the floor, I turned and screamed but there was nothing there. I took a deep breath, looked down and picked up my key. I unlocked the bolt and then the handle and pushed but Melissa had the door chains on.

"Melissa. Can you come let me in?" She didn't come.

"Melissa, please come open the door." Finally I heard little feet pattering toward the door.

"Tara?"

"Yes, I'm sorry to wake you so late. But the chains are on and I can't get in."

"Oh." She quickly unlocked the chains and I was safely inside locking the door up behind me. "Hmm, not sure what we can do about that. You'll just have to wake me up I guess. Are you okay?"

"Yes, just a little freaked. I hate that hallway, it's so long. I always feel like someone is following me."

"Girl you are just tired. Come on let's get some sleep."

I was tired but first I decided to Jake's advice and call mom and dad. "Just a sec I need to make a call home." Melissa headed down the hallway and I grabbed the phone making myself comfortable on the couch.

"Hello" I heard my mom's tired voice on the other end.

"Hi mom, it's me, Tara."

"Tara! Oh my God, we've been so worried about you. Why didn't you call us sooner?"

"Mom, I told you I would call when I got settled."

"I know but you could have called when you got there. So you are in New York?"

"Yes. I found a place to stay and I actually found a job."

"Wow. Is it acting or singing?"

"More like acting. I'm waitressing at a bar."

"Oh. They don't know you very well do they?"

I laughed, "I already tripped and dropped drinks on some customers."

"And you still have the job?"

"I know amazing huh?"

"So are you doing okay?"

"I'm fine mom, just tired. I've been having some bad dreams and they've been keeping me from getting some good sleep."

"You always were one for talking in your sleep. Maybe it's the stress of the move?"

"Probably. Well I just wanted to check in with you. I'll talk to you later."

"Okay sweetie. Hey don't forget you've got family upstate New York, you get a chance you should make a trip up there and visit them."

"Yeah, yeah I know. I will."

"I'll call your Uncle and let him know to expect you soon."

"Mom! I said I'd go you don't have to make plans for me."

"Baby, they haven't seen you since you were a little girl. Practically your whole family lives on the reservation. You have cousins you've never even seen before."

"Mom, stop it please. I didn't say I wouldn't go, just don't force me okay."

"Fine, but I will mention to your Uncle Gerald that you are in the City. He'll want to know you are close by. He's the chief now you know?"

"Yes, I know. I'll talk to you later, okay."

"Bye dear."

"Bye."

I hung up and went to bed grouchy.

Chapter 5: The meeting

As the weeks passed I tried out for various roles and auditioned for some commercials but still no call backs. I was getting very frustrated. I was also getting better and better at being a waitress. Not exactly my goal but I'm sure the customers at the Kilt were happy I was no longer spilling drinks on them or screwing up their food orders.

Jake and I continued our late night talks. For one thing I was sure of and that was I loved him and his music but this I would never tell him. I hung out with him as much as I could. Work seemed to be the most logical place for us to spend time together however I did make it to a few of his other gigs when I wasn't working. Our relationship wasn't official but I considered him mine in my own mind.

I woke on a Saturday morning after another long Friday night at the Kilt. Surprisingly enough it was a dreamless night. I was thankful for that. No dreams about murdered girls last night. It had actually been awhile since I last dreamt of the little girl. Maybe my prophetic dreams were coming to an end. The light was shining brightly in my eyes. I yawned and looked over next to me; Melissa was already gone. I couldn't believe it was so late in the morning.

I warmed up a cup of coffee in the microwave and grabbed the paper to look for auditions. There were a few for a local play, non-paying, next week. Then I read they were looking for understudies for various Broadway shows but the auditions were today at 3 p.m. I was hoping I could get down there and back before work. This would be a great opportunity for me. I wish I had a chance to redo my pictures. Oh well, either I get it or I don't.

It was an interesting trip downtown. I took the subway, well a couple different trains. I got a little lost but who says New Yorkers aren't nice. I was able to get some directions and I finally made it before they closed up shop for the day.

"Tara Mason?" I heard my name and walked out onto the stage, nerves racing through my stomach. They handed me the music and the piano started to play. Thank goodness it was something I knew. It was "Honey Honey" from Mama Mia. I really played it up and acted out the song as I sang. Once I finished singing I thought they would want to hear some acting too but all I heard was, "Okay thank you. If we can use you we'll give you a call."

And that was it. It took me two hours to get here and it was over in less then five minutes. Next time I'll be sure there is more than one audition before I spend this much time traveling to the city. I chose to take it in stride and chalk it all up to a learning experience otherwise I'd be on the first bus back to Arizona. Right now I needed to get on the subway and get back to my neck of the woods so I wouldn't be late for work.

Starving and a little depressed I headed into the Kilt. I've pretty much been eating one meal a day, saving my appetite for when I was at work and taking advantage of my employee discount. Often times that discount amounted to free because Jim the cook would usually just bring me out something and I would eat it on the run and that way I wasn't really ordering so I didn't really have to pay.

The usual crowd was there at 4:30 p.m. Devin was at the bar talking with creepy Ed. That was my new nickname for him. That or Edzilla. I usually try to like everyone but Ed was just plain weird with his long lanky legs, white complexion, greasy black hair and piercing black inkwells for eyes. Him and Devin were such a huge contrast it was weird that they seemed to be such great friends. To each his own they say.

Since the place wasn't too busy I decided to sit and eat. Jim came out of the kitchen, saw me and walked over.

"I'll take "The best burger in town" again Jim." I smiled at him. He was a cute kid.

"No problem Tara, it will be out in a jiffy." He scuffled off to the kitchen.

A young girl not much older then I sat down across from me. She had beautiful dirty blonde straight hair with bangs and blue eyes.

"Hi I'm Jamie. I'm one of the other waitresses here."

"Oh. I'm Tara. I didn't know there was someone new. What a relief." I sighed, I was quite happy there were more of us. Each night I felt like I would drop dead from exhaustion. It always seemed like someone was calling in sick.

"Well I'm not exactly new I've just been off while. Actually I was supposed to train you but I just couldn't bring myself to come in after hearing about Sam."

I was confused. What did Sam have to do with training me to be a better waitress?

"I'm sorry but I'm not sure I follow."

"Her parents called Patrick asking if they knew where she was because she's missing."

Oh, is that all. Well I knew where she was, she was in the Hamptons with her professor.

"Didn't you know that she ran off to the Hamptons and is staying with her professor?" I wasn't sure I should say anything but I didn't want her to think she was missing.

"Well that's what we all thought too but apparently she never made it there."

"But that was months ago?" My eyes widened.

"I know." She leaned closer to me over the table.

"And they are just now looking for her, why didn't the professor say anything?"

By then my food had arrived but I was so entranced in our discussion that I barely touched it.

"Well apparently the professor is married and he assumed that Sam had changed her mind and didn't want to make a big production out of his mistress not meeting up with him for fear his wife would find out."

"But her parents, didn't they worry when they didn't hear from her."

"I guess they only recently started calling the apartment but there hasn't been any answer. Sam told them she was going on vacation after classes ended so they waited awhile before they started to get worried."

"So the police are involved now?" I was really starting to fear the worse for the girl I didn't even know except for in my dream. Even then I wasn't really sure it was her, I just heard the name Sam.

"Yes, they are questioning everyone that knew Sam." Her head hung down and I could tell she was upset.

"You two were friends?" I reached out and touched her hand.

"Yes. I begged her not to go but she wanted to get away from the bar scene here and was ready to" --finger quotes-- "settle down."

"I'm really sorry."

"Well just keep an eye and ear out. Listen to the customers and see if you catch any conversation about her."

"I will." By now my burger and fries were cold and it was time to get busy before Patrick busted me for sitting around. I took my plate to the bar and Devin smiled at me. "I heard you had an audition in the city today. I didn't know you were interested in being on Broadway?"

Was nothing private in this place? I snottily replied, "Why do you think I would move here from Arizona?" The day's events were forcing me to take my frustration out on Devin when all he was doing was asking a question. Even if it was a dumb question, it didn't mean I had a right to be a brat about it.

He sat up straight and arched his eyebrows, "Well I wasn't sure exactly why you moved to New York but I was going to say that I have a couple friends in the business that are actually working on getting a play financed. I'd be happy to introduce you to them. I'm sure they will be holding auditions soon."

Now I felt like crawling under a table. Here he was doing me the biggest favor ever and I was giving him attitude. My eyes lit up, "You're serious?"

"Of course, I wouldn't bring it up if I wasn't."

I was ready to jump out of my skin from excitement. The break I needed was sitting at the bar where I worked, what were the odds? I gave him a big hug.

"Thank you!" I whispered in his ear.

I went to back up but he held me a little longer. Under normal circumstances that would have freaked me out a little but he smelt so good, I could feel his strong arms around me, it was so comforting and he was so handsome and *Tara what about Jake,* my little angle snuck into my thoughts. I quickly pulled back but the smile was still on my face.

"When do you think I could meet them?" I said quickly trying to clear him from my mind.

He grabbed my hands and held them in front of him and smiled.

"Actually I was going to meet up with some friends tonight in the Village. I could give them a call and tell them I have someone I want them to meet and have them join us."

I smiled and then disappointment swept over me when I remembered, "Yeah but I have to work, it's Saturday night."

"Jamie is here. They'll be fine without you for a couple hours."

"Well let me see what Patrick says, okay?"

I immediately ran down the back hallway to Patrick's office. The door was closed and so I gave it a quick knock.

"Who is it?" Patrick's voice bellowed through the door.

"It's me, Tara." I sounded so meek.

"Come in!"

I slipped in.

"What's up Tara?"

"I was wondering if I could leave a little early tonight."

"How early?"

"10pm"

"10! That's when we get our second rush!"

I gulped down my nerves and continued, "Well Devin offered to introduce me to a couple contacts he has for a play in the city and it would really help me a lot to meet some of the people in the business."

"We got a stage here. You can act all you want up there and even do some singing."

I stood there, silent, he couldn't be serious.

"Agh! Go! You young girls all think you're going to make it big."

I left quickly before he could change his mind.

Devin was still sitting at the bar when I returned wrapping my apron around me.

"You're smiling. He must have said yes."

"Yep!" I squealed.

"Great! We'll leave from here."

Oh great I was going to meet these people smelling like the bar and looking like crap. Seeing my worry, Devin interrupted my thoughts, "Don't worry. You look great." He flashed those jade green eyes at me and all my worries disappeared. I heard the bar door open but it didn't break the gaze I had on Devin as I was caught up in his mesmerizing good looks. However, Devin's eyes flicked over to the door and his smile faded, his gaze turned to stone. I turned to see who could change his demeanor so drastically. Walking in wearing his checkered jacket, black knit hat and guitar on his back was my Jake. Why the fury in Devin's face?

"Miss, can we get some service?" Someone called out.

I needed to get to work so I didn't have time to dig deeper into this mystery.

I felt like a pro tonight compared to how I started in the beginning. Devin stayed at the bar nursing his drink and Jake began to play his guitar. I headed to the bar to get Jake a water.

Desperately wanting to know what the connection was between Devin and Jake I asked nonchalantly, "So Devin do you know Jake?"

My question seemed to take him by surprise. He didn't answer me right away.

"Hey, Ed can I get a water please?" I waited and looked at Devin. Finally he took a breath and looked at me. "We used to hang out when we were younger."

"Oh." He didn't offer anymore and it seemed like a pretty lame answer. I guess I was expecting more after the reaction I saw on his face when Jake walked in tonight. I didn't have time to pry so I took the water and walked to the table closest to the stage. Jake really was an accomplished musician. I was surprised he chose to spend his evenings playing here. I was sure he could find better gigs then this place. I set his water down and he glanced over at me and smiled. After 15 minutes more of playing he took a break and I timed my break at just the same time and headed to his table.

"I've got great news!" I was practically bouncing in my seat from excitement. I couldn't wait to tell Jake about my new connection and tonight's meeting.

He smiled at me and took a drink of his water. I waited patiently. He sat back, "Well spit it out, what's the news?"

"Devin is taking me tonight to meet some friends of his that are producing a play in the city," I squealed with excitement that quickly diminished when I saw the smile fade from his face.

Jake looked over my shoulder toward the bar. He didn't say anything but I could see in his eyes that he wasn't even happy for me. His eyes continued to stare off, no smile in them.

"Jake, isn't that great news?" What was wrong, why wasn't he happy for me?

"Tara, are you sure that's the best way to get in the business? I mean you don't even know who these people are?" He looked at me with all seriousness.

"Jake, how else do people get in without a little inside help? Devin is going out on a limb for me with these people. He hasn't even heard me sing or seen me act and he's going to introduce me to the producers of a play!" I was still very excited and Jake's coldness wasn't going to take that away.

"Exactly, Tara. Now ask yourself why would he do that? Don't be so naive." Jake stood up and slammed his chair into the table and headed to the bathroom. He was angry. I've never seen him act this way before. I sat there dumbfounded. I thought for sure Jake would be supportive. Now I was angry. I got up and started back to work. I hustled around fueled by my fury over Jake's reaction to my news. Who was he to judge why someone would do something nice for me. He was just jealous.

Jake began his next set and it was already 9:30 p.m. I told Jamie about my plans to leave early and she was fine with it. She said that Devin did have connections in the city and was even working with Sam but she really wasn't that serious about becoming an actress she just wanted to go to all the cool parties.

At 9:45 I headed to the bathroom to freshen up as best as I could. I took my hair out of my pony tail and tried to brush the bump out. Ugh! It was useless. No matter how hard I tried I still looked like I just came from work. Jamie came in when I didn't come out after 15 minutes.

"Everything okay?" she asked nicely.

"No! I look like crap and I'm supposed to make a good impression. I'm about ready to just cancel." I slumped up against the bathroom stall.

"Here let me help you." Jamie took out her makeup bag and began applying make-up, something I hardly ever did.

"Just a little, I'm not used to wearing make-up." I was a little apprehensive. I didn't like other people making me up. Next she took the top layer of my hair and began braiding it and it fell over my bump.

She smiled. "There now it will stay out of your eyes and cover your bump." I turned to look in the mirror. I couldn't believe the transformation.

"Oh Jamie, how can I thank you! This is wonderful" and I gave her a big hug.

She pried herself loose of my bear hug, "No problem! Now go knock'em dead."

I headed out to the bar and stole a glance at Jake and caught him looking at me. He stopped playing which stopped me in my tracks. He jumped off the stage and was walking towards me just as Devin was headed for me. Devin reached me first.

With his green eyes gleaming he smiled. "You look beautiful. You ready?"

I smiled back at him nervously, his overt attention always made me a little weak in the knees.

Jake jumped between us, his back to Devin. I hadn't realized that Jake was actually taller than Devin. I guess it was because Devin was so much more muscular I assumed he was taller too.

He placed both hands on my shoulders. "Tara you don't have to do this." I could see the pleading in his eyes. Why was he acting like this, for goodness sake, it was dinner and a meeting. The bar immediately turned quiet as all eyes were on us.

"Jake, please stop it, you're embarrassing me," I urged.

"I think the young lady has made up her mind." Devin reached around Jake and grabbed my arm. Jake didn't move and I was forced to pull away from his grasp and walk around him. I couldn't escape the anger in his eyes.

We walked out of the bar and I glanced quickly back to see Jake standing at the bar, his gaze full of rage. Was it directed at me? Why was he so angry?

The evening air was cool and Devin directed me to a red Ferrari parked two spots down. Why would anyone hang out at the Pipers Kilt when you had the money to drive a hot car like this? So far the people in this city made no sense to me at all. Devin, being the gentlemen that he was, opened the door for me and I slid down into the soft supple leather seat. Once I was settled he closed the door and walked around to his side. I was still pondering Jake's reaction. He acted like a jealous boyfriend. Why was he acting so protective?

Devin slid into the driver's seat with ease as if the car were molded to his rock hard body. My gaze wandered up from his strapping legs to his taut stomach, up towards his chest which was better defined under his tight t-shirt that was covered by another button down shirt which was open midway. This allowed me to see some of his six-pack abs protruding through his t-shirt. My gaze sauntered past his chest on up to his face and I caught him smiling at me, those green eyes burning into me and my face turned beet red, my stomach flipped, as I just now realized he was watching me the whole time as I sat here boldly checking him out. How embarrassing.

To assuage my embarrassment he did not respond to my ogling but just started the car, and the radio blared classical which was totally unexpected.

He hit the gas and I was forced back into my seat. I'd never, ever been in a car this cool. The ride was a bit rougher then I had imagined but I knew how cool we must look and this was way better then riding the subway. Devin filled the drive with small talk, asking me about my hometown. Since he asked most of the questions I did most of the talking. It wasn't long and we were at the restaurant. I was trying desperately not to let my nerves get the best of me. I needed to be calm, cool, collected and klutz free.

Devin held his arm out for me and I linked mine through his. He looked so debonair even in his causal clothes. We walked into the restaurant, through the dining room and out onto the patio where there was a large group of people gathered outside enjoying drinks and appetizers. Devin squeezed my hand and I glanced up and saw him smiling confidently at me. "Don't worry, you'll do just fine." He was very reassuring.

We walked out onto the patio, the breeze made the temperature just perfect. The atmosphere was quite elegant, with lit lanterns, white lights and green garland with white roses draped across the railings. Each glass table held a beautiful white rose centerpiece. The table settings included black square plates with the napkins folded into a fan. No one seemed to be eating a main course just snacking on appetizers. There was some light music playing in the background and everyone seemed to be having a nice time.

A waiter offered us both some Champaign. I wasn't much of a drinker but I decided to fit in with the rest and took a glass. Devin stopped to talk to a few people and I stood there smiling, not really knowing what to say. I glanced around at the people and noticed that they all seemed to be staring at me. They were probably wondering who I was or why Devin was hanging out with someone so young.

Finally my thoughts were interrupted. "Ah Devin you come at last," an older gentlemen held out his hand and greeted Devin. He looked to be around 60, with white hair and a nice tan that made him look extremely healthy for his age. "And this must be your newly acquired talent you so anxiously wanted us to meet." He held out his hand to me. I took it and he brought my hand up to his lips, looked me in the eye, and lightly kissed the back of my hand. Only in the movies have I ever seen anyone do this, I bowed my head and blushed slightly. "Oh she is a beauty. I believe she will find work in this city." He dropped my hand but continued to look me in the eyes "Your name sweetness?"

My voice, I was so nervous I was afraid nothing would come out when I spoke. "Tara."

"Yes, Tara, beautiful name." Then loudly he said "Everyone I would like you to meet Tara, she will be joining us this evening, she is our guest." I was stunned at the loud announcement.

"Please join us won't you?" He motioned to the table. I couldn't move. I looked up to Devin. He looked down at me expectantly. Devin had his arm around my back and gently pushed me forward. I sat at their table. They were all mostly aged 40 and older. Devin and I were the youngest there.

"So how do you like our great city, Tara?" another guest at the table interjected.

"Um, it's wonderful and overwhelming. I just moved here."

"Yes, Devin tells us you are from Arizona."

"Yes."

"Well this hopefully is an exciting time for you as it is for us, having you join us this evening."

What was so special about me joining them? I was the one that was trying to make a good impression and it seemed they were more eager to meet me.

The drinks continued to flow, Devin never left my side. He held me close to him almost like he was my protector, his arm around me. It felt nice to be watched over. Occasionally he would run his fingers along my arm. I would catch him smiling down at me. Everyone seemed very interested in where I grew up and hung on my every word. Devin kept pouring me Champaign which tasted amazing. Usually I didn't like alcohol but this was really good. I wasn't sure how many glasses I had drank since Devin kept refilling my glass before it was empty. I was beginning to feel a little loopy.

"Excuse me please; I need to use the restroom." I got up and could feel the effects of the alcohol. Devin followed me into the main dining room. I turned to him. "Devin really, I can go alone."

"Yes, Tara, I know, I was just showing you where it is. It can get a little confusing in here." He pointed me in the right direction and I concentrated very hard not to stumble on my way fighting the affects of the alcohol.

Normally my danger signal would be going off but the affects of the Champaign were too strong and I was feeling quite comfortable among the odd assembly of characters. But I knew it was time to go home. My face was flushed from too much alcohol and I was so tired.

I took my time in the bathroom, contemplating splashing cold water on my face but not wanting to ruin my make-up so I took a deep breath and decided I would tell Devin I was ready to go. I opened the door to head out of the bathroom and Devin was standing right there.

"Devin, I said I could go alone." I was getting a little perturbed with his protective nature. He grabbed my hand and pulled me into the corner.

My coldness didn't seem to damper his mood, he was smiling. "I couldn't wait. Guess what?" He tucked his finger under my chin to bring my face up towards his.

"They loved you and want to give you one of the main parts in their play." He was smiling down at me full of excitement.

"Oh my god, no way?"

"Yes Way" He dropped his hand and wrapped both arms around me to give me a big hug. "I told you they would love you and not to worry."

I hugged him back. I didn't know how I could repay him. This was amazing. The alcohol was making me feel so comfortable in his arms and he pulled me closer to him. I looked up and his lips were right there. *Tara, no.* But I couldn't help myself. I stood up on my tiptoes and kissed him.

He kissed me back and he smelled sweet and musky he took my breath away. I reached my hand up and wound my fingers in his hair and his mouth pressed violently against mine as he hungrily kissed me. Instinct took over and I pulled him harder against me. He leaned into me, pinning me against the wall of the hallway to the bathroom. This startled me slightly as I had never, ever been in this situation before. His kiss was intoxicating, his lips were hot and moist, and I heard a low groan as he slid his tongue inside my mouth. I could barely move his full weight pressing against me. He moved his leg between my thighs and my stomach flipped, my heart was pounding out of my chest. Both of his hands cupped my face and he continued to kiss me deeply. His thigh rose higher between my legs so that my groin pressed hard against him and the jolt I felt was enough to make me catch my breath. I thought I was going to faint the feelings were so overpowering and for the first time in my life I felt as though I would give of myself freely. I wanted him more than anything to take me, the feeling was exhilarating and then he stopped and pulled away. I opened my eyes barely catching my breath, searching for an answer to why.

He creased his eyebrows together as if he were in pain. "Tara, I'm sorry. I just. I know it's the Champaign and I just don't want you to regret kissing me or more. As much as I am loving this, tonight is not the right time."

I couldn't argue with his logic but it didn't make me less hurt or embarrassed. I dropped my hands and my head, pushed him away and walked out of the hall.

"Tara, please don't be mad at me. That's the last thing I want is for you to be angry with me." Devin grabbed my hand and tried to stop me.

I whipped around on him, "Please Devin, I'm ready to go." I continued to walk towards the exit. Honestly I wasn't mad at him, I was thankful for his obedience, I was mad at myself. Give me a little Champaign and I'm ready to give away my virginity and forsake Jake in the process.

Once outside, Devin opened the car door for me and I plopped down. I could still feel the effects of the alcohol, my head was spinning. I knew Devin was right and he was being a total gentleman. I should be relieved I was with him and not some other more dangerous man like the frat boy from my first night. Devin hopped in the car and we were on our way home. I couldn't believe I was just kissing Devin. I haven't even kissed Jake yet.

It was a silent ride home. I was ashamed and felt like I betrayed Jake even though I had made no promises to him. Devin turned on the radio and the late night talk show was on. The D.J. was taking calls about all the recent murders and missing girls in the city.

"I think this city is going to hell. The police need to get busy and start finding out who is behind these young girls' murders. We're tired of living in fear!"

"I think it's some sort of cult or serial killer."

The D.J. cut in "Well the police have reported that there isn't a connection between neither the murders, nor the missing person cases so it doesn't seem as though there is one person or group responsible."

Devin changed the station. I thought of poor Sam and wondered if she was now one of their missing person's cases.

It was 2 a.m. when we arrived at my apartment. Devin pulled up in front and cut the engine. I reached for the door handle but Devin reached over and put his hand on my thigh.

"Wait." His voice was husky.

All I wanted to do was go bury my head in my pillow and not wake up for a couple days but I turned to look at him, his face was right next to mine.

"What?"

"Tara, I really do think you are special and what you think of me is important. I don't want the evening to end with you being angry at me." He really did sound sincere. But he was misconstruing my anger as directed towards him when actually I was just angry at myself. Now I felt guilty that he thought I was angry at him when actually I was thankful for his gentlemanly behavior otherwise my first time would have been in a bathroom hallway. Ugh!

"No I'm sorry Devin. I shouldn't have kissed..." Devin leaned forward, pulled me to him and kissed me. Now it was my turn to be shocked. The ride home had given me time to think about what I had done and how wrong the kiss was and now it was happening again. "No!" I pulled away. "You're right Devin, we shouldn't, not now." I turned to open the door but again he stopped me and held my arm. I was beginning to feel a little scared. "Devin let me go." When I looked at him he was smiling his devilish grin and those jade green eyes were dancing with excitement.

"Tara, just a little kiss goodnight?" He tilted his head and smiled sweetly. I couldn't resist. I leaned in to give him a quick peck on the cheek and he turned his mouth towards mine and grabbed me behind my head. He kissed me hungrily. All the nerves in my body caught on fire. I was both excited and scared. "Come home with me" he whispered as he kissed me along my neck. His kisses were leading him down my chest and I gasped for breath. I leaned back trying to get away from him but this actually gave him more access. He moved his hand from the back of neck and pulled my shirt aside as his mouth searched for my breast. Now the danger signals were hard to miss. I knew I could not be alone with Devin. I shot straight up.

"I have to go!" and with that the car door was open and I was headed to the front door of my apartment building. Once inside I turned to see the taillights of the Ferrari speeding away.

I let out a big sigh.

"I see you made it home safely."
I screamed and turned around. Jake was standing in my lobby. Oh my God, how much did he see? "Jake! What are you doing here?"

"I just wanted to make sure that you made it home safely." He was leaning up against the wall in the lobby with his arms crossed over his chest.

"Oh really? Well your concern is not needed; I'm perfectly fine thank you." I blasted past him. How dare he check up on me? Actually I wasn't worth his kindness, not after tonight.

He followed after me. "Tara. Please. I just don't think Devin has your best interest in mind."

I stopped and turned to look at him. "Well I beg to differ. He happened to introduce me to some very important people tonight that have offered me a leading role in their play."

By now we were face to face. "What play Tara? What's the name of it? What role is it?" I saw anger in his face for the first time directed at me.

"Jake, if you have a problem with Devin why don't you just come out with it instead of insinuating that there is some ulterior motive to his being nice to me." Actually I was beginning to think there was an ulterior motive myself but I wasn't ready to admit it just yet.

I stood there and waited. No answer.

"Well?"

Still, no answer, he just looked down at his feet. I felt for him. He seemed torn, like he desperately wanted to tell me but something was keeping him from it.

"Fine, until you can give me a good reason not to associate with Devin then he will continue to be my friend. Good night."

Where I got my courage to be so mean to him tonight I have no idea. I decided I would take the stairs, I was so angry. I needed to work off my extra energy.

I heard the lobby doors close and assumed Jake had left. Would I regret this conversation in the morning? I hoped not.

I climbed the stairs, struggling on the last few flights. I opened the door to floor 5. The door opened up close to our apartment, no walking down the long corridor. Mental note: Definitely taking the stairs from now on.

I knocked on the door because I knew Melissa would have the chains on and have to come unlock the door whether I used my key or not. We were going to have to figure out a system of some sort, I really hated waking her up like this. After repeated knocks no one opened the door. I tried my key and the door handle moved but the bolt was keeping me from opening the door. I knocked again.

Behind me I heard footsteps. I didn't want to turn around. I knew I was awake so why was I having these visions and hearing things when I was awake. The steps got closer. I knocked on the door harder.

"Sam! Get back here!"

"No, leave me alone Devin!"

My eyes widened. Hearing Devin's name took me by surprise. What did he have to do….

Click

Clank

The door suddenly opened and interrupted my thoughts. Melissa was standing there, hair disheveled.

"I'm sorry to wake you Melissa. I'll think of something so I don't keep doing this to you each night."

"It's okay. I feel bad that I keep you waiting out here. I honestly didn't hear you."

I quickly walked in while our conversation progressed. I headed to the kitchen looking for something to eat. In all my nervous excitement I realized that I didn't really eat anything at the dinner, just drank Champaign and that made me incredibly thirsty. I still couldn't believe what I heard out in the hallway or was it just in my head? The voices I heard brought back the conversation I had with Jake and now the seed of doubt had been planted. Did Devin have something to do with Sam's disappearance?

Melissa followed me to the kitchen in my hunt for snacks. "Melissa, did you know that Sam is missing? Her parent's haven't heard from her and I guess Jamie at work says the professor guy didn't hear from her either."

"Yeah, I got the message from her parents. They had been calling but I didn't return their calls in the beginning because I knew Sam didn't tell them about this guy. I feel really bad for them and wish I knew more."

By now Melissa was sitting on the counter and I was warming up a slice of cold pizza in the microwave.

"So where were you out so late?" She looked at me suspiciously.

"Nowhere I shouldn't be if that's what you're getting at." I took a bite of my pizza. Mmmm. I'd never tell Patrick but he may have the best hamburgers in town but next door Pizza Haven had the best pizza in town. "Devin took me out to meet some of his contacts and they are considering me for one of the lead roles." I could hardly keep in my excitement.

"Wow! That's great! What play is it?" Melissa was genuinely excited but her question bummed me out since it reminded me that Jake asked the same thing for which I had no answer.

"Well I don't know exactly but it's off Broadway but not too far off." I smiled. "Once they get financing I will find out." I finished up my pizza.

"Well good for you Tara. Good luck…or is it break a leg." She winked at me.

"I'll take either one at this point." I yawned and headed to the bathroom, Melissa jumped in bed.

Tomorrow was Sunday, my first day off. Of course I've only worked a couple days but each night was so late, later then I was used to staying up. I was looking forward to sleeping in and not doing anything. By the time I finished in the bathroom and headed to bed Melissa was snoring. I pushed her arm and leg over to her side. I curled up under the blanket. It was quiet, well just Melissa's snoring. I was happy. I was living my dream, almost. I hadn't found an acting job or singing gig but I was working and I had my own place. Jake was on my mind, I was feeling a little guilty for taking my anger out on him.

I knew I was over tired, the sleep grabbed me and held me down. I had to talk myself through it: *breath, be calm, and let it take you Tara.* It was so dark, I was paralyzed, and the force was pulling me down past the darkness into a scene of which I had no choosing. Finally the darkness released its hold on me and I opened my eyes. I was standing in some sort of dark, cold, chamber.

"This could be the chance of a lifetime Sam. You will be perfect for the role."

I thought I recognized the voice but I couldn't see the face.

65 Dream Catcher by Tricia Currier

"I told you I didn't want to perform here. This place gives me the creeps."

Was that Sam? I'd never seen her before so I had no idea but I could only assume.

"It's a special performance for some very important people. If you do this you will have your pick of the best roles."

It was if I were speaking to her, once again I was inside the body of someone else. I tried to look around but it was dark. Around the windowless walls were lit torches.

"I told you I wasn't really interested in acting anymore and besides I'm leaving soon." She pouted and swung her head around.

I could feel the rage building inside me. "I spent all this time trying to get this organized and you just want to walk out on me."

I reached out to touch her shoulder and she pulled away from me.

"Sam! Don't do that!"

The anger in my voice caused her to turn and look at me. She was afraid now just how I liked them before it was time to end our relationship.

She began walking away.

"Sam."

She began to run. "Just leave me alone."

I started to run after her. "Wait Sam"

She was heading toward a dark corridor. Statuesque black robed creatures lined the walls. Their arms began reaching out pulling at her as she tried to run through.

"Stay away from me!" She was scared; I could see it in her face.

I slowed to a walk now, knowing she wouldn't go far now. "I won't hurt you if you just come back and do what I say." I was close enough to smell her fear. Oh this was just how I planed.

She turned to me. Finally surrender. "Never!" She spat in my face.

"You Bitch! Your choices are gone and you will be our sacrifice tonight!"

The arms holding on to her were bright white against the black robes. Menacing groans escaped from under their hoods between incoherent chanting. Sam's eyes were wide with panic.

"Sacrifice, you said you wanted me to do a play for you, what's going on?"

Though she struggled the robed monsters easily forced her into the cavernous room of shadows and red flames. She screamed but it was muffled.

"Sam, you were given a choice. Perform or be our sacrifice. You made your choice and now you must die for it."

They strung her up between two wood poles that seemed to magically appear atop a cement and rock slab. She was crying and yelling "Please No, I'll do what you want, I promise!"

"Yes exactly Sam, you are doing what I want. We had wanted a little entertainment before the main course but I believe my guests are hungry now and tired of waiting."

I looked up through the darkness and under one of the hoods I saw the familiar silver hair and healthy tanned face of the same gentlemen I met this very night. Loudly the hooded monsters began chanting again; they were giving praise in some other language or tongue. What was going on?

"I'll make this easy Sam and take only one thing from you…your heart."

Then he wielded a knife straight into her chest and her blood spilled.

I sat straight up in bed. I was soaked with sweat. These dreams were going to be the death of me. I was hardly getting any sleep and I was so full of anxiety over the possible meaning of these dreams. Was any of this possible? I looked over next to me and the bed was empty. I looked at my clock and it said 8am. Man that was a fast night. I rolled over and tried to go back to sleep but it was useless.

Melissa already had coffee brewing. I got up and poured a cup and made myself comfortable on the couch along with the paper. The news section was reporting on the latest developments on the murders which were basically nothing. No new leads. I kept seeing that knife go into Sam's chest. Hungry guests, were they going to eat her heart? It's only a dream Tara I had to keep reminding myself.

"Melissa I was thinking of checking out that park you sold me on and going for a run, want to come?" I had to yell as she was headed into the bathroom.

She came out brushing her teeth. "You're serious?" She mumbled, toothpaste bubbles dripping down the corners of her mouth.

"Yeah, it's nice outside and I haven't been on a run since I got here."

"Uh, not to hurt your feelings, but I'm not a runner. Actually, I don't exercise. The most exercise I get is shopping in SoHo. When you're ready to go shopping I'm there for you." She held up a big thumbs up and walked back into the bathroom.

"Okay, well if you change your mind I'm going around 10 a.m."
Ring, ring.
"hello"
"Hi, it's Devin."
"Hi!"
"I just wanted to call and make sure you weren't still mad at me."

I had forgotten about our uncomfortable moments last night, now I was feeling a bit embarrassed after the alcohol was out of my system I was remembering more of my actions.

"Of course not, if anything I should apologize."
"Tara, it's not necessary. What are your plans today?"
"I'm thinking of taking a day off and going for a run."
"Oh, well give me a call later and maybe we can get some dinner."
"Okay, we'll see." I still felt weird. I mean he was totally hot but for some reason it just didn't feel right now and I think last night it was just the alcohol. My heart still belonged to Jake.

I hung up and decided to get my running gear on. I took off down the stairs and out of our apartment. I knew I could find this park; hopefully it wasn't too far away.

I clicked on my Ipod and let the music fill my head. What a nice release, nothing but music, no bad dreams, no stress, no guys, no murders. I began my jog while searching for the park; I just couldn't help it once the music started.

Jogging on the sidewalk wasn't the best but it wasn't long before I spotted the green trees. The park was huge and there was a nice running path. People were walking and riding their bikes and in the open field a bunch of guys were playing soccer. It was a wonderful sunny day but a bit muggy which was more difficult for me to catch my breath then jogging in Arizona. It felt so good to break a sweat.

I made it once around the path and was heading for my second lap when up ahead I thought I saw Devin. Had he come here knowing I would be here after our phone conversation? Then I saw Jake and started to slow down. What was he doing here with Devin no less? I slowed to a fast walk and tried to peek into the trees where they were standing. They weren't looking my way so I wasn't sure if they even knew I was here. From what I could see they looked like they were arguing.

I began to jog again then I saw Devin push Jake and I started to run faster. Jake shoved Devin back and now I could hear them slightly.

"Get away from me or you'll be sorry!" I could hear Devin yell.

"Devin, I'm not trying to start anything. I'm just asking you to please stay away from her," Jake pleaded.

"Why Jake, you afraid she'll want me instead of you?"

"You know that's not it. There are plenty of wannabe actresses out there for you to get your claws on you don't need Tara too!"

"Jake, I offered my assistance and she wanted it, now if she wants a little more than that, how can I help that?"

Jake threw a punch and the fight began. By the time I reached them they were wrestling on the ground.

I was close enough now to yell at them both "Stop it, NOW!"

Their surprise stopped them from throwing anymore punches and they both turned to look at me. Devin smiled and Jake looked at him.

"Jake what are you doing?" He turned to look at me with disbelief on his face.

"Me?"

"I'm a big girl I don't need you looking out for me."

I started to run again, I couldn't believe they were fighting over me. As I ran off I could hear Jake.

"You knew she was here, that's why you said to meet you here. You're such an ass!"

Had Devin set Jake up trying to make him look like a jealous boyfriend? My nice relaxing run was turning into more stress. I headed home. Melissa was gone when I got home. The light on the machine was blinking. I pushed play and headed to the kitchen to grab some water.

"Tara, its Jake. I'm sorry about today. I'm not trying to look out for you, well I am but I'm not trying to…, I don't know what I'm trying to do, I just want you to be okay and I'm sorry if I'm interfering in your life." Click.

Now I felt bad. There was a note stuck to the fridge from Melissa. *You and I are going out tonight! My treat!*

Hmmm this ought to be interesting. Who goes out on a Sunday night? Well really it would be the only night I could go out. I decided to spend the rest of my day just chilling getting ready for my big night out. But first I had to call Jake back and tell him I was sorry.

Chapter 6: Big Night Out

"Pleeease Tara. Let me help you get ready. You can't wear jeans and a t-shirt to these places. They won't let us in!" Melissa's urging was giving me a complex. Were my clothes that boring? I just didn't like the attention but I suppose one night of letting someone else take control of my wardrobe wouldn't hurt.

"Okay, but not too over the top."

"Yeeeeah!" She squealed like a little girl.

We were getting ready for our venture into the city, well the out-skirts of the city. Melissa was going to give me my first clubbing experience. She was over the moon and I was a nervous wreck. For one thing I was only 19 and she was 20, so I had no idea how she thought we were going to get into these places. Plus as much as I wanted to sing and act I was a little nervous about being in front of people, especially dancing.

"Here it will take the edge off," she stood there with two shot glasses. I took one and she held the other up in the air.

"To our first night out in New York together!" Our glasses clinked together and I threw my head back and let the liquor splash into my mouth. I really wasn't much of a drinker. I tried to look cool but it was just impossible as the hot liquid burned as it slid down my throat. I grimaced and squeezed my eyes shut. Melissa just laughed.

She shoved me towards the bathroom. "Come on lets get started, this may take a while." She giggled as she tugged on my shirt.

Two hours later what emerged was someone I did not even know existed. My dark brown hair was unclipped and allowed to fall down my back in wild curls, my face was made up to make me look as though I were a runway model and my clothes well that's another story altogether. Melissa convinced me that in order to fit in yet stand out at these clubs I had to wear something of hers. She had me wear a backless halter top, shiny silver, with black shorts and here's the kicker, black thigh-high velvet boots. My mom would die if she saw me. I blushed when I peered into the mirror at the stranger before me; I looked like I belonged in a magazine. Melissa was beside herself with pride over her masterpiece and couldn't stop fidgeting over me.

"You look so hot Tara! Just wait until you see how many guys fall all over you tonight." Her smile was beaming with satisfaction.

To be honest with you I really only wanted one guy to fall all over me and that was Jake. However that wouldn't be happening tonight because Jake was playing at some club. I text Jake and told him I was going clubbing with Melissa and all he said was "Be Safe." I'd wished he begged me not to go so I could give Melissa a reason for me to stay home. I really wasn't the clubbing type but now after Melissa's magic touch I sure looked the part.

Our subway ride to the first nightclub was uneventful. Everyone pretty much kept to themselves. I thought for sure we would stand out and people would stare but I'm pretty sure that I could have walked down the isle naked and no one would bat an eyelash. After 40 minutes we were outside the first club.

"Would you calm down, they won't let us in if you act guilty." Melissa was a pro; I on the other hand was a panicky mess; practically sweating my make-up off. We got to the front of the line and the bouncer asked us how old we were.

"22, 23" I tried to smile but it looked more like a grimace. He looked me over and smiled. Could he see right through me, did he know I was only 19?

"Okay, you're in."

We both walked in, heads held high, like we just pulled off a major heist.

The music was so loud we had to use hand signals to communicate. The first stop was the bathroom. We had to see what affect our trip down here had on our appearance. I was a little worried since I couldn't seem to stop sweating.

Once we freshened up we headed to the bar. I really had no idea what to order this was all so new to me. When Melissa ordered and the bartender looked at me I just pointed to her as in I'll have what she's having.

Alcohol was alcohol to me, it all really didn't taste that good. We grabbed our drinks and found a table. The music was more punk. The people were young but the garb was a little more Goth looking. We finished our drinks and headed for the next club.

It was pretty much the same routine for most of the evening, dancing now and again, saving some money with guys buying us drinks. I was really starting to get drunk and Melissa was pretty drunk too. I was glad we were taking the subway home. The last place we went to was a little trendier. Young people with money to burn showed off their riches in designer clothes, shoes and purses. I really started to let lose here either because I felt safer for some reason or maybe it was the alcohol that was making me feel less inhibited. I saw Melisa leave the dance floor with a guy and I kept dancing with my partner. When she didn't come back after about five minutes I went to our table and sipped on my drink. Where is she? I decided to check the bathroom. No Melissa. I headed back to our table and someone had bought me another drink, this one had an umbrella in it. I loved those umbrellas, they were so cute. I took a sip and this drink had a hint of salt mixed with some kind of fruit concoction. I almost downed the whole thing when a couple guys came and sat next to me.

"Hey sweet thing, you want to come party with us?"

"No. I'm waiting for my friend." I was starting to feel really dizzy. I hope Melissa comes soon. I really need to get home.

"You okay sweetheart. Do you need us to take you home?"

"I'm fine and no I don't need your help thank you very much." I tried to get up but fell back down. My legs felt so heavy.

"Here let us help you." They both stood up and each grabbed one of my arms.

I struggled against them and yanked myself out of their grasp. I saw the exit sign and willed myself toward the light. I bumped into other people as I tried to make it outside. I couldn't believe how drunk I was, I couldn't walk straight, and I felt so dizzy and sleepy. I turned and the guys were following me.

"Stay away from me!" I yelled as loud as I could.

That stopped them in their tracks as other party goers stared in their direction. I was able to make it outside. I took a deep breath but I still felt terrible. I stumbled to the sidewalk and leaned up against the light post. I wrapped my arms around it and held on for dear life. I could feel the weight pulling at me again, sleep was inevitable but I was fighting it, then my eyes closed.

Suddenly I was back in the bar. It was if someone had pressed rewind. But it wasn't me doing all the partying and dancing it was some other young girl. What am I doing? Why was I watching her, watching her dance? I was targeting her. I didn't want to move but I couldn't help it. I walk up to her and try to talk to her, buy her a drink. I look down and again the boots and hands that aren't mine. She agrees to a drink. I go to the bar and order a mixed drink that I've never even heard of, reach into my jacket pocket and pull out a vile and pour in a powder and mix it with the straw. I walk back to the blonde, cuddle up close to her as I hand her the drink. She sips at it and I wait anxiously for the drug to take affect. I could see she was drunk. I lightly caress her face with my hand and she smiles. Her eyes close. I stand and pull her up next to me and she leans heavily on me as we walk out of the bar.

Next we're in a candle lit room. It was still so dark that I didn't see the other people come out of the shadows wearing black robes. They took the girl and lay her on a concrete slab surrounded with even more candles. It looked stained with blood. *Oh my God, please, please wake up. The weight against me was too heavy and I didn't have the strength to push myself out of my dream. I was stuck, forced to take part in this person's sick world. What is this place, what are these people?*

They began chanting and the girl who was barely lucid tried to get up. I reached over and slapped her and she smacked her head on the concrete. I grabbed the neckline of her dress and yanked it, ripping it from her, exposing her breasts. She just lay there, unable to move from the power of the drug. One of the cloaked figures moved next to her and began feeling her breasts with bony white hands and then started kissing her. Soon others joined in and I just sat back and watched. I couldn't pull myself away. I was disgusted and frightened. Then I felt a warm excitement and I could only assume it was from the body I was in. Watching them caress and fondle the young lady was more then I could bear. I tried to look away but suddenly I saw crimson on their faces it glowed in the candlelight and the young lady moaned. They were biting her! The chanting grew louder and the blood flowed faster. I thrust myself forward and finally I was free from the body that held me prisoner that forced me to watch this heinous act.

I had a voice now "STOP! PLEASE STOP! YOU'RE KILLING HER!" No one could hear me and I knew that even if they could they wouldn't listen. I had to wake up. I needed to get out of this horrid place. I looked around to find a way out and standing in the doorway was the little girl.

"They killed her and now you must kill for her."

"What does that mean? Why do you keep telling me that? Can't you say anything else? Get me the hell out of here!"

The girl turned and ran and I ran after her.

"Tara, is that you? Tara?" I could vaguely hear a voice. I couldn't believe I was still standing. Where was I? I could barely open my eyes and then I saw Jake's face.

"Jake?" My grasp on the lamp post slipped apart and I fell back towards the sidewalk but Jake caught me before I could hurt myself.

"Tara, what happened?" I could hear the concern in his voice but I couldn't see it on his face because I just couldn't keep my eyes open. "Tara, wake up. Where is Melissa?"

My eyes opened then. Melissa, where was Melissa? She left the dance floor with a couple guys but I hadn't seen her since.

"Swe….were dancing" I couldn't get my mouth to move right. "Shwas with guys. Didn't come back." I was getting very scared now.

"Did anyone touch your drink Tara?"

My eyes shot to him my brow furrowed, "What do you mean?"

"I mean did anyone drug you? I think something more is wrong then just too many drinks tonight."

"Mmmm. Don't know. I went to the bathroom…" My head fell back and my eyes closed.

"Tara!" Jake shook me violently. I opened my eyes wide, trying to concentrate.

Slowly as if I were trying to remember something from weeks ago, "When I came back new fruity drink with an umbrella" I had a big smile now as I remembered the pretty, fruity, drink. But Jake wasn't smiling, his eyes were piercing right through me; the reality of my words hit me like a ton of bricks. I rolled my eyes "I'm stupid." I hung my head.

He cupped my face in his hand gently tilting my head upwards. "Tara, you promised me." I could see the pain in his eyes and he pulled my head to his chest and wrapped his arms around me. "What if I hadn't shown up? I think we better call the police."

"I thought I was being safe."

The police showed up and took my statement. I was definitely more coherent now but still no Melissa.

"Is this normal behavior for her?" The Detective looked at me.

"Really, I don't know. I just met her this week and this is our first time out." Just then Jake cut in.

"Detective, I believe someone slipped a drug in Tara's drink and might have done the same with Melissa's. I just happened to run into Tara outside, barely coherent.

"Is this true miss?"

I shook my head up and down.

"Well there's not much we can do about your friend. She's over 18 and she hasn't even been missing for more then a couple hours if she's missing at all."

"But…"

"You on the other hand need to come down to the E.R. and get tested to see if indeed someone tried to drug you."

Instead of giving us a ride he called in an ambulance. I was mortified. It wasn't serious. Jake on the other hand was acting like I had been attacked. He hadn't left my side and he kept whispering "it will be okay." I was more worried for Melissa. What if the person in my dream was Melissa, what if right at this very moment Melissa was going through what the poor girl in my dream was going through?

The ambulance arrived and two ER personnel got out and started taking my blood pressure, temperature, and asking me a bunch of questions. I couldn't believe all the attention they were paying me. The people coming in and out of the club were staring. My face was flushed.

"We need to get you to the hospital right away!" One of the technicians yelled and broke me out of my pity party. "Get on the stretcher miss."

"What? Why?"

"Get on the stretcher miss!"

I turned to look at Jake and he gestured for me to move and get up on the stretcher.

"But why? Nothing is wrong."

"Miss I believe that you were given a drug called Gamma-hydroxybutyrate (GHB). Your temperature is 104 and right now you need to be under observation at the ER."

I still wasn't moving, how could this be? Who would drug me, why?

"Miss, people have died from taking this drug!" I could see the seriousness in his eyes and I began to get scared.

"Tara, please just go. I'll be right here with you." Jake's eyes were pleading with me. I felt hot but I thought it was from the embarrassment I felt from all the stares. I stood up from the curb and immediately fell back down. Jake quickly grabbed me before I could do any damage and lifted me right up in his arms and placed me on the gurney. I think maybe he was getting a little impatient with me.

"I could have done it myself." I huffed. The technicians pushed me back so that I was laying flat on my back. Through the crowd I thought I saw Ed. I tried to sit up and see.

"Please miss, you need to get to the hospital." The technicians began buckling me in like I was going to fall off.

Jake began raking his hands through his hair. I was surprised by how worried he looked. This can't be because of me, he must be wondering about Melissa. He slid his hands down the sides of his face and joined them together in front of his mouth, he was whispering into them. Was he praying?

"Can we please get her in so we can go?" Jake's loud impatient voice made me jump and they slid me into the back of the ambulance. Jake hopped in and we were on our way.

It didn't take long and we were at the E.R. I was forced to lay there since they still had me strapped onto the gurney like some mental patient. Jake held my hand the entire way. I couldn't help wonder what happened to Mellissa. And why was Ed there and why didn't he come over? Soon I was in a curtained off room and a few orderlies were pushing and prodding taking my vitals and asking a 100 questions. I was feeling better as more time passed. After a urine and blood test they confirmed that someone indeed drugged my drink and that I could have been in a lot of danger had Jake not shown up. Maybe I was too naïve for this big city after all?

After a few hours I was released. Jake and I shared a cab to my apartment. It was very late. I was hoping Melissa would be home once we got there. We walked into the lobby and I went straight to the stairwell and Jake headed to the elevator. He turned to look at me.

"Tara, please take the elevator. You don't need to be walking up 5 flights of stairs."

"But I don't like our hallway." I must have sounded like I just came out of the loony bin.

"Okay, but you're still not going to take the stairs." He grabbed my hand and led me into the decrepit elevator.

Chug, chug, chug, the elevator slowly crept upwards as the light buzzed off and on. I had no idea what time it was but it was quiet. The elevator stopped on 5 and Jake pushed the iron gate open and I quickly slid out making a bee line for my apartment door.

"Tara, wait, what's your hurry." Jake was shuffling behind me. He just didn't understand, I wasn't in the mood for creepy footsteps, yelling, and murder, I just wanted to get home.

I reached my door and pulled out my key. I risked a look down the hallway and only saw Jake slumbering toward me, no click, click, click sounds of other people's footfalls. I sighed in relief and the door was open by the time Jake was by my side.

We were safely inside and I locked the doors.

"Melissa?" I yelled but no answer. I wandered to all the rooms calling her name but no one was there. I returned to the living room and Jake was sitting on the couch.

"Do you want something to drink?"

He jumped up from the couch "Tara rest, please." He pointed to the couch. "Let me get you something to drink. Would you like something to eat as well?"

I slowly walked towards the couch. I was really tired but I was so afraid to go to sleep, the dreams were horrifying and I just couldn't go back there again. It had been weeks since I dreamt of the little girl and now she was back. Usually my dreams showed me of what was to be and I fear now they were showing me what had already been. I felt so empty, what could I do now for these women, if they were already dead?

I hadn't realized that I was just standing there in front of the couch, in a daze as I hashed out my thoughts. Jake took my hand and pulled me to him. "Don't worry, they'll find her." He was misinterpreting my misery however I did worry for Melissa I was deeply troubled by how I was to stay awake.

Jake sat down on the couch and pulled me onto his lap. He held me and I immediately felt comforted. He pressed his lips against my head and I leaned against his chest. I could hear his breathing, his heart beat, his warmth surrounding me like a blanket. My eyes began to flutter; my eyelids were so heavy, the rhythmic beat of his heart was rocking me into a deep slumber.

"Get her! She mustn't escape!"

I turned to see the gruesome scene behind me. The little girl grabbed my hand and pulled me forward. "Please Tara, you must hurry!"

I looked down at the little girl and her eyes were pleading. I knew there was nothing more I could do for the women laying on the cement slab. The others in the dark hoods began to move away from her and started to come towards us. We started running through the fire lit corridor.

"What is this place?"

"It's where he holds us prisoner."

"Hold's who?"

"Tara, there is no time. You have to help us before he captures you too."

I took a chance and glanced over my shoulder. I couldn't see anything in the blackness since the darkness closed off the tunnel we were running through. Before I could turn back around the uneven cobble stone tripped me and I flew to the ground. My knee took the brunt of my weight and I screamed out in pain.

"Tara, are you okay?"

I was rocking back and forth holding my knee. "No, I don't think I can walk."

"He's coming Tara, you have to try, we need to hide." The little girl was pulling at me but I couldn't raise myself the pain was too intense. I could hear footsteps getting closer. My heart began to race. I started to drag myself to the side of the corridor, pushing myself with my good leg. She opened a door and I was able to scoot inside just as I heard voices.

"She couldn't have gotten far."

"Demitri, I thought you had the entrance blocked?"

"I did, I don't know how she got through."

"Well don't stop looking for her. I have plans for her; she's special, very special. I need her, do you understand."

"Yes master."

With that the footsteps ran away. I thought I recognized the voice, it reminded me of Devin's husky tone but I knew it couldn't be. My eyes adjusted to the darkness and the little girl was balled up next to me with her arms wrapped around her knees.

"You've been following me, how come?"

"I was sent to warn you. He's a very bad man. He's not of this time. He's of many histories."

"I'm not sure I follow what you're saying."

"He's evil and appears through time to take of the innocent to feed to the devil."

The Devil? I needed to get out of this place. She placed her hand on the side of my head and pictures of her death flashed before my eyes. Her pretty little dress stained with blood, ripped apart, her heart cut out. I screamed.

Jake was shaking me. "Tara! Tara! Wake up!"

Once again I found myself peering up into those crystal blue eyes. Always my savior, my Jake.

"What's wrong, is Tara okay?" The door slammed.

Both Jake and I looked up to the door and there stood Melissa. I bolted up.

"Am I okay? What about you, where have you been?"

Melissa took a step back. "Whoa, back off, I'm fine and I've been out looking for you. Well I started looking for you. Anyway, I told you I was going to get a drink with those guys." She smiled now and looked at Jake. "Jim and Ed" She looked back at me, "I told you I would be right back. When I came back you were gone from the bar, I looked for you all over the place. I figured you must have found someone you wanted to hang with so I continued to party." She flauntingly walked into the kitchen.

"Well at least you're okay." I rested back on the couch however, Jake look at me like I was out of my mind.

"At least you're okay…what? Melissa, do you realize the danger you two were in tonight? Tara was drugged, that's why you couldn't find her. I found her outside barely hanging onto a light pole. She had to be taken to emergency."

Melissa glanced over her shoulder "She looks okay to me."

"The point is Melissa, there are some dangerous people out there and you two should have stuck together no matter what." Jake was flustered and by now he was up off the couch pacing back and forth. I tried to grab his hand but he snatched it away.

I got up to join Melissa in the kitchen, I was starving. I took a step and the pain shot through my knee brining me to the floor. I screamed in agony. Jake ran to my side to help.

"What did you do, are you okay?"

"My knee." It was the same knee I fell on in my dream.

"Did you twist it?"

"No, I just took a step."

Melissa ran over in concern too. "That must have been you I heard from the hallway screaming. I'm sorry I left you Tara, are you okay?"

"I'm fine. It's just my knee."

Jake picked me up and sat me on the couch.

Melissa looked down at me quizzically. "Why were you screaming earlier?"

Jake looked over at her "She was sleeping and she just started screaming. I was trying to wake her up."

"Oh, another one of those dreams, huh?"

Jake looked at me, worry in his face. "You've had these types of dreams before." I really hated all this attention.

"Jake, I'm really hungry can you find me something to eat please?" I had hoped the request would get the focus off of me for a moment so I could figure out why my knee was throbbing.

Chapter 7: The followers

I wracked my brain trying to figure out the meaning of my latest nightmare. I wasn't sure how long Jake stayed on the couch but he was gone by the time I woke. My head was pounding. All I wanted to do was stay in bed and enjoy some dreamless sleep. Melissa was gone, her first class was at 10, and I was alone.

Ring

Ring

I stumbled to the living room to grab the phone. I didn't recognize the caller I.D.

"Hello."

"Hello, Tara Mason?"

"Yes."

"Hi. I'm calling because you auditioned for a commercial and we were wondering if you would be interested in coming in for a second screening."

I could hardly believe what I was hearing on the other end. I had been waiting months to get a break in this town. I had been pinning all my hopes on Devin's group of stage friends but I was open to anything at this point.

"Sure I would love to."

She gave me the information, where and when to meet and I hung up. Immediately I shirked my clothes off and flung myself into the shower. They wanted to see me today. I was supposed to work tonight but hopefully I could get out of it if I needed to.

I wasn't sure what to wear or how to fix my hair. She didn't say what the commercial was for just that it was for several local spots that they were working on. I decided to go casual, wearing jeans, button down blouse, tennis shoes and my hair in a ponytail. Failing to eat again, not enough time I thought, I grabbed my phone, my purse, and my keys and headed out the door. I should have left a note for Melissa but I didn't have time. I made a mental note to call her later.

I was feeling pretty confident about my sense of direction. I was pretty sure I knew where I was going and if I felt I was getting lost I could always hail a cab. That was one thing this city was not lacking. I've never walked so much in my life since I moved to this city. I headed down the block to the train station passing a local grocer and remembered that it was my turn to pick up groceries. We were totally out of everything with sustenance in our place. I didn't work everyday so saving my one meal a day for my employee discount at the Kilt didn't work on my days off.

I paid my fare and took a seat by myself on the train. I rattled off my grocery list in my head "milk, bread, peanut butter, ramen, toilet paper" then I decided I had better find a pen and paper because my list was getting way too long. I was rummaging through my purse when the train stopped at the next station to pick up more passengers. Riding the train was so convenient. Arizona needed to really look into getting something like this. I pulled out the paper with my audition instructions and a pen and began writing my items down on the back. I hoped I had enough money to cover the basics.

As I was pondering my financial status a young man sat down across from me. He was relatively attractive, probably 22 years-old. I was noticing his necklace; it was a star with what looked like a goat head inside. It was very unusual and actually pretty creepy. I couldn't take my eyes off of it. My eyes traveled upward and he was staring at me, smiling, but it wasn't a friendly smile, it gave me the chills. It reminded me that I was supposed to call Melissa and tell her where I was headed. I decided to text her since the train was so noisy.

'headed to audition, then to wk.'

'k'

'home late'

'k'

Then I decided to text Jake.

'headed to audition, c u 2nite'

'b careful'

'k'

The train stopped and I noticed that it was time for me to get off and catch the subway. I draped my purse over my shoulder and across my chest. It was only a couple blocks to the next subway entrance. It was hot out and my stomach was really growling now but I didn't have time to stop and eat. I looked behind me and saw the same guy from the train following me. I talked myself out of that possibility explaining to myself that he could just be going the same way as me but my gut was telling me I was being followed. I hopped on the subway and when I was seated I looked around and found that he didn't follow me. I looked out the window and he just stood there on the platform staring at me with that creepy smile. I sat back, let out a sigh, relieved that he wasn't on the subway with me, but it was by his choice. I looked down the cab full of people and my eyes fell upon another young man dressed similar, but more notably he was wearing the same necklace. He slowly turned his head in my direction, I couldn't pull my eyes off of him and he caught my eyes and began to smile. My heart was racing. Who were these people and why were they following me? Thank God I only had to go a few stops before I was at my location. Once the subway stopped I raced out almost forcing the doors open. I ran up the steps and when I turned to look behind me he wasn't following me. Relax Tara, maybe it was a coincidence. I took a deeper breath and let it out slowly. I found the building I was looking for and took the elevator to the 24th floor. After I signed in I was told to wait and so there I sat, and waited, and waited, and waited. Any minute now they'll call me I kept telling myself. I was afraid to leave my seat because I knew as soon as I did they would call me. Then finally at 4:30pm they called my name.

"Tara Mason."

I gathered my audition sheet and purse and quickly walked into the office. An older gentleman was sitting behind a desk and a younger man was fidgeting with a large camera.

The man behind the desk stood and walked towards me "Ms. Mason, glad you could make it and I'm sorry for the incredibly long wait."

"That's okay. Thanks for calling me back." I couldn't help but sound eager. I hadn't had a call back in all my auditions over the last several months.

"What we're going to do is have you provide us with a screen test. We have reading roles and a few emoting roles and we just want to see which we think you would be best at." He was smiling and moving me to a spot in front of the camera. My stomach was in knots. I surmised that I did get a role it was just a matter of which one.

They had me repeat the same line a few different times; it was for a cereal commercial. Not really knowing how the commercial was going to take place I had to figure it out in my head and try my best to sound realistic. It was a lot harder then I thought it would be.

"Very good Tara, now I have another part I want you to test for. This is actually a T.V. movie."

My eyes bulged but I tried to stay calm. He walked in front of me and smiled. "Don't worry, you will do fine." He started to unbutton my blouse. I sucked in my breath. "Just a few, the part you're playing is a wild teen and it will help if you look the part instead of miss goody-two-shoes."

He unbuttoned the top 3 buttons of my shirt to expose my cleavage. I was very uncomfortable but was desperately trying to hide it; a TV movie would be an excellent opportunity, one I didn't want to waste because of my bashfulness. He came around behind me and placed his hands on my shoulders.

"How does she look?" The camera guy looked into the lens.

"A little more."

He put his hands on my chest and pushed my blouse apart and down. I swear he felt my breast and squeezed them on purpose.

"Pull the shoulders down some."

Now he pulled my blouse off my shoulders.

"Should we leave the bra straps?"

"Yeah, it looks trashier."

He gave me my lines to read; when I reached for the paper my hands were trembling. I tried to focus. I did the reading and I thought I did okay. I thought we were done when he moved toward the camera.

"Okay, I'll man the camera; you get in there and play the guy. Tara, there's a make-out scene and we want to see how you project on camera."

"Action"

The younger man started kissing me and I didn't know what to do. I didn't kiss him back and so he just stopped.

He peeked his head out from behind the camera, "Tara, darling, what's wrong?"

"Well I don't know what the scene is about and I don't know what I'm supposed to do?"

"Just make out with him. You are a wild child so go for it. We need to capture this on camera. Let's try this again. Action!"

This time he placed his hand inside my blouse and squeezed my breast. This just didn't feel right. He started kissing me and his lips traced my neck, and the whole time I was thinking of the night with Devin and how wrong this was.

"I'm sorry but I just can't do this. I guess I don't want the part." But the guy didn't stop and the other guy behind the camera didn't say anything.

The younger guy ripped my blouse open exposing my breasts and clasped his mouth around my nipple sucking hard and biting it. I screamed and pulled back, tripping and landing on the office couch. He grabbed my hands and lay on top of me and began trying to kiss me again. I was so embarrassed and shocked.

"Stop it! NO!"

At that moment the older gentleman interjected, "Cut!" as if this was all part of the act. "That was perfect! Tara you nailed it."

I sat up and grabbed my shirt together. Tears were welling up in my eyes. I snatched my purse and walked out. I could hear laughter behind me and "You'll be hearing from us."

Would I ever learn to trust my instincts? Getting a part on a TV show was not more important than my dignity. I took the elevator to the lobby and walked out onto the sidewalk. I wondered how many other girls they had done this to. I'm sure it was a real call back but the second half of my screen test was only for their benefit. Bastards!

I began my long trek back home and remembered that I still had a shift at the Kilt to deal with and the only upside to that was that I was going to see Jake. Jake and I had really never officially said we were dating but I considered him my boyfriend and I hoped he thought of me as his girl-friend. All I wanted to do was curl up in his arms and cry. Men were such pigs except for my Jake.

I was walking in a trance all the way to the subway, not really pay-ing attention to my surroundings. I hardly noticed that it was getting dark. All I knew was that I was late for my shift and Patrick was going to read me the riot act. I jumped on my train and found an empty seat. I felt like someone was watching me and I looked around to see who but no one was paying me the least bit of attention. My switch was coming up and I man-aged to squeeze through the throngs of people to make it off. I waited on the platform for my next train to come. I couldn't get the image of the days earlier events out of my mind; I was engrossed in my thoughts when I heard a familiar clicking noise of footsteps behind me. I waited for the fa-miliar dialogue between Sam and now to my surprise Devin. But the click-ing stopped and I heard no talking. I turned around, my curiosity piqued, and there stood a young man wearing a black shirt with the same star neck-lace with a goat's head inside. My chest tightened, my pulse raced and I started to back up away from him. He stood still, not following me and smiled. I heard the train come to a stop behind me and the hustle of the evening crowd swarm around me. Too afraid to take my eyes off of him for fear he would follow me, I continued to walk backwards towards the train, bumping into strangers as they made their way home not realizing the fear I felt.. When I reached the door to the train I turned and ran on. I looked back over my shoulder and he was gone as if I had only imagined him. He couldn't have vanished so quickly he must have been in my mind only.

This time the train was packed and I had to stand but I found a pole to wrap myself around to keep from falling as the train swayed from side to side. Quitting time was the worst time to be on the subway. I could hardly see around the sea of suited men and women. It was stifling hot. The sweat was dripping down my back and I was finding it hard to breath. My stomach was rumbling and once again I found myself having gone all day without eating. I couldn't wait to get back to work so I could eat. I glanced around the cabin and caught a glimpse of the necklace. No way! I licked my lips and swallowed the lump in my throat. He couldn't have made it on here, the doors closed right behind me. I struggled to see the face but my view was blocked. The train rolled and rocked and people shifted and I caught the familiar face from the platform. Dark eyes peered at me between two polyester clad bodies, his lips curved up into a devilish smile.

Oh my God, how did he get on here? My thoughts were racing. Did he mean to harm me? Should I get off? Will he follow me? What did he want? Was he just picking me out of the crowd to torment and scare?

The train screeched to a halt at the next platform and I was hesitant, my hands sweating. My plan was to hide amongst the tall suited business-men and sneak off the train. The doors opened and with my heart pounding so loud I could hear nothing else I practically clung to the man next to me and walked off the train. I looked back over my shoulder expecting to see him but he wasn't there but up ahead I saw the other two men from earlier. I stopped and ran back to the train squeezing through the doors as they slammed shut. The train began to move and relief flooded over me as all three of them stood there staring at me from on the platform. I was still trembling, the vision of those evil grins seared into my memory. The whole incident made no sense to me. I just wanted to go home and hated the fact that I had to go to work.

A few more stops and I bolted off the train and ran for work. I for-got my top was ripped apart and the stares I received brought it to my atten-tion. I was mortified. I was still so scared and now I was crying. I slowed my run to a walk. The sobbing took over not really caring what a mess I must look like and the pity party began. At night I'm plagued with horrible dreams and now during the day I'm stalked by creepy guys and groped by middle-aged men.

I continued to walk the sidewalk, my arms clasped around me, tears streaming down when a red car pulled up beside me.

"Where you going good looking?" It was Devin. As much as I wanted to avoid him, right now the familiar voice was a godsend.

I stopped walking and turned to look at him. His eyes widened and his mouth dropped open. In one fall swoop he put his car in park, jumped out and was holding me.

"Tara what happened, are you okay?"

"I'm fine, just late for work."

"I'm sure that's not the reason for all those tears." He backed up and let me loose to peer down at me.

"No really, I'm fine. I just had a really, really bad day."

"Well come on get in. I'll give you a lift." I wasn't about to refuse a ride but once again I found myself alone with Devin. The sooner we got to the Kilt the better. He glanced over at me and I was still holding my blouse together with both hands. I caught his eyes as he examined my predicament.

"Should I be worried?" I could hear the concern in his voice but he was the last person I wanted worrying over me.

"I'm fine."

I made it to work by 6:30 p.m. three hours past my starting time. Before I even walked in the front door I could hear Jake's beautiful music. I just wanted to curl up in his arms and lay in bed forever. I walked in with Devin close behind me. Jake was sitting on his stool with his guitar, no knit hat tonight so his hair was all tousled and messy. He was so beautiful. I don't think he knows how beautiful he is and that makes it even better. When he saw me the music stopped. He hopped off the stage and started walking towards me and I saw his eyes move above me and he stopped. Devin. Did he really think I was gone all this time with Devin? Jake's eyes were back on me and I watched as they traveled down to the blouse I was clinging around me. Could he see the missing buttons and the ripped material? It happened so fast that I hardly had time to say anything. Jake reached around me and slammed Devin back against the front door which gave way and both of them disappeared outside.

I ran outside to explain to find that they both landed on the sidewalk.

"Jake stop, it wasn't Devin!" I couldn't believe I was actually sticking up for him. By now they were both standing, fists raised.

Jake was the first to speak. "I told you to stay away from her!" I must have missed the first punch because Devin's mouth was bleeding.

"Man, I didn't do anything. She was walking along the sidewalk crying and I picked her up."

Jake looked over at me and I shook my head up and down. Jake put his fists down and Devin decked him right in the face. Jake fell to the ground and I ran to his side.

I shot a murderous look at Devin, "Why did you do that?"

"I was just getting him back for punching me for no good reason." And he walked back into the bar licking his lip.

I helped Jake stand as he was rubbing his face.

"Do you want me to get you some ice?"

"No, it's okay."

All the spectators went inside since the action was over and I began to follow but Jake pulled me back by the arm.

"I'm sorry Tara. I overreacted when I saw Devin with you and your face and shirt, what happened?" His hand was softly caressing my face trying to wipe away my long dried up tears.

I looked down at my feet. I wasn't ready to tell this story yet. "It's a long story and I need to get changed and begin my shift before I get fired. I'll tell you later but I'm fine." He pulled me to him and kissed me softly. I brought my arms up around his neck and he kissed me deeper. With all my being I loved this man. He pulled away and held my face, gazing into my eyes.

"I worried about you all afternoon and when you didn't answer your phone I thought I would go crazy."

With my brow creasing and a bit confused I answered. "I had my phone." I reached into my purse and noticed that the battery had died. "Well it would help if it were charged." I smiled meekly.

"Tara, you will be the death of me." He turned me toward the door and patted me on the butt, my punishment.

We walked back in and Patrick was already yelling at me to get busy.

The night moved at a fast pace. Thank goodness we sold shirts so I didn't have to run home to change. My t-shirt was black with green clovers over my breasts. It read "Find a 4-leaf clover & get lucky!" How embarrassing. Patrick thought about making these shirts our uniforms. I really hoped he didn't. Tonight the crowd was manageable but all I could think about was eating, I was famished. With no time to sit and eat I grabbed a few fries while picking up a food order. Jake surprised me, coming up behind me for his food.

"Don't you have time to eat tonight?" I jumped like 10 feet almost dropping my food orders.

"Jumpy tonight are we?" He was only joking but it was the truth. The day's events had me on edge and I hadn't had a chance to even talk to Jake about what happened. Actually I wasn't sure I really wanted to tell him. Jake seemed to read the worry on my face. "You sure you're okay? Why don't you take a quick break with me?" His pleading blue eyes were enough to make my heart melt. Did he know I loved him?

"I can't. I was in late and we're short a waitress." Jamie was working tonight but that was it, so I really didn't have time to sit, not that I didn't want to hash out my horrid day amongst a bar full of rowdy drinkers.

I stole a couple more fries from his basket with my free hand and walked off to deliver my orders. I didn't know what it was about him, I just couldn't think straight when he was around. I headed to the bar to place more orders. Ed was working tonight and he and Devin were deep in conversation when I interrupted.

"Hey can I get three shots of peppermint schnapps and three drafts." Devin moved closer to me and wrapped his arm around me pulling me close to him.

He whispered into my ear "How you hanging in there?" Why he felt the need to pull me so close to ask me such a mundane question I'll never know.

I instinctively pulled away from him, "I'm fine Devin, thank you for asking." Ed leaned across the bar and placed my drinks on my tray. For the first time I noticed that Ed was wearing the same exact necklace that the three men from earlier were wearing. Was this some sort of gang or a new fashion that I was unaware of? I was in such a haze that I barely noticed that Devin let his arm fall from my shoulder and slide down my back and across my backside. I turned and caught Jake's stare. I saw now whose benefit this little show was for. I rolled my eyes trying to make light of the situation. I could see in Jakes steel gaze that it didn't work. I couldn't let the jealousy between these two get in the way of my figuring out the mystery of this necklace. What did the necklace mean? I wanted to ask Ed but I was too afraid. What if it was something sinister and they found out through Ed that I worked here.

After delivering my drinks I stepped into the bathroom for a moment alone but I ran into Jamie.

"Hey girl, how are you?" She was fixing her perfect hair in the mirror.

"I'm fine. Have they found out anything new with Sam?" I headed for one of the stalls.

"No. The police are adding her case to all the other cases that can't be solved." I could hear the desperation in her voice.

"Well Melissa never mentioned if they called her down for questioning. I thought they said they wanted to question everyone Sam knew."

"I think they've just got too much to deal with that they don't have enough people to look into all aspects of the case."

"I can't believe she's been missing for over three months."

"Yeah, I know."

I washed up and headed back to work. By now the place was almost empty and it was time to clean tables and wash dishes. Finally I would be able to go home. Home? How was I going to get home in the dark? I couldn't ask Devin for a ride. Usually I just walked home, no big deal, but tonight was different. I was afraid to be alone and Melissa text me earlier that she was staying over at her boyfriend Jeremy's house tonight. I looked over to Jake. I often wanted him to stay the night with me but the good Catholic girl kept rearing its prudish head, keeping me from what I really wanted. But tonight was different. I needed him to be with me.

I nervously walked over to Jake as he was putting away his guitar. A couple girls were hanging around waiting for him to join them. Oh if they only knew that he made plans with me each night. I sat down at the table and he was bent over snapping his guitar case shut. His hair fell over his face and he glanced up at me his blue eyes peering through his golden brown locks. He took my breath away. He raked his hand through his hair forcing it out of his face as he sat up and smiled at me. I was so lucky.

The girls waiting lost their patience and headed for the door and as usual practice Devin quickly met up with them to assuage their hurt feelings. Jake could tell I had something on my mind.

"Out with it."

"Can you walk me home tonight?"

"I always walk you home, well almost always." He pinched his eyebrows together.

I nervously tapped my finger on the table and bit on my lip. He reached over and grabbed my hand. I looked up at him and took a deep breath.

"And will you stay the night with me? I mean, not for that, not that I wouldn't like that, that's if you even wanted to…"

"Of course I'll stay" he interrupted my nervous banter. I put my head in my hands. Could that have gone any worse?

"Tara, what's really bothering you?"

"I really don't want to talk about it, can I tell you when we get home?"

"If that's what you want." He smiled and I knew he meant it.

I finished up the rest of my duties. Jake finished up his beer and we were on our way. The night was always so nice. I didn't know what I was going to do when winter got here. I can't imagine it would be so nice walking home at night in the freezing cold. No, I like the summer nights. It cooled everything off and it wasn't so humid. I still couldn't get used to all the wetness in the air. I felt like I was always sweating, which I hated.

Jake grabbed my hand and we walked silently down the sidewalk to my apartment. I felt safe with him. Even though it was 2 in the morning there were still quite a few people roaming about. It was hard to get used to the constant hustle and bustle. It wasn't as noticeable in our little city but the closer you got to Manhattan the busier the nightlife became. I had often heard of people that only came out at night, almost like nightlife vampires.

My apartment was only about a 30 minute walk from work. Before I knew it, I took out my key and we were safely inside. What a day. The light on the answering machine was flashing.

"Make yourself comfortable Jake, help yourself to anything in the kitchen." He took a seat on the couch.

I pushed play on the answering machine and continued to settle in for the night, taking off my shoes, hanging my purse and remembering to use the key hook for my keys so I could find them again.

"Hi Melissa Smith, this is Detective Garcia. Can you please call me at 555-343-9932? I need to discuss your acquaintance with Samantha Davis. Thank you." I found a pen and paper and played the message again so I could take down the number.

"Ms. Mason, this is Mr. Randolph from Talent 1 scouting agency. You did a screen test today for a commercial and I would like to let you know that you received a part. Please come to the studio at 6am Monday. You will be paid $30 a hour." I tried to smile. I was happy but wasn't sure I wanted to work for these guys but I needed the money. Jake jumped up after hearing the message.

"Tara! That's excellent news!" He gave me a big hug. He pulled back revealing a grin from ear to ear. "Why aren't you happy?"

I sighed; it was time to tell him. "I am happy. I just had a really bad experience with their agency today at the screen test."

I sat down on the couch and he sat facing me. I swallowed and told him what happened at the screen test and the impromptu make-out scene. As I progressed, his face became red. I tried so hard not to cry, I wanted to be brave and act like it didn't bother me so I wouldn't upset him but my traitor tears spilled over and the more I tried not to cry it seemed like the more tears fell. When I finished Jake didn't say a word. He pulled me in his arms and I leaned my head against his chest. He wasn't as muscular as Devin but he still had a well defined chest and I felt at peace lying in his arms. When I stopped crying Jake finally spoke.

"I'm so sorry they did that to you Tara." He kissed me on top of my head.

I felt so much better but I still wanted to tell him about the three guys and the necklaces but maybe I should save that for another night however that was the real reason I had him over tonight.

"You don't have to take the job Tara. But if you do I won't think any less of you."

"I'll have to think about it." I stood up and headed to my bedroom to change. I needed a moment to compose myself and shake the awful memory from my head, mainly the memory of the three men stalking me. I changed into a tank top and shorts and walked back out into the living room. Jake had already made himself comfortable on the couch, his shoes and socks aligned straight against the couch, his jeans folded neatly and placed on the chair. He was so the total opposite of me, I was a slob and he was Mr. clean. The T.V. was still on but he was already sleeping, lying there in his white t-shirt and boxer shorts. He was like an angel. His face was masculine and feminine at the same time. His dark eyebrows were full and with a perfect arch, his eyelashes long and lush, what any women would die for, his cheeks were often stained red, I loved that the most. He lay here on my couch, his lips slightly parted, barely making a noise and he was here because I asked him, here because of me. I quietly knelt next to the couch, next to him, staring at him, watching him sleep. He was so peaceful; I wished I could sleep with such peacefulness. His head turned slightly toward me and he licked his lips. I should just let him be, let him sleep. But those lips, I had to kiss them goodnight.

I slowly and quietly moved in and softly placed my lips upon his. His lips were warm and lush, I pressed just a little harder. Like a flash his arms wrapped around me and he pulled me on top of him. I let out a little squeal.

"Gotcha!" he was smiling.

"Hey! I thought you were sleeping."

"How could I sleep knowing you were in the next room?" He rose his head up and kissed me. I sat up and he stood up and picked me up in his arms with him.

"What are you doing?" I wrapped my hands around his neck.

"Tucking you in, it's past your bedtime." He carried me carefully down the hallway and into the bedroom. He laid me on the bed.

I patted the bed next to me, "Stay with me for a little while."

A smile crept across his face. I scooted over and he got in next to me. He turned the light off but I could still see him because of the moonlight through the window. He turned towards me on his side. My stomach was doing flip flops. All the nerves in my body were tingling. He propped his head up on his hand, his other hand brushing my cheek and then he ran it down my shoulder and the length of my arm. When he reached my hand he took it and pulled me toward him and wrapped it behind him. My face was now only inches from his. My breath started to come out unevenly. His hand cradled my neck and he pulled me to his lips. There was a quiet hunger in his kiss. This was our very first serious make-out session and I was incredibly nervous. Usually there were so many interruptions, like work, so our kisses were short. Now his kiss was hot and probing, his tongue tickled the inside of my lips, he was making me want him more than I should.

I was always taught that abstinence was the best policy but if I didn't stop now there was no way that was going to work. I hated to push him away. The taste of his kiss was making me heady I had to remind myself to breath. Instead of pushing him away my body betrayed me. I reached my hand up behind his head, raking my fingers through his hair, forcing him to close the space between us. I pressed my lips against him harder, no playing around now, and his tongue delved into my mouth, so hot, I could feel an electric charged race through me causing me to catch my breath, a small gasp escaped a startled reaction to his kiss. I felt like my body was going to catch fire and I had never felt like this before. "Stop… stop…stop" Was that my voice? I pressed my body against his but then Jake gently caressed my shoulders and pulled back. Maybe he realized I wasn't ready for this. My mind was telling me to stop but my body was aching for him to go further.

"I'm sorry if I moved too fast" his breath was labored and his blue eyes searched my face for any sign that I wasn't ready.

"You didn't. I just," I dropped my eyes as the honesty boiled over and the heat rushed to my cheeks "I've never felt like this with anyone before."

"So I'm your first?" he cocked his eyebrow.

I pushed him away and turned towards the window, "Don't look so smug." I hated how my body betrayed me when he kissed me. It was like I had no control. I'm sure the rush of emotions were one sided as he seemed every bit in control of this relationship.

"I'm just foolin' with you. Please don't be mad at me." He wrapped his arms around my stomach and pulled me to him. I could feel his warm breath on my neck as he bent his head down next to mine, his chin moving my hair aside so he could press his lips against my neck. Just this small touch made my stomach flip.

"You better go now." I wanted him to stay, I wanted so much more but it wasn't right. Pretty soon I wouldn't be able to be strong enough to tell him to stop.

I turned to look him in the face but the reaction I was expecting wasn't what I got. He looked sad, like I had broken his heart. If anything I thought he would be mad, like other guys that took me on dates thinking they would score but often times didn't even make it to first base.

"I don't understand. Did I move too fast? I'm sorry really, please Tara tell me what I did wrong?" He tried to look into my eyes but I looked down.

"Honestly, it's nothing you did, it's me." I looked up at him pleading. Why was he making this so hard? Usually when they don't get what they want they just get pissed off and bolt.

He brought his hand up under my chin and turned my face toward him "Tara, please you can tell me, what's wrong?" I just couldn't resist him; those penetrating blue eyes could get me to do just about anything.

"It's embarrassing."

He continued to stare at me and just wait.

"Ugh! Alright," I turned to sit up on the side of the bed. "When you kiss me I can't think straight." I turned to look over at him. He just laid there staring at me.

Then, "That's it, you can't think straight. That's what this is all about?"

"Well, it's slightly more then that. I feel like I don't have any control when you kiss me that way and it's really hard for me to tell you to stop." My face had to be beet red it was so hot. I was happy it was dark. I bowed my head into my hands, hid my head was more like it, from sheer embarrassment.

Jake scooted closer to me. "You know its okay to like kissing me, I like kissing you. Actually I love kissing you and touching you, holding you, holding your hand and just being with you. If all you ever wanted was for me to be by your side then that would be good enough for me."

"That's just it Jake, I want more from you when we're kissing but my mind is telling me no. I was brought up to wait until marriage and since I've never been in a relationship before it's never been an issue for me, until now."

"Oh, I see. This is a predicament. Well you'll just have to marry me then so I can keep kissing you," he said with a big smile.

"You're making fun of me."

"Tara, please. You seem to think that you are the only one dealing with self-control issues. It takes all my strength not to bend you to my will every time I have you alone. The last thing I want to do is scare you off so I try to rein myself in but I feel like I'm going to jump out of my skin I want you so bad. I promise to try hard to keep myself under control and watch out for you as well." He hugged me then and pulled me back into bed. Could he really be saying that he felt as strongly for me as I did for him? My beautiful blue-eyed guitar player liked me above all the Barbie college girls at the bar?

"Tara," he pulled back so he could look into my eyes, "I love you and I don't want anything to happen to you. I want to be here for you and do my best to make you happy." He leaned in and kissed me, just as before but this time his fingers curled up in my hair pressing me hard against him. I was dizzy. He literally took my breath away. I thought I was going to pass out. I wanted to tell him I loved him too but again I couldn't think straight. His kiss ended with a soft peck on my nose. I lay my head on his chest and finally I was where I had longed to be all day, curled up safely in his arms for the rest of the night.

The grip on my arm was like a vice. I couldn't see anything up ahead it was so dark. The air was cool and damp and smelled of death. I was being pulled over uneven ground, the sound of my footsteps echoed, the walls seemed close. I stumbled often but the grip on my arm never loosened. My eyes slowly adjusted to the darkness and I looked to see that the shackle on my arm was actually a bony white hand. It was so pale it glowed against the darkness but that was all I could see, it looked as though it were floating through thin air.

Up ahead I could see fire-lit torches on the walls, I was in a tunnel similar to others I had been in before. I could see I was being led by a robed minion of this morbid place. Finally after what seemed like a mile of walking we entered a large room, this was different then the other place from earlier dreams. Prominently displayed above an altar was the circled star with the goat's head protruding through the middle. The eyes were wide and red, the horns were curved up and sharpened to a point, and the mouth hung open to reveal fangs.

Torches surrounded the altar, a long table covered in a red satin fabric. Who were these people and where was I? I tried to pull away from my sentry but the grip grew stronger the pain shooting through my arm making my cry out in pain. It forced me to look at the claw on my arm and I saw the fingernails digging into my skin, blood dripping down my arm.

"Stop! You're hurting me!"

Another hand slapped me across the face with such force that it knocked me to the cold stone floor. I could taste the blood and knew my mouth was bleeding. I needed to get out of here. I looked around but could see nothing outside of the ring of firelight from the torches. I squinted, trying to make out an escape route when I heard footsteps coming toward me.

"Ah great, our audience is here." Again a voice eerily similar to Devin's but different. I just couldn't explain it. He was walking with a young lady, her arms bound behind her. He was covered in a long red robe with the hood pulled so far over his head that I couldn't see his face. He led the girl to the altar and sat her down.

I heard him whisper to her, "I want your blood so I can offer a toast to my maker."

The young girl screamed and he just patted her reassuringly on the shoulder "Now, now. I didn't say I wanted all of it." Her eyes widened at the possibility that she might be kept alive. I looked down at my hands. The blood on my arm had dried and I was no longer restrained, I could help her.

I quietly felt around for something I could use and came across a few rocks. When I found one large enough I grasped it in my hand and waited. He moved closer to her and brandished his long steel knife swiping it across her cheek. It seemed to hardly touch her but the dripping blood and her gasp confirmed he did more than just touch her. He reached around behind the altar and came out with a golden chalice.

"Fill this cup and you will please me." His tone reeked of seriousness.

He untied her hands and took one hand, palm up. He began to mark her with the knife. She didn't say a word or make a sound. When he was done he held up her hand to reveal a 5 pointed bloody star carved on her palm. He walked closer to me.

"Kneel!"

I sat up on my knees and he placed her hand on my forehead. Flashes of her death exploded before my eyes. The five pointed stars were carved into her skin and covered her body. Blood was dripping from every wound but this wasn't to be her death sentence it was the heart she was missing, as it was carved out of her body. Her eyes were open.

"Please stop!" I tried to pull myself away but a force was locking me in place.

He glared at me, "This path has already been chosen."

"No it hasn't. I will save her. I will kill you! I will kill you!" I threw the rock as hard as I could, striking him in the head. I jumped up, grabbed the girl by the hand and ran through the darkness. I couldn't see where I was going and ran into a wall, nearly knocking myself out. I felt someone pull me up.

"Hurry there's not much time."

I ran faster down the dark tunnel but the faster my legs moved the slower I moved. I felt a strange force pulling me back. I could hear him behind me.

"Where do you think you are going Tara? You are the one I really want and you are the one I will get. Come to me my sweet Tara."

I turned and the robed man was pulling an invisible rope, reeling me back in towards him. I had no strength against him, no ability to change my situation, I felt hopeless, defeated and conquered. This couldn't be the end.

"NO! I won't come to you! This isn't my chosen path! "

Immediately the air felt different, it smelt different, the hold on me loosened and I could hear someone calling my name.

"Tara! Tara!" Jake was here?

"Jake?"

"Tara! Wake up!" I looked into his eyes and could see the anguish and I began to really worry.

"What's wrong Jake?" He grabbed me and held me. "Jake, please tell me what happened, are you okay?" He pulled away from me the look of confusion on his face.

"Tara, come follow me please." Now I was confused but followed him to the bathroom from the living room. All the lights were on. He stood me in front of him and then turned me to the mirror. My face, oh my god. The right side was swollen, my lip was split and dried blood was smeared across my cheek, lips, and chin. I looked down at the pain in my arm and saw four half-moon punctures surrounded with dried blood. I looked back into the mirror and caught Jake's reflection. His eyes were red and wet with tears. What had I done, I brought the misery of my dreams to life.

I turned to hug him, "I'm so sorry Jake."

He looked at me, so hurt and confused, "Sorry. Tara, please, the last thing you need to be is sorry, but you have to tell me what's happening. Something was attacking you and I couldn't stop it. I couldn't wake you, all I could do was watch." He held me again, resting his forehead on my shoulder and began to cry. I didn't know what was happening; I didn't know what to tell him. Hearing him cry was scaring me.

"I'm sorry," it was all I could say.

His head shot up, and he clasped his hands on my shoulders shaking me, "Tara, if you say you're sorry one more time! I saw wounds appear on your body when no one was touching you; I saw blood drip from your face after what appeared like someone had hit you. Now I don't know what's going on but I'm scared to death. I couldn't make it stop, I couldn't help you. You were walking into the living room yelling and screaming." He stood there, tears escaping down the side of his face, his hair messy, and his eyes were wide with fear. My heart was breaking.

I couldn't take it anymore, the sight of him breaking down. I walked to the bedroom and curled up in bed. I wanted to hide from it all. This was too bazaar for words. I couldn't understand it myself let alone explain it to

Jake. He was soon by my side trying to comfort me. I fell back to sleep and dreamt of nothing.

I woke an hour later to the smell of eggs and bacon. I hadn't eaten a real breakfast in months. My stomach was definitely telling me to run to the kitchen. I got up and took a trip to the bathroom. I peered into the mirror at my swollen face and busted lip. I still couldn't believe how this could happen from my dream. None of my injuries were severe enough to warrant a visit to the doctor. Just a band aid and they would heal with time. I still didn't know what to say to Jake, I was just as shocked as he was. This was the first time my dreams had ever been this extreme.

I walked into the kitchen and he smiled at me. He handed me a plate of breakfast and I brought it to the couch to devour in front of the T.V. We didn't speak, we just sat and ate. I don't think we knew what to say to each other.

Knock, Knock, Knock

It was too soon for the landlord so my curiosity had me hurrying for the door. I unlocked it and opened it to find Devin standing there grinning from ear to ear, a grin that quickly disappeared once he got a good look at my face. I had completely forgotten about my swollen cheek and split lip until his shocked expression brought back the image I saw of myself in the mirror. I tilted my head and smoothed my hair down the side of my face trying to desperately to hide the evidence.

"What in the hell happened to you?" He took a step forward reaching his hand to move my hair out of my face. I stepped back turning my face to the side blocking him.

"Nothing." I wasn't about to let him see the extent of my swollen face.

"What do you mean nothing? Tara your cheek is as big as a chipmunk!"

I heard Jake walk into the living room. Devin's eyes looked over my shoulder.

"What happened to you Tara?" His tone was unmistakably harsh now.

"It's not what you think Devin."

His eyes were back on me, pleading for more answers that I just couldn't give him. "What do you want Devin?"

"Well I came to tell you they want to you start work on that play in two weeks. They got the financing."

I forced a smile, "That's great Devin. Thanks for coming over to tell me."

"Yeah, well you deserve it." He flashed another look to Jake. "I'll see you later then?" It was a question rather than a statement.

"I guess so, I'm working tonight."

"Okay, bye."

I shut the door but was afraid to turn and look at Jake. I took a deep breath and turned around. Jake was gone. I walked into the bedroom and he was sitting there on the edge of the bed. I stood in the doorway. He looked up at me with deep sorrow in his eyes.

"Great, now everyone is going to think I beat you up."

"What? That's ridiculous Jake."

"Is it? Look at you? And did you see the way Devin looked at me as if I were some sadistic girlfriend beater. And it didn't help that you didn't have an explanation."

Now that ruffled my feathers. "What was I supposed to say? I was attacked in a dream?" Jake jumped up and darted to my side.

"I'm sorry Tara; I didn't mean to blame you. I know it's not your fault. I'm just frustrated."

We still had over four hours till we needed to be at work so I decided that now was as good a time as any to tell him about my dreams.

"Jake, I need to tell you something about me that never seemed to be much of an issue until I moved to New York." I moved to the bed and sat down. He followed and sat down facing me.

"What is it Tara."

"First let me say that what happened last night, has never happened to me before. However, I am a vivid dreamer." I glanced up at him to see his reaction. He was staring at me intently.

"What exactly does that mean?" He seemed to pause between each word as if it were a struggle to say them.

How to say this without it sounding like I was crazy? "Well when I was young it started out with me sleep walking and talking in my sleep. I would wake in the morning and not remember anything I did. Then as I got older I would have repetitive dreams and sometimes these dreams would scare me and they would be about unfamiliar people and places. It felt as though something or someone was trying to relay a message to me. Once I became a teenager these dreams evolved into premonitions." I had to stop here. It just sounded too crazy and he had already been through so much.

He continued to look at me, still serious. I had to give him credit. I'm not sure I would still be sitting here if the shoe were on the other foot. Since it seemed he wasn't going anywhere I continued.

"More then once I would have a dream and not long after the same situation would either play out before me or I would read about it in the paper or see it on the news. I never told anyone. I always kept it to myself but I used my ability when it affected those close to me, which was more often then I realized. The dreams weren't easy to understand, they were like a puzzle or a mystery to be solved. Sometimes it would take me days to figure them out only to find that the result was perfectly harmless. However there were times that I was able to keep myself and my family out of danger by postponing trips, altering driving routes, or changing plans. Sometimes the dreams were frightening and not knowing the people in the dream I wasn't able to use my ability to warn or help them. It became quite depressing at times when I would see the tragic outcome on the news knowing that I knew that it was going to happen ahead of time but not be able to prevent it. These dreams didn't happen every night. I would have them maybe once a week but I would dream every night. I had to learn to decipher the difference between a prophetic dream and a regular dream." Now to how this whole process has changed since I moved to this city.

"I began having explicit nightmares a month before my move here, basically when I set a date to move here, when it was set in stone that I was definitely coming. I began dreaming of death and murders of young women. I thought it was because my dad was scaring me into not coming to New York by showing me news articles on crime in the city. I also kept dreaming of a young girl who I believe has been my guide through these dreams but I'm not sure what her role is yet in all these murders." When I paused Jake took a breath.

"Do you think I'm crazy?"

"No. But just so I'm clear, you have been dreaming about the murders in the city before they happen?"

"Yes. It's not the exact method of how they are killed such as in my dream the murderer cuts their throats and their hearts are cut out but in real life they were stabbed." I said it so matter of fact that the words seemed to come from someone else. Jake looked at me in disbelief.

"You've been dreaming of people being murdered?" His blue eyes were deep blue now, they must change color with his emotions.

"Well not only that but for some reason I seem to be taken over by the murderer and I find myself in the body of the murderer and I wake up feeling as if I had just committed an actual murder. It's quite terrifying." Jakes eyes widened at this confession. I knew this was too much for him to take. He ran his fingers through his hair and then bent over and put his head in his hands.

I was afraid to go on. "There's more."

He sat up and looked at me.

"I dreamt of Sam before I knew it was her. I've been dreaming of her and the fight she had with her boyfriend before she disappeared." I paused not wanting to confess my hallucinations but I figured I was revealing my soul now I might as well let it all out. "I heard their arguments when I wasn't sleeping." I looked at him, squinting my eyes, waiting for what, I don't know. He was silent, probably shocked into silence. "When I would walk this corridor to my front door I would hear footsteps behind me and then the argument would begin. And the day of my audition downtown when I came back with the torn shirt, that wasn't the only thing that happened that day." He looked at me confused and then drew the wrong conclusion.

"Devin?"

"No, not Devin. I was followed onto the subway by someone but I managed to lose him but after my audition the same person followed me again along with two others. They were all men wearing black and all three wore a necklace with a 5 pointed star with a goats head in the middle."

"Tara, that's the sign of the devil or witchcraft. How come you didn't tell me about this sooner?" He held my hand.

"I was afraid and I was trying to figure it out on my own. I didn't want you to think I was crazy. Well I noticed that Ed wears the same necklace."

"Well he's pretty disturbing; maybe he's into that kind of stuff." He stared off not looking at me.

"Well what I don't understand is why me? Was I just picked out of the blue or did it have something to do with the murders and my dreams? I wonder this because my last dream, last night, I was lead into a huge room with that same symbol up on the wall but it was real, made of iron and centered with a mutated goats head. It was sickening. And then the leader carved the symbol into the lady's hand and pressed it against my forehead. Jake, I had never seen this symbol before until the necklaces the other day." I was really beginning to get anxious now.

"Is that the person you were yelling at? Is that who hit you?" He brushed his hand lightly across my swollen cheek.

"Well yes I was yelling at him but it was another man that hit me." The look in his eyes was like I had just ripped out his heart.

"When I first met you I knew you were special." He smiled. "I guess I didn't know how much." He took his finger and followed the outline of my lip stopping just before my cut. "I swore to myself that night after the frat boy incident that I would protect the naïve sweet girl, my Tara, but I can't protect you from your own dreams." He dropped his hand. I didn't want him to feel like this, for it would be his strength that I would draw from to figure this mess out. I sat forward, closing the space between us. I swept my lips across his cheek, he turned his face to me and his lips touched mine. He smelled so beautiful; it was like he was meant just for me. His kiss was so sweet it made me crave more. I maneuvered myself so that I was straddling him. The shock on his face made me feel like I was doing something wrong but then I realized the compromising position this put us in. His hands reached around behind me and pushed me towards him, I could feel how excited he was, which in turn took my breath away and made my stomach tingle. I closed my eyes and arched my back and Jake's hand slid up my back and around to the front and cupped my breast. I sucked in my breath so quickly it made a loud whooshing sound, which was soon cut off by Jakes lips over mine. I thought I was going to catch on fire. My body, once again, was betraying me, as I gently moved my hips back and forth on him because it felt so good. I heard what almost sounded like a growl come from Jake and with one arm around me he picked me up with him and turned me on my back laying me on the bed with him between my legs and him on top of me kissing me deeply. Oh my God help me to breath. I wanted him so bad.

"Jake"

He kept kissing me and his lips moved down my neck, then down my chest.

"Jake"

"Tara, please."

His mouth found my breast and I could stand it no longer. I grabbed Jakes shirt and pulled it up over his head. He pulled my shirt up over mine. I couldn't believe I was about to do this.

The pause gave both of us a moment to think a little clearly. We stared into each others eyes. Jake was the first to speak.

"I'm sorry Tara. I promised that I would be strong for both of us and the first time I'm tested I'm just about to blow it." He dropped down on the bed beside me, propped up on his elbow.

"Jake, please you have nothing to be sorry for. I just can't seem to control myself around you." I could feel the heat rise into my face. He turned my face towards his and kissed me softly again. "I'll take that as a compliment. I can't seem to control myself around you either."

Just then Melissa was plowing her way in, racing into the room.

"Oh! I didn't know you guys were here." I grabbed my shirt and quickly threw it on.

Jake was always so formal with her even without his shirt. He stood up to greet her. "Hi Melissa."

"Hi Jake. I got to hurry, I have a ride to the Wash-Emporium and I need to grab my dirty clothes." She hustled to the closet. We always made up funny names for the laundry mat.

I jumped up to help and started shoving clothes into her net bag. We were almost finished and something tripped me up and down I went. Melissa grabbed my arm to pull me up. "Hurry, there's not much time."

My face went white and I just handed her the bag. I'd heard those words before, the voice in the dark. Someone was helping me up and they said those exact words. Would it be Melissa that was trapped in that place that I was trying to help escape? Jake took notice of my sudden change of expression however Melissa was already off and out the door.

Jake was immediately by my side, "What's wrong Tara?"

"I dreamt of her voice telling me to hurry and then she grabbed my arm and helped me up but it was in the darkness and I didn't see her so I didn't know it was her. I still don't know if was her, hopefully it's just a coincidence."

"So what's wrong if it was her? You act like someone died or something?" He was shaking his head not understanding my reaction.

"Jake, the place I was at was where all the girls were being held captive and then tortured and killed. If Melissa were there too then it's possible that she may be one of those girls. You see what I mean about how my dreams are like a mystery? Let's just hope it's all a coincidence."

Jake kissed me on the forehead and we got ready for our shift at work. I tried to cover up my bruises. The swelling had gone down some on my cheek but just in case I wore my hair down so I could hide it better. It felt weird now that Jake knew my secret; I had never told anyone about my dreams not even my best friend. I guess I didn't have much choice after last night but I felt so much closer to him now, especially since he didn't walk out thinking I was off my rocker.

111 Dream Catcher by Tricia Currier

Chapter 8: My first time

Like a robot, I mechanically walked through the paces at work. I didn't remember doing anything. I knew Devin, Ed, and Jake were there along with Jamie and Patrick. I didn't remember eating, waiting on tables, taking orders, but I'm sure that I did. All I could think about were my dreams and how out of control they were and how I felt that I was out of control. I couldn't figure out what the little girl wanted me to do besides kill the bad guy which I had no way of knowing how to do since I didn't know who he was, I hadn't even seen his face. I had no way of stopping this evil. I needed help and decided that it was time to look towards my heritage for answers.

My Uncle Gerald was Chief of the Mohawk people on our reservation in upstate New York where most of my family was from. If anyone could help me understand my dreams and help me it would be him. In order to fight this evil I needed to know what tools I had available to me. I asked Patrick for a few nights off and he agreed to Sunday and Monday, our two slowest days. Now all I had to do was tell Jake I was taking off for a few days. We sat at our favorite booth unwinding from the long night. I decided to just come out with it.

"I'm leaving town for a few days." I'm such a coward I couldn't even look him in the eyes.

"Oh really, where to?" I could feel his glare but still I could not bring myself to look him in the eyes.

"Upstate to visit some family." Jake didn't know that I was three quarters Mohawk Indian we never really talked about it before only about my family back in Arizona. Come to think of it I didn't know anything about his family.

"How are you getting there?"

"I'm renting a car." What did it matter to him?

"Hmm. When are you leaving?"

Now I looked at him, he was sitting erect staring right at me, "Jake, I'm just going out of town for a few days."

"And I'm just wondering when you're leaving?" His eyebrows rose up in frustration. I didn't want to worry him more but I had a feeling this trip alone was going to do just that, worry him to death.

"I'm leaving on Sunday and I'll be back on Tuesday." I fumbled with the straw in my soda not looking at him.

He looked around and took in a deep breath, "You ready to go home?"

That was it, no more discussion?

"Yeah."

We walked home holding hands. It was another hot evening.

"Why now Tara, why do you have to go now?" I was wondering when he would bring up my trip, I guess he didn't want to talk about it in the bar.

"My family is Mohawk Indian and we have different views on dreams and premonitions. I'm going to visit my Uncle Gerald; he's the chief on our reservation."

He stopped walking and turned to me, "But you don't look Indian?"

"I know, I'm three quarters, my mom is half Mohawk half Canadian and my Father is practically full Mohawk. I guess I just have more of the Canadian traits, plus I try to stay out of the sun. I have a little color on my own but when I'm in the sun I get really dark."

"Wow, that's so cool. I'm Caucasian, European decent." He smiled.

"I pretty much figured that out paleface." It was all in jest but the conversation turned serious.

"So you are going to consult with your Uncle about your dreams?" He raised his eyebrows.

"Yes, I need to find out what's happening to me and learn how to control it, or something bad could happen to me and the people around me."

"You mean me."

"Yes, you." I punched him in the shoulder.

"Would it be too much of an intrusion if I asked to accompany you on your trip because honestly I don't know if I can handle having you out of my sight for two whole days?" Frankly I was hoping he would ask this very question the moment I had come up with the idea of going upstate.

"Yes, No, I mean yes you can come, I would be very happy if you did." He took me in his arms and lifted me up off the ground. He was so much taller than me and I only seemed to notice it during times like this.

We were in front of my apartment complex; it was the fastest I could ever remember arriving here before. I wasn't ready for him to go. "Jake where do you live, you are always over here I should come to your place sometime." I smiled thinking maybe he would get the hint.

"Let me walk you to your door." He turned me toward the front door. How does he do that, just ignore my questions. That's not fair, when he wants to know something of me he doesn't take no for an answer. Defiantly I stopped.

"No. I want to go to your place." He practically ran into the back of me.

"Tara, we're here let's just go upstairs. We'll go to my place another time." He was probably right and it made no sense but still I wanted to know where he lived.

"Where do you live Jake?" Defiance in my voice.

"I live about 20 minutes north of here." Both eyebrows were raised in that 'is that enough' kind of look. I decided not to push it. I headed for the stairwell.

"So the footsteps, is that why you would rather take five flights of stairs?"

I smiled, "Yeah." He must think I was crazy now.

We got to the door and I unlocked it. No bolt or chains so Melissa must have decided to stay at her boyfriends again. My excitement rose at the prospect of Jake staying longer then just making sure I was safely inside. I was so bad. I'm not sure I would be able to wait until marriage unless I kept a distance from him and I knew that wasn't going to happen. I realized then that I hadn't been to church since I arrived in New York and decided right then that I would have to start going because I had plenty to confess and I could use all the prayers I could get.

It was so late. Jake followed me in. I'm not sure he interpreted the clues of Melissa's whereabouts and I would have to be bold and spell it out for him before he turned to leave. My heart started to race, this wasn't something I was used to doing being brazen and bold. I dropped my purse on the couch, my keys on the coffee table, kicked my shoes off and headed to the kitchen for a glass of water. I needed to settle my nerves. I turned around to see Jake hanging my purse up, hanging my keys on the key rack and lining my shoes along the edge of the couch. That guy! I rolled my eyes.

"Are you done straightening up?" I teased.

He just stood there caught in the act like he wasn't doing anything out of the ordinary. If only he knew how funny it looked to me. He was the total opposite of me at least on the organization and cleanliness front.

He walked over to me, his hand caressed my cheek softly and combed through my hair to the back of my head arching my face up towards his. He brought his lips down to mine and kissed me with passion. It took me so off guard that I almost dropped my glass. His tongue explored my mouth, it was so hot. I wrapped my arms around him pulling him closer to me and that actually pushed me backwards towards the kitchen. I hit the edge of the counter and I set my glass in the sink. He lifted me onto the countertop and now we were almost eye to eye. He continued to kiss me and I wrapped my legs around him squeezing him to me.

"Stay with me tonight." I whispered.

"I thought you would never ask." With that he lifted me again and walked me to the bedroom. It was amazing how safe I felt in his arms, I wished I could stay there forever. Here I was just thinking I needed to go to church and now I was ready to commit one of the biggest sins. It was just so hard to keep pushing him away when I wanted Jake to be my first. To my surprise Jake laid me in bed, undressed me to my undershirt and panties, then stripped himself down to his boxers but then to my disappointment he just got in bed. Why did he have to pick now to be so damn strong! I couldn't be mad at him for honoring my virtue; obviously I couldn't have it both ways. I turned onto my side away from him; I was angry and didn't want to look at him. I wasn't being fair and I knew it. He pulled me close to him and kissed me on my neck and bit my ear and immediately my body burned with desire.

"Jake what if I don't want to wait until I get married anymore?" I couldn't believe I was saying this but right now I wanted him more than anything.

"It's just your hormones and I don't think you know what you are saying. I don't want you to be mad at me if you become remorseful if we make love, I'm not sure I could take it." Why did he have to be so damn self-righteous?

"Well I'm mad now because you aren't making love to me." I was being daring for the first time.

"Tara, that's hardly fair." He leaned over me and turned my face towards him. "Don't be mad at me, please."

I started to cry. Why was I crying, oh my god. I was a mess. He kissed me and I quickly wrapped my arms around his neck so he couldn't escape his hair fell across his face. He was so hot. He tried to pull away from me but I pulled on him harder.

"No don't go." I kissed him harder even though the pressure was hurting my lip.

"Tara, stop. You know you will regret this in the morning." He sat up. "Can't we just lay here and let me hold you without it leading to sex?"

Now I felt like a slut. Like on of the Barbie girls from the bar. I should be so lucky to find a man like my Jake and here I was ruining it.

"Yes, of course Jake. I'm sorry. Please don't be mad at me and my stupid hormones." I smiled at him. I was back in control. He turned to look at me and we both lay down for the night. For him it would be a restful evening holding the girl he loved and for me it would be a night filled with sorrow, shame, and agony.

The darkness enveloped me like a cloak – gripping me tightly forcing me down so the metamorphosis could take place. My panic squeezed my lungs empty and I had to remind myself to relax. Immediately I could feel that I was in another person's body, it was a women's. I was getting ready to go out, hustling about looking for something to wear. I tried to catch a glimpse of myself in the mirror hoping I would recognize the face but before I could a crashing noise came from outside. I walked down the hallway toward the offending noise and observed the living space to be rather narrow and long like a trailer. The bedroom from where I came was in the back, then I passed the bathroom, and into the kitchen and finally I was in the living room. I peeked out the window but it was dark outside except for the orange glow of the streetlight. I walked back towards the bathroom and another crash, this time it sounded like someone knocked over a garbage can. I tried to ignore it and looked into the mirror to finish putting on my make-up. I was young, maybe 24. I had brown hair, pale skin, thin, about 5 foot 7. I had beautiful blue eyes. A knock came at the door and I ran to get it. She was expecting someone, I could feel her excitement. I opened the door but instantly knew this wasn't the person she was waiting for.

"What's wrong? You were expecting someone else?" It was Devin.

"Who are you, what do you want?" She backed up mistakenly letting him in. I tried to fight against her and make her do my will but she didn't -- I was trapped in her body with no control.

"Well if this is the only way I can have you then this is how I will do it." He closed the door behind him and she ran towards the bedroom. What did that mean?

She slid closed the door but there was no lock. I looked around for a weapon, nothing. Here it goes again, another victim, but Devin? Could this be right?

He slid the door open and grabbed my dress, pulling me close to him and kissed me hard on the mouth. "Stop! Stop!" she yelled.

"Please just do as I say and everything will be okay. No one will get hurt."

Maybe he was right. Maybe if she just gave in and gave him what he wanted he would go away. He pushed her on the bed, his hands ripped her underwear off and he slid his hands up over her hips.

"You see, just relax and I will be on my way."

It was him alright. There was no mistaking his green eyes. Buy why would he be in my dream, did I bring him here?

He stood up and took off his pants. The sight must have spooked her because she tried to get away. He grabbed her by the hair and was on top of her with his other hand around her neck. With his powerful grasp he flipped her on her back. He was looking me right in the eyes, this was a nightmare. I felt exposed, like he knew it was me and I couldn't hide within this other person, he was too close, too intimate, too Devin! He was choking me with his hand around my neck. I could hardly breathe.

"I've been waiting a long time for this Tara." And with that he forced himself inside me; the pain was so immense that the fact that he said my name was lost on me. The act didn't seem to ever stop. I screamed from the pain, this wasn't how I imagined sex to be. He seemed to be lost in his business and I began searching for a way out. I tried to keep from looking at his face because all I could see was Devin.

"Oh Tara, you belong with me. You know you want me to. Don't just lay there make love to me." He rolled over and sat me up on top of him. He grabbed my breasts and now he was further inside me. The pain was unbearable I could feel I was losing consciousness. I knew it wasn't supposed to bet his way, he was doing it on purpose. The tears were streaming down my face and I was screaming in protest. He sat up and held his arms around me.

"Why are you crying Tara. This is what you wanted right? You wanted to be made love to right? This is what I'm doing, you are my love and I'm making love to you."

I tried to struggle away from him but he held me tighter, he was so strong. The massive pain between my legs was more then I could bear, I tried to lift myself off but he dug his hands into my hips and pulled me harder onto him. I felt like I was being torn inside. There was no way out of this, I just gave up. I stopped struggling, I stopped moving, and I just went limp. He flipped me around on my stomach and came at me from behind. My piercing screams were all that kept me lucid. I knew I had to get out of this body; I had to find the strength somehow to end this torment—this nightmare. With as much fight as I could muster I pushed against the force that bound me, I could feel its grip loosen, I pushed harder and harder and like a bolt of lightening I shot free of the body. It was unnoticeable by everyone but me. I turned to look behind me as I walked down the hallway and saw that Devin was still having his way with the girl. I could no longer feel the pain but I knew the memories would be burned into my brain forever.

I hid behind the chair in the living room. I began to quietly sob until I heard another scream and then a gurgling sound. Devin walked into the kitchen and sat down a bloody knife on the counter. He washed his hands. The girl must have fell off the bed or moved somehow because the noise had Devin running back into the bedroom. I went for the knife. I grabbed it and ran outside. It was a trailer park. I crawled under the trailer and hid it on top of one of the steel joists.

I slid out from underneath, the tiny rocks jabbing into my legs and the little girl was standing there smiling.

"Oh my god, you scared me. Where have you been?"

"I've been trying to find you."

"Well I think I'm closer to figuring this out."

"Be careful Tara. You can't let him know of your powers or he'll use them against you."

"What powers."

"Your ability to control your dreams."

"But I can't control my dreams."

"You just did."

I thought about it for a moment and she was right. It took all my might but I was able to free myself from the girl and then do what I wanted in the dream.

"When you visit your Uncle you will learn more how to use your powers and develop your ability." She hugged me now and the darkness lifted.

It was morning and I was still in my own bed. I was thankful for that, no roaming the halls and no waking Jake in the middle of the night. Jake rolled over and kissed me good morning.

"No dreams?" He looked so delicious in the morning.

"Oh just a few," that I wasn't about to share with him.

I turned to put my arms around him and a thousand jabbing knives sliced through the bottom half of my body and I froze.

"What's wrong?"

I couldn't answer only a small squeak escaped my lips. When I left the girl's body the pain was gone but now it was more intense then I remember from last night. My endorphins kicked in and the pain subsided but I was afraid to move—afraid to pull the blanket back for fear of what I might see. But Jake wasn't as patient or as understanding.

"Tara, I asked you what's wrong."

"I just had a really sharp pain." I didn't want to explain why.

"Are you hurt, where's the pain?" The urgency in his voice was unavoidable. Experience told him he had a reason to worry.

I didn't know how to explain where the pain was nor was I ready to move so I could show him where. I was too afraid the pain would return. But before I had a moment to contemplate further he threw the blankets back and I heard him suck in his breath. The contorted look on his face forced me to look. I also drew in a sudden breath when I saw the source of my pain.

My underwear was torn half off of me revealing scrapes along my hips and blood stained the sheets. My legs were full of bruises; purple hand prints lined my thighs. My shirt was gone and my breasts were also bruised. Jake jumped from the bed as if avoiding a deadly plague.

"Tara! What happened to you? How did this happen?"

"Jake, please. Don't make me answer that." I knew how Jake felt about Devin. I just couldn't believe it was Devin or maybe it was me putting his face in there subconsciously.

"Why? Who was it?" After my silence he gave up. "Actually it doesn't matter we need to get you to a doctor." He moved to pick me up.

"No! I can't see a doctor. I'm fine. I don't have anything to tell them to explain to them what happened." I tried to move my legs and I could feel the pain travel through my whole body. I hurt too bad to be embarrassed that I was practically naked in front of him.

Jake grabbed a housecoat for me and helped me up. I slowly walked to the bathroom. The more I walked the better I felt. I turned the shower on and once I could see the steam I got in.

The water was so hot it stung my skin but I had to get the images out of my head and the pain helped erase my thoughts. The blood swirled around the drain as the water washed it off my body. Why, why was this happening to me? The heat relaxed my muscles, I no longer had the strength to hold onto my strong exterior and soon I was overcome with emotion. I lay down in the bathtub, curled up and began to cry. I didn't think I would ever stop. I heard a knock at the door.

"Tara, are you okay?" It was Jake. I didn't answer, I couldn't answer I was crying so hard. I heard the door open and felt the water stop pulsing against my skin. He covered me with a towel and lifted me out of the tub. The tears still weren't dried up yet, I think I was in shock. Jake sat me on the bed; he had changed the sheets while I was in the shower. He put a nightgown on me, dried my hair and laid me down. I couldn't speak. I was trembling. I felt as though I would never be able to sleep again. I needed to figure this out before it was too late, before I was the next victim.

I decided that I wouldn't sleep until I was prepared to fight against my enemy and right now I didn't know how. I would have to stay awake until I talked with my Uncle Gerald. Three days.

Chapter 9: The Eagle

I wasn't much of a coffee drinker but it wasn't too bad when you added cream and lots of sugar. I started to drink monster drinks, rockstar, and anything with caffeine that I could get my hands on. After the first night of no sleep I felt pretty good and realized this would be easier then I thought. Jake seemed a little concerned that I just seemed to brush myself off and go on about my business as if nothing had happened. Once the pain wore off, albeit with a few pain pills from Melissa, I was back to my normal routine, minus the sleep and that just had Jake confused. The only thing that did throw me was Devin. That very night he was there at the bar and very excited to see me.

"Tara! Guess what? I'm taking you to a Broadway show, whatever show you want to see! It's all on the producers of the play." He grabbed me around the waist and I cringed. I wasn't smiling.

"Why aren't you excited?" His green eyes were so close to mine that the memory of him flashed before me.

I pushed him away and headed towards the bathroom. "Yes, I'm excited. I just have a lot going on." It had to be my subconscious putting his face in my dream; he wasn't a killer and a rapist. Now it was ruining my friendship with him. I felt horrible for treating him like this when he was just trying to be nice to me.

I returned to work and decided to take a break. All the caffeine I had been ingesting was beginning to make me feel sick to my stomach. I needed some food to help even me out. Jamie joined me and we shared a plate of fries.

"So I hear you are going out of town for awhile." She dunked her fry in ranch dip and inhaled it.

With my eyebrows pinched together, "How did you know?" This place was a rumor mill.

"Oh people talk. I also heard that you and Jake are on the rocks." She arched her brow.

"Now that's ridiculous. We're fine." I stuffed another fry in my mouth.

She eyed my bruised cheek, "Are you now?"

"It wasn't Jake, I fell. You know what a klutz I am." Hopefully this would dispel the rumors.

"Well Devin sure seems to have takin' a likin' to you." Her voice was sweet as saccharin. Where was she going with this?

"He offered to help me with some contacts that's all. Plus he seems to keep himself pretty busy with his own flock of girls, he doesn't need me." And that was the truth. He was always after some young hot thing that walked in here. I grabbed the newspaper to interrupt our conversation and pretended to be deeply engrossed in the latest celebrity gossip. Eventually she got bored and got back to work. I was happy she gave up and I was about to get back to work too when a headline caught my attention.

"Broadway Starlet found Raped and Murdered" My pulse raced as I scanned the article. There was no picture but they mentioned that she was a relative newcomer and was about to embark on her first big break. She was found night before last murdered in a mobile home park in New Jersey. This was the same night that I experienced my dream. My dream was not a premonition because it was happening at the same time. Was I really there, did I really hide the knife?

"I don't pay you to sit around reading the paper and eating fries" I jumped 10 feet in the air at the sound of Patrick's booming voice. "Now get back to work!"

I hurried to clear the table, the caffeine had me bouncing off the walls, and I tripped as I came around the table. When I fell to the ground I landed on the glass plate with a loud crash. I felt the jagged edge pierce my skin and slice open my hand.

"Damn it Tara!" Patrick was right above me. "Get up!" I scrambled to get up. What was his problem? "Pick up this mess and get back to work." I knelt down, tucked my hair behind my ears, this is why I usually wore it up it was always in my face, and began picking up the pieces. I noticed the large slice across the palm of my hand and the blood was really dripping.

From behind the bar Ed came with a white bar towel. I guess he noticed my performance too. He grabbed my arm and wrapped the towel around my hand. His hand wrapped around my arm flashed the memory of my bony shackle; it was so pale against my tan skin.

"That ought to help stop the bleeding." He was so tall and gangly but nice in his own way, I felt bad for teasing him in my mind.

"Thanks Ed."

"You might want to wash your face, you got blood on it." He gestured with his fingers across his cheek.

"Oh, thank you." I glanced over at Jake and his eyes widened when he saw me. I practically ran to the bathroom, I didn't want Jake to worry over me again.

Too late, he was standing outside the bathroom when I exited.

"What's going on? What happened to your hand?" He had his arms crossed in front of him. His constant supervision was starting to irritate me.

"It's nothing. I tripped and fell on my plate. I just cut my hand. Ed gave me a towel and now it's all better." I showed him but since I didn't have a band aid the cut was wide open and it still oozed blood.

"It's all better huh? You scared me half to death. I look over to see Mr. Death standing over you and you have blood across your face." He sighed deeply. "I wish Melissa would just stay at her boyfriend's so I could stay over. Being apart from you is driving me crazy."

"Jake, I'm fine. I need to get back to work before Patrick yells at me again. I can't afford to lose this job." I was on my second night of no sleep and starting to get a little irritated.

"Just promise me you will try and be careful." I heard this last part as I was walking away back into the crowd of people that had just come in from a winning co-ed softball game. It was fixin' to get real busy.

"Ed, what do you recommend to get me through the night?" Ed shot me a look of surprise and Devin walked over to me.

"How about some coffee with Baileys and Cream?" Ed began to make me a cup.

"Sure whatever." I was trying to hurry up and grab some menus to avoid Devin but I wasn't able to slip away fast enough.

"What's going on Tara, are you okay?" His green eyes stopped me in my tracks, that look, that face, I just had to get away. I turned around to deliver the menus to the new bunch of patrons without saying a word. I thought he would get the hint but realized when I reached the table that he was right behind me. I passed out the menus and took drink orders still ignoring the fact that he was standing right there. Not another scene tonight, please. I turned around but he wasn't there he was up at the bar, I could have sworn he'd followed me, I could feel his presence; feel his warm breath against my neck. I stood there dumbfounded, confused. I walked back to the bar to give Ed my order but came up next to Devin.

"Devin, did you follow me just a minute ago?" I bit my lip trying to hold in my nervousness.

"Tara, darling what is the matter with you? I just asked if you were okay and you walked away from me. I've been standing right here the whole time." He smiled wryly and took another drink of his beer.

"Here you go Tara; this should grow a little hair on your chest." The sight of Ed smiling gave me the chills but I willingly took the cup of coffee. I took a sip and the creamy flavor was delicious. It didn't take long and the cup was gone and I was onto my next. It did perk me up however me being the light weight that I was the alcohol made me a tad bit clumsier then normal. I spilt a couple beers, not on the customers thank god and I ran into a few people but they were dancing so it didn't seem too out of place. People were having a great time and getting pretty drunk myself included. I decided to skip the Baileys this time around and just go with cream and sugar. Again I felt the presence of Devin right next to me but when I turned he wasn't there and seeing him far away at the bar no where near me resulted in a chill that never seemed to leave me.

It was time for last call and most people had left for the night all but a few diehards and those were always the fun ones. I wasn't looking forward to telling these yahoos that the party was over. It was the guy half of the co-ed softball team.

"Hey guys, it's time to wrap things up. Last call."

"Come here little lady, come take a seat next to us and take our order." He patted the booth next to him and I decided it wouldn't hurt to be friendly. I went to sit down next to him but he grabbed me around the waist and pulled me down hard upon his knee. Under normal circumstances this probably would have been fine but after my tortuous dream the other night the pain shot through me so hard and so fast that the scream that escaped my lips was impulsive. Jake bolted to their table and grabbed me up in his arms and I just fell, it hurt so badly. The poor guy had no idea what he did wrong.

"Man I swear I didn't do a thing." His hands were raised in a sign of surrender.

"No problem, I understand." Jake took me outside so we could have some privacy. I was thankful there weren't many people inside.

Once we got outside Jake grabbed my face between his hands "You're white as a ghost Tara, I knew you weren't okay, why did you feel the need to hide it? You could have taken a few nights off." He looked as though he were in as much pain as me.

"I took some pain pills of Melissa's but they wore off. Plus I wasn't expecting to be slammed against some man's knee." I wiped away the tears. I was so ready to just give up, I couldn't handle this anymore. Everywhere I went, everything I did was just a catastrophe. "I just want to go home." I started slowly walking down the sidewalk, the pain still reverberating through my body.

"Tara, wait, please. Let me pack up my stuff and I'll walk you home." I just kept walking. Maybe whatever was out there would just get me now and end it all. "Tara, I don't want you walking home alone." I still ignored him. I heard the front door open. "I have to get my stuff will you please stop her."

Running soon followed, it was Jamie. "Tara, wait up!" I turned and she slowed her pace to a walk. "What's going on?"

"Nothing, I'm just ready to go home." I started to turn but she put her hand on my shoulder.

"Tara, just wait for Jake. He said he would walk you home."

With a big smile I told her "I'm a big girl, I can walk myself home, it's only 20 minutes away." I turned again and began to walk down the path to home.

Behind me I heard, "You're being ridiculous! You shouldn't walk home alone at night."

I knew I should just wait for Jake but I was done with all of this, all of these nightmares, these visions, and I was just ready to give up and let whatever was after me just get me if it wanted me. Jake was treating me like I was some breakable little piece of glass and I was tired of feeling like he had to look after me like a child. Only two more nights and I would be upstate where hopefully I would be able to figure this mess out. In the meantime if whatever was out there wanted me then fine it could have me.

I continued to walk down my sidewalk. It was a warm night. I noticed that the streets were deserted, no one was around. I knew it was late but people were always hanging around, that was one cool thing about the city, even our little place, people were up all hours of the night.

I was so tired and sore. I wasn't sure I could make it another night without sleep but I had to try. I continued walking. The warm air massaging my whole body put me in a state of relaxation.

I heard footsteps coming up behind me and knew Jake must have really hustled to get all his stuff put away to catch up to me this fast. I really needed to give him a break; he was only looking out for me. I stopped and took a deep breathe, calming myself so I wouldn't overreact to his over protectiveness.

I turned around expecting to see my Jake but there was no one. No one was running towards me to walk me home, no one was running towards me to see if I was okay. I was standing their by myself. I turned back around in disbelief. I moped forward and noticed that the sidewalk surface was changing to cobblestone. I blinked my eyes and it was back to normal. I looked up ahead and it was very dark like the tunnel from my dreams. I shook my head trying to erase the vision from my eyes. I turned and glanced up at the eves of the apartment buildings and standing in the entryways were the dead women from months past. The lady in red with her throat slit, the young lady from my first dream, next the blonde with the pentagram stars carved into her skin and her heart missing. They just stood there, starring at me with empty eyes. My heart raced and I started to tremble. They aren't real, I chanted to myself as I continued to walk down the cobblestone pathway using my hands as blinders to block out the revolting images. I peaked over my hand to see if they were still there and saw Sam with a blood stained shirt. This was impossible; they were all hallucinations because I was so tired, they had to be. The footsteps started again behind me but this time they were quicker, they were coming after me, I knew it. I had to get away. I stepped off the cobblestone, away from the morbid scene but I could still hear the footsteps, they were getting closer. I closed my eyes, squeezed them tight and wrapped my arms around my head. Make it stop, make it stop, make it stop. I repeated in my head. A bright light pierced the darkness behind my eyelids. Was it the morning sun, had I been dreaming all along? I heard my name being yelled but I didn't dare turn to look. Suddenly there was a loud blaring noise and I was lifted off the ground. I felt arms around my waist and I was practically thrown from the spot I was standing in.

I forced opened my eyes to discover Jake standing before me, tight lipped, steel jawed, and just glaring at me. It wasn't morning after all. I was confused, a minute ago I felt I was back in the dark cobblestone tunnel with dead girls lining the walls and now here I stand on the sidewalk, everyday people going about their business, sitting on their eves drinking and smoking. My eyes darted from doorway to doorway, no dead girls, just living breathing people. But they were just there, no, no, I know what I saw. I turned and continued to walk home. Jake huffed and without saying a word, walked next to me all the way home.

We were home in a matter of minutes and I unlocked the door. Jake followed me in to my surprise; I had assumed he wouldn't want to stay. I wanted to tell him I was sorry but I had no words to explain what happened.

"Tara, why couldn't you wait?" He stood there, fists clenched.

"I, I was ready to go home," I said meekly, I knew he was right and I should have just waited but I tried to hang on to my defiance.

"I just don't understand you sometimes." His voice was rigid with anger.

I walked into the kitchen trying to ignore his glare. "What's not to understand?"

"Tara, you do realize you were standing in the middle of the road, you were almost hit by a car! Didn't you see it? You act as though nothing happened." He had closed the distance between us. I tried to move away from him but he caught my arm and held me there. "No, you will answer me."

"No I didn't see the car. I'm sorry." I yanked my arm away from him and headed to the bathroom. I took down my pants to go to the bathroom and the purple bruises were turning greenish now. When would this nightmare end? I hadn't seen the car, I thought I was being chased through a dark tunnel but I wasn't about to admit this to him. I washed up and went straight to my room and only then did I realize that Melissa wasn't here. I assumed she was staying at her boyfriends again but that meant Jake would want to stay over but he didn't know that I wasn't sleeping, that I was trying to stay awake.

I pulled on my nightgown and Jake showed up in the doorway.

"Tara, don't be angry with me, it just seems like every time I turn around something is trying to take you away."

He was so lovely and beautiful, it was hard to resist him and I wasn't angry at him. I came to him and gave him a huge hug and kiss. "You'll stay then?"

"If you don't mind?" He looked down at me through his wispy bangs.

"Never."

We got in bed and I thought I was safe from sleep since I had drank more than enough coffee to at least keep me up after he went to sleep and then I could get up and watch some T.V. to distract me from how tired I actually was. Jake pulled me close to him and held me tightly. I loved being in his arms, he was so comforting, strong, and all mine. My eyes were heavy; the sleep weighing them down, will alone was unable to keep them open. Jake's body was so warm against mine; he was like my personal heater warming me up and lulling me to sleep. His soft breath was quiet and soothing and soon the darkness was all around me and the familiar tight paralyzing grip surrounded my body. It was too late now, there was no going back. I was locked into my dream, no choice of where it would lead me.

The wind was blowing leafless branches, tiny tornados of garbage and leaves rustling around me. I was standing in the middle of a field. I could hear the rumble of thunder in the distance. My hair whipped at my face, I tried unsuccessfully to keep it out of my eyes so I could see. I was waiting, waiting for the darkness of the tunnel or to sink within another body to experience the excruciating murder I was sure to commit but nothing, I just continued to stand there in the field as the distant storm moved in on me. Haunting pine trees loomed around me circling the field where I stood. The wind screamed through the trees bending them forward to the point that I thought they would snap. The field grass sliced at my legs stinging my skin. I looked up into the ominous sky and the deep purple and black clouds streaked across the heavens, lightening bringing them to life. A high pitched screech pierced through the whistling of the wind and towering above me on a leafless lifeless branch sat a stoic eagle his feathers ruffled by the wind. He screeched again as he stared, I thought, right at me. I looked around me to see what he could see that was forcing the high-pitched siren from his throat, but there was nothing, no rabbits, no vermin, no snakes, no danger to warn me of. I looked back up at the eagle and behind him flashed the glowing red eyes of the satanic goat's head branded into the now purple and red clouds. I looked away with fear. Behind me the storm was moving faster towards me, I could see the outline of a tornado. A rustling through the trees was growing louder until it sounded as though it were right upon me, pounding, crashing and breaking branches. Bursting through the forest wall a herd of buffalo trampled the field grass and came bounding right towards me. The only difference was these buffalo had not their usual heads they had been transformed into riling mutated goat heads.

I could see the steam blow out of their nostrils as they charged towards me. The eagle screeched again but then flew off leaving me alone to be trampled. The panic set in, was this how I was to die? Something dark out of the corner of my eye flew in from off to my side and snatched me up, moving me out of the way just as the herd was about to take my life. I was being carried higher and higher above the open field. As I looked down I saw the buffalo continue on their dangerous path trampling the life out of all that lay before them. The eagle must have swooped in and saved me from sure death. I looked behind me to find Jake holding me; he was flying with immense wings. He flew me high into the sky above all the danger and I felt like I was free, like I was floating. It was the best feeling, one I hadn't felt in so long. I felt safe and I felt strong. The sky began to clear and the wind died down and up ahead I could see my eagle. Jake landed and carefully placed me in a field of wildflowers. I turned to look at him and he wrapped his arms around me and his large wings enveloped me.

I woke feeling at peace for the first time since I moved to New York. I felt rested and I felt strong.

Chapter 10: Unlucky four-leaf clover

Only one more night till I would be on my way to see my family on the reservation, I knew I could make it through the day now. I thought I better call my Uncle and let him know to expect me. I rang him on my cell phone.

"Uncle Gerald?"

"Yes."

"It's Tara, your niece from Arizona."

"Tara! Wow, how are you?"

"Umm okay."

"What say you?"

"Well I'm living in Inwood New York now; I have been for the last three and half months."

"Yes, your mother called to tell me you would come see me soon."

"Well yeah, that's why I'm calling. I was thinking of driving up tomorrow if that's okay with you?" I bit my lip, nerves were taking over. What if wasn't a good time? I never figured this into my equation. I needed to see him now, I couldn't wait.

"Sure, Tara, I'll be here this weekend."

I let out a big sigh of relief. "I also have a friend that's coming with me."

"Sure, the more the better. We'll take him out on the boat and show him our beautiful water."

"Okay. Wait how did you know it was a boy?"

"Oh someone here mentioned a white boy would come visit us with questions on his face and I just assumed when you mentioned a friend, well we don't get many visitors with questions except which way is the casino?" With that he let out a big laugh. Normally I would laugh too but the thought that someone saw us coming had me excited and I realized that I might not be alone in my special ability.

"Okay Uncle I'll see you tomorrow night probably."

"Onen"

"Onen"

I hugged my cell phone as if it were him; I didn't think I could make it through another night. Jake came up behind me and hugged me tightly. Well maybe I could make it through another night with Jake by my side. I turned around in his arms and circled my arms around his neck and kissed him softly. His lips were like two rose petals, just the sweet smell of his breath made my stomach tingle, I loved him so much. I never thought I would ever find someone I would fall for like this.

"You're smiling; you're in a good mood." His sapphire eyes were smiling down at me.

"That I am Mr. Jake and nothing is going to ruin it. Tomorrow we will be with my family and that's all I'm thinking about."

We didn't have much time till our shift started, actually till my shift started. Jake didn't really need to be there until later but when he was with me he would walk me to work and just hang out until it was time for him to play. Some nights I wished I could just sit back and listen to him play. I often wanted to ask him to play for me but I figured after long nights of playing he wouldn't want to take requests from me.

The walk to work was pleasant, a little warm for me but it always was. It was mid August and muggy. I could feel the sweat dripping down my back under my t-shirt. So much for the shower I took. It was Saturday night so I knew my shift would go fast. Saturday's were always a mad house. As we were closing in on the pub I could see Devin's red car parked out front. I swear what did this guy do for a living? He was always out drinking; did he even have a job?

Before I could pull the door open Jake stopped me.

"What?"

"Promise me Tara, that if you feel like it's too much" I sighed and dropped my head, "I'm serious." He held my face in his hands. "Don't push yourself, if you need to go home early just tell me and I'll walk you home. Don't leave me again like last night." He bent down and kissed me passionately. I wasn't expecting my exploding nerves and my knees went weak. He wrapped his other arm around my waist and held me to him and the closeness took my breath away. I really hope I had the same affect on him. One of these days I would have to really try and work my magic on him instead of the other way around. He released his hold on me and we walked into work with me a little fuzzy in the head.

I canvassed the place and saw the usual suspects except for a couple new guys standing next to Devin. I walked back to the kitchen to get my apron. Walking back to the bar Devin called me over to him.

"Tara, I want you to meet Mr. Julius Wayne and Mr. Thomas Henry. These are the financiers of the upcoming play you will be performing in." They stood there in their black suits and wide grins and here I was in a t-shirt and jeans, bar apron, with my hair in a ponytail.

"Hi! It's nice to meet you. I'm very excited about the play and thank you for hiring me."

"No thank you Miss. Devin's told us nothing but wonderful things about you and we're very happy about the story line and think this will be a success." They both shook my hand their heads bobbing up and down like bobble heads, staring at me and then each other.

"He has, has he?" I shot a look to Devin as he stood there admiring me with those jade green eyes of his, he really could do no wrong. "Well sometime Devin will have to tell me a little about the story since I don't know anything about it; I guess it's some mystery to the cast. You'll excuse me. I have to get to work." I smiled as nicely as I could.

"Sure, no problem." Devin's smile seemed to tarnish slightly but not for long. He ordered more drinks for all of them. Why he would bring them here, they stood out like a sore thumb, hardly a place they would normally hang out.

I took some orders and turned them into the kitchen and then placed more drink orders. I noticed that Devin and his friends weren't just drinking beer they were on to the hard stuff to include shots.

"Ed, can I get a couple waters please."

I took the waters over to Jake's table. He was sitting way on the other side of the pub reading the paper. He didn't even look up at me when I set down his water.

"So what are Devin and his loons up to now?"

"I guess he brought in the financiers of that play to introduce me to."

Jake flipped down one side of the paper to peer up at me.

"You're not still seriously thinking of doing that play are you?"

"Why not? It's a job."

"Whatever." He flipped the paper back up and continued reading. I hated when he did this. He just didn't trust Devin and I didn't know why. I wasn't going to have a bad night I swore to it, so I left Jake to sulk by his self.

I was correct in that the night would fly by. We had a packed house and Patrick even called in extra waitresses. Jake had help with music tonight. He had been working with a band and they were playing a set that was more rock. I knew it was a little out of his comfort zone but they sounded amazing. The band talked Patrick into adding more speakers and so it was extremely loud. Patrick said that if it went well then he would advertise them next week. He knew that he got more business when Jake was playing.

Around 7 p.m. Patrick started calling each of us waitresses back into his office. At first I was worried but then I saw Jamie come out and I rolled my eyes. Then one by one each of the other girls came out in the new uniforms that Patrick picked out for all of us to wear.

He still hadn't called my name and I thought maybe I would get out of having to wear one, wishful thinking. "Tara! Come here." Great it was my turn.

I walked back to his office, slowly, dread in every step. I pushed open his door and Patrick stood in front of his desk where four samples of shirts were spread out before me. I couldn't believe I was supposed to fit into one of those, they looked like little girl shirts they were so short. I read through my selection:

"Find a 4-leaf clover & get lucky!"

"Show me your Kilt...I'll show you mine!"

"Piper's Kilt Girls do it better!"

"Find your pot-o-gold at Piper's Kilt" This one had a rainbow that ended right at my boob.

"You're kidding right?"

Patrick stood there, arms across his chest and eyebrows raised. I snatched a t-shirt off the desk and walked off in a huff. I heard Patrick's voice trailing behind me.

"I want you wearing that tonight!"

I made an immediate left into the restroom. This was ridiculous. I locked myself in the stall and sat on the toilet contemplating my job over a stupid t-shirt. I figured I would just wear the t-shirt until I found another job. I pulled my shirt up over my head, then grabbing the white t-shirt I forced it on with contempt. It was snug and came down a couple inches above my bellybutton. There was no way I would even wear this in the privacy of my own home let alone in public. I came out of the stall and stood in front of the mirror. The white stood out against my tan skin or the other way around. The form fitting shirt showed off my bosom which wasn't as small as I thought, I guess I was always hiding under baggy shirts so they seemed smaller to me. I let down my hair thinking maybe it would cover the words on my chest with no luck. Of course there was no mistaking the large 4-leaf clovers covering my boobs. I figured I might as well get this over with and swung open the door. Leaning up against the wall and blocking the hall was Devin.

"I was wondering which uniform you were going to choose." He tried to brush my hair off of my shoulder to better see my shirt but I shrugged him off.

"Move out of my way Devin." I stared straight ahead trying to avoid his eyes but I couldn't help but see him in my peripheral vision.

"Tara, that's no way to show your appreciation for someone who got you your big break." He was smiling that devilish smile that tended to melt my insides but not tonight. He was drunk.

"You've been drinking Devin, you had better go home." I tried to make a move around him but his arm caught me around the shoulder and pushed me back with a little more force then I think he planned and it knocked me into the bathroom door. His lack of concern scared me.

"Devin, I need to get back to work." I said this forcefully but then decided on another tactic and turned sweet as honey. "Why don't I get you another drink, come on, come with me." I grabbed his hand but that wasn't what he wanted. He slid his other hand down my side.

"Devin, no, come on let's go to the bar." I said trying to move away from him. The muscles in his jaw hardened to stone, his gaze dripping with lust, his breathing intensified and his hand clutched my side. I knew then that I had lost the upper hand and things were going to get out of hand very quickly. The memories of him from my dream kept flashing before my eyes and I had to push away the panic to try and stay in control. He pushed me back into the bathroom door which opened behind me. I walked backwards to keep a distance but he kept pushing me until I was flat against the bathroom wall trapped by Devin's roaming hands. He reached both hands around my neck forcing my chin upwards with just his thumbs then kissed me hard. My head was racing, trying to figure out how to get out of this.

"Devin, stop." I mumbled between kisses.

"You wanted me before, so here I am." He dropped his hands down to my hips, grabbed my thighs, lifting me up, forcing my legs apart and around him. He pushed himself up against me and held me to the wall, kissing my neck.

With more command in my voice now I yelled at him "Devin! I mean it, stop!" The music vibrated the walls and I realized now that no one could hear me. The terror rose up into my chest and took away my breath. He held me against the wall with his body so hard I couldn't move, freeing his hands to grope me. His lips traveled down my chest and I clawed at his hair and head to pry him off of me. Thank God the door to the bathroom opened but when whoever it was got a look at the scene before them they quickly turned and ran out.

"No! Come back! Help me!" My screams were lost in the music.

Devin leaned back to undo his pants and again I tried to push him away but it was like hitting a brick wall. His pants were undone but then realized he would have to undo mine before he could go any further.

"Tara, please help me here. You know you want me." He flashed those dazzling green eyes up at me and I slapped him as hard as I could, my hand stinging with pain. He grabbed both my wrists and pinned them hard against the wall.

"Don't ever hit me again!" He hungrily kissed my lips, which were sore from the brutal assault they had already taken. By now my legs had dropped down and I was standing on both feet. The bathroom door swung open and Ed stood in the doorway.

"Man, save it for later, let her go!"

Devin loosened his grip slightly and turned to look at Ed. I took advantage of the distraction and kneed him in the groin. Immediately I was free as Devin doubled over in pain and I ran past Ed and out of the bathroom. I knew Devin was going to be pissed with me. I could only hope that he would be too drunk to remember anything.

Disheveled, I came around the corner, smoothing my hair down. I looked over to the stage to find Jake staring at me. He raised his head as if to say what's up? I nervously shook my head back and forth, forcing a smile and grabbed some menus to hand out. I turned to see Ed walk out with Devin behind him. Devin's golden hair was a mess and he was walking with a limp. He yelled something at Ed then bent over as if to catch his breath. I turned back around to try and ignore it but didn't have the courage to look at Jake because I knew he just saw what I had. I can only imagine what he must think and now to see me prance around in this ridiculously skimpy shirt. Well the day did start out good.

I wasn't able to take a break tonight so by the end of the night my feet were burning and sore. The only thing that kept me going was the fact that I had a couple days off and I would be on my way to see my Uncle in the morning.

Devin avoided me like the plague for the remainder of the evening which wasn't long for him because Patrick told him to leave once he found out how drunk he was. Thank goodness the financiers had already gone so they didn't have to see his gross display of immaturity.

Jake wasn't quite ready to sit down for the night by the time I was, he was busy putting away all the extra equipment from his big night with the band. They were really good and they had the groupies to prove it. A whole bunch of young 20 something's were hanging out waiting for the band and I'm sure some of them had their eye on my Jake.

I sat down in our booth with my diet soda, propped my feet up on the seat across from me and watched the display of affection the girls showered on the band members. Jake took off his knit hat and his tousled hair tumbled down across his forehead and I thought I could hear a collective sigh from the girls down front. He smiled quietly to himself, his head down, almost as if embarrassed by the constant admiration. If only he knew that that's what the girls seemed to like the most, his humble, I'm not good enough for you, I don't deserve your affection persona that he gave off. Oh well, what did it matter when all his love and affection was directed towards me anyway. I guess I just got a little jealous when they forced themselves on him. I didn't like them to touch him, even in the smallest of ways such as now. One of the girls grabbed him around the neck to pull him closer to her so she could whisper something in his ear all the while her breasts rubbed oh so gently against his chest. I could feel the heat rush into my cheeks even after I told myself to remain calm. Weren't these girls taught anything about personal space?

He brought his head back up and I thought I could hear him say thank you. He was finally finished packing up his stuff and he headed to the bar to get a beer. He scooted into our booth, took a big drink, and smiled at me. He grabbed one of my legs and started to rub and squeeze it, he knew they were tired and sore. I was in heaven and I knew that I was very lucky. The girls started to disperse once they realized that he wasn't going to leave with one of them and there was no Devin tonight to take his place.

"What did she want?" I just couldn't let it go I had to let the green-eyed monster out.

His eyebrows creased together, "What did who want?"

"That girl whispered something in your ear, I was just wondering what she wanted." I tried to act like I didn't care so I played with my straw too cowardly to even look him in the eye.

"She said that we sounded really good." He titled his head as he said this to me with a half smile. "And I said Thank You."

I took a drink of my soda, I felt like a fool.

"What did you think of the music tonight?"

"Me? I thought it was awesome, you sounded great!" I couldn't hide my excitement not that I wanted to.

"Well your opinion is all that matters to me." His smile was wide and crept up into his blue eyes.

I smiled back at him. He was older than me and it was during moments like these that you could really tell. I wasn't used to dealing with jealousy and I've never been overly confident about my looks so this match of ours always seemed to throw me for a loop. From the very first moment I saw Jake I never thought that he would feel for me the way I feel for him.

I stood up to go and Jake followed suit. He handed me his black and white checkered jacket. It wasn't cold out but I knew why he handed it to me it was so I could cover up. "What, you don't like my new uniform?" I rolled my eyes.

"Everyone likes it, that's the problem." He looked around from under his eyelashes as if he were embarrassed.

"Everyone?" I stared right at him.

He smiled. "If you were wearing it just for me I would love it but your not so would you please put on the jacket?" I grabbed the jacket out of his hand and put it on. I tried to push the sleeves up over my hands but they wouldn't stay and Jake huffed and patiently began to roll them up for me. I felt like a little kid.

We walked outside and the air was sticky and warm. I could hear thunder in the distance and it reminded me at once of my dream. Drops of rain began to fall and we quickened our step. Soon I was holding his jacket up over my head to keep from getting drenched but poor Jake was soaked.

We slopped into the lobby of my apartment complex and decided to take the elevator as wet jeans made it pretty difficult to climb stairs. The elevator climbed slowly up the 5 flights and chimed our arrival. Jake shoved the iron gate open and I dug for my keys as we walked to my door. It had been a while since I last walked this hallway. No voices, no footsteps, I felt pretty safe tonight.

I turned the key and I was in, no bolt or chain which meant no Melissa. "I hope you will stay the night again Jake, you wouldn't want to walk home in the rain."

"Well I need to take a shower and I need to pack some clothes. So I'm thinking that I may have to pass tonight."

"Must you really go?" I tried to pout as best I could.

"Tara, I don't have any clothes with me and I still have to pack for tomorrow."

Time for another tactic I thought. I took off his jacket to reveal my new uniform and sauntered up close to him.

"Who says you need any clothes tonight. Come take a shower with me." I licked my lips and started to kiss him. He started to kiss me back but then pulled back.

"Tara, that's not fair, you're cheating." I wasn't letting him off the hook that easy. I was tired of being the one left all hot and bothered, it was going to be his turn. I shimmied down the front of him and began unbuttoning his jeans. Jake grabbed my arms and pulled me up almost lifting me off the ground like I was light as a feather.

"Tara, please, what are you doing?" His face was more shock then sexual frustration. This wasn't going like I had imagined. I had hoped he wouldn't be able to control himself but he seemed to have some sort of super human control power that was really pissing me off.

I decided to try something else so this time I kicked off my tennis shoes and started unbuttoning my jeans. Jake's eyes widened. Ah, so maybe this was my best maneuver. I gradually unzipped my jeans and turned to the side. I bent over slightly and grabbed my jeans tugging them downwards shaking my hips from side to side. They were almost over my hips, my bikini underwear were peeking through when Jake made a move towards me. Ha! Gotcha!

Jake picked me up in his arms and carried me to my room. He laid me in the bed, sat down next to me and kissed me on the forehead. "Goodnight Tara."

"Jake!" I sat up so we were eye to eye.

"Tara, don't be angry with me, I want you more then you will ever know but not tonight."

"But…" He placed his finger over my lips.

"Please don't Tara, I can't handle any more temptations, and I won't be able to resist you any more tonight." He stood up to leave but I caught his hand.

"Then stop trying. I said it was okay." His face looked as though he was in torment. Did I do this to him? Was I being unfair? I pulled him back down and he sat on the edge of the bed. His head hung down and his shoulders slumped. It was then that I decided that tonight would be the night since it was all this frustration that was making him so distraught.

I straddled him, placing his hands around me on my hips. I lightly brought his face up to meet mine and kissed him fully on the mouth. His kiss was intoxicating, there are no other words to describe it, he simply takes my breath away. Before it could be too much of a distraction I reached around him and grabbed his shirt and pulled it up over his head. I sat up higher on him so I was taller then him now and tangled my fingers in his hair arching his head back. I heard him groan and I knew he was mine. His kiss was hot. His hands pressed me harder against his groin and a shockwave pulsed through me. Damn, I was supposed to be in control. I pushed him back and he fell on the bed. He opened his eyes to me taking off that stupid uniform top and me unhooking my bra. His eyes dropped down to my breasts and then shot back up to my eyes. I knew he was asking me again if I was sure. He sat up and wrapped his arms around my lower back swinging me back around onto the bed. He stripped off his jeans and took off mine.

Jake knelt over me, 'This is it.' I thought to myself. Then I heard the front door open and Melissa's loud voice yell down the hall "Hey Tara, hope I'm not interrupting anything but I'm home and I'm staying here tonight."

Jake just lay on top of me and groaned. He didn't have to say I told you so I could read his mind. "If it's any consolation, I'm feeling just as frustrated as you." He brought his lips up to mine and kissed me deeply and he flexed his hips between my legs. I sucked in my breath and then shot him an evil look, how dare he make me want him so badly when he knew I could get no fulfillment tonight. A big grin spread across his face.

"You're simply evil Jake. Now get off me before Melissa comes in here." He jumped up and got dressed. I donned a t-shirt and sweats and walked into the living room.

"Long time no see roomy." I found Melissa in the kitchen making a sandwich.

"Yeah, well Jeremy's roommate's parents were coming to visit so I decided I wouldn't stay the night again."

"Well I'm going to be gone for a few days myself so you guys will have this place to yourselves at least until Tuesday." Jake walked in and grabbed his coat.

"I'll see you in the morning Tara. Melissa."

"Bye Jake" Melissa said in her sing song tone.

I hurried to catch him before he closed the door.

"What no kiss good-bye?" He turned in the hallway.

"I thought that's what that was in the bedroom."

"Oh, well good-bye. I'll see you tomorrow." He walked up to me and kissed me on the forehead.

"Goodnight sweet devilish Tara." His smile was beautiful; it was hard to believe that he wanted only me. With that he turned and got into the elevator. I closed the door and locked all the locks and headed to the bedroom.

Chapter 11: Trip up north

That night I lay in bed thinking of our evening and how I should have just let him go and not try to seduce him. I must have fallen asleep by the time Melissa made it to bed because I was already deep into another dream, one similar to the night before.

Jake and I were driving in a car with the storm chasing us and an Eagle was showing us the way through the storm. I felt the presence of evil following close behind, it wasn't just the storm. I checked my rearview mirror and the little girl was sitting in the back seat. I whipped around to find the seat empty. I peered back into the rearview and she was there looking at me through her blonde stringy hair. I felt desperation, her soul lost. The rumble of thunder forced me to look up into the sky and again the purple and red clouds were exploding across the sky, the wind was whipping the trees in all directions. I turned to look at Jake next to me but the red hooded man sat next to me and I screamed. His head turned to look at me and the hood slid off to reveal a mutated goats head with razor sharp horns and fiery red eyes. I heard the screech of the eagle and I tore my gaze away from the gruesome head to see the sun's blinding rays piercing through the dark sky, my ray of hope?

I blinked my eyes and I was in my room, Melissa snoring next to me. I looked out my window and the sun was shining and a little bird was hopping on my window sill. I smiled at the thought of the day's journey and the answers I was hopeful it would bring. I jumped up and rushed into the shower not even glancing at the clock. It was morning and that was all that mattered. I knew I didn't want to sleep more. When the knock came at the door I was packed and ready to go.

I quickly unlocked all the locks and with a big smile on my face I pulled back the door. My face dropped. Devin.

"Tara."

"Devin."

"I know it's early but I wanted to catch you before you left." I tried to shut the door but he held his hand out.

"Please Tara, hear me out?" His jade eyes were sorrowful as he looked up through long lashes.

I stood there with my arms crossed over my chest, defiant. The memories of last night were still fresh in my mind. I wasn't ready to forgive him no matter his excuse.

"I'm sorry, truly sorry about last night. If you never forgive me I will understand. I just had to come here and let you know that I don't know what got into me and it will never, ever happen again."

"Fine Devin, now if you will excuse me I need to get ready, I'm leaving soon."

He took a deep breath, "Sure. Will you still come to the get-together next week with cast and crew? It's sort of like a pre-cast party for the play."

"I guess so." I still didn't even know what I was getting into or what I was getting paid.

"Great! I'll touch base with you when you get back and we'll hash out the details of the contract." And with that he was on his way.

I shut the door and to be honest he took a way some of my good mood but it wasn't long and there was another knock at the door. I opened it and Jake was standing there with a backpack.

"Tara, didn't you lock the door?" His face was puzzled.

"Oh, yeah, well someone was just at the door, I guess I forgot to lock it. You ready?" I didn't want to give him a chance to ask who it was visiting at this hour; actually I was surprised they didn't run into each other. His face was still questioning but I think he just chose to drop it.

"Yep, I'm ready."

The phone rang and it was the cab I called to take us to the car rental agency. I scribbled out a note to Melissa, leaving her my cell number in case she needed me. The ride to the rental center was quick. I was so excited I could hardly sit still. I headed to the counter to retrieve my rental car.

"Your name please?""

"Tara Mason."

"Yes, you have an economy reserved, would you like to upgrade to a standard, you'll have more leg room?"

"Naw, that's okay." I shuffled my feet behind the counter, impatient, ready to begin our drive upstate.

"I'll just need a credit card and your driver's license."

"Credit card?"

"Yes, to pay for the car?"

"Oh well I have cash." I quickly dug into my purse to grab for my wallet.

The pertinent young man behind the counter interrupted me, "Well we still have to have a card to keep on file incase something were to happen with the car."

Already a snag, I didn't have a credit card. I did have a bank card though.

"I have a debit card." I handed him my bank card.

"Um this won't work; you need a credit card in order to rent the car."

Jake was standing back and when he saw me turn to look at him he walked up and quietly asked "Is there a problem?"

"They say I need a credit card to rent a car."

"Yes, of course you do." He smiled at me. Did he have to sound so smart? What was I the only one who didn't know this? I have cash. What they don't want my cash?

Jake's smile faded fast when he realized that the credit card was the problem. He reached into his back pocket and took out his wallet and handed the agent his credit card and his driver's license. In what seemed like seconds the agent handed us a set of keys and we walked to C-12 and got in a cute little blue Ford Focus.

"I'm sorry." I felt bad and grateful.

"Sorry for what?" I thought I could see his chest pop out a few inches, proud as a peacock, saving the damsel in distress. Well actually I did need him and I think my dreams were telling me he meant more to me then I let on.

He jumped into the driver's seat which I wasn't expecting. "Okay navigator, tell me where I'm going."

I punched in the address and directed us towards the George Washington Bridge. It seemed like just yesterday when I stood there my first day calling around looking for a place to stay. We crossed over into New Jersey and eventually ended up on North 87. What a week I thought to myself. I was so happy to have Jake on this journey with me.

It was a beautiful drive and I felt the most relaxed I've felt in weeks. Jake reached over and held my hand which brought my thoughts back to us.

"You know Jake you never told me where you grew up and about your family." Seemed like a good time to bring this up seeing that he was trapped in this car with me with no where to escape.

He flashed his crooked, knowing smile as if he were waiting for this, not surprised at all. "That didn't take long."

"Well you always say we'll talk about it later or another time, seems to me like we have plenty of time." I glanced out the window trying to hide my enthusiasm. I have been dying to find out a little about Jake's past. Something always seemed to get in the way when the conversation turned in that direction.

"Well, I was born in New Jersey. My parents still live in the same house I grew up in."

"Do you have any brothers or sisters?"

"I had a younger sister."

"Had?"

"Yes, she died."

"Oh. I'm sorry. How old was she when she died?

"She was 17."

"How old were you?"

"I was 20."

"What happened?" I couldn't help myself the questions were firing out of my mouth like a reporter, no thought to the emotional toll they must be taking.

He sighed heavily and then I realized that this conversation must be very difficult.

"You don't have to answer if you don't want to, I'll understand." I would try to understand but I was dying with curiosity. I stared out the window waiting, hoping he would start talking. Only silence.

Just when I was about to ask another question he began.

"It was summer and she was walking to her car after working a late night shift at the local restaurant. A group of guys confronted her. She had her cell in her hand and she called me. I could hear the voices. I knew where she was and so I drove as fast as I could to the restaurant while I called the police but by the time I had got there they had already raped and beaten her. I went crazy trying to go after them and they held me down and beat me up pretty bad. We were both in the hospital for a couple days but a blood clot formed on her brain. She had to go into surgery so they could remove it but she never woke from the anesthesia. It was supposed to be a somewhat routine operation but they said the combination of the blows to the head she received there may have been a lack of oxygen I don't know, she didn't wake up and that's all that mattered. I couldn't stop what happened."

"Did they catch the guys?" The tears were threatening to spill over but I was trying to remain calm.

"No. I was told that if I said anything they would come after the rest of my family. So I never gave a report."

"What? So you knew who they were and you've never said anything?"

I could see his knuckles turn white as he gripped the steering wheel and he stole a murderous glance at me and then back at the road in front of him. My tears spilled over now. He looked at me like I just accused him of killing his own sister.

"I can't say anything because I truly believe he will come and murder the people I love."

"He? I thought you said there was a group of them?"

"There was, but there was a leader."

"So who was it?"

"You don't want to know Tara." He was shaking his head back and forth. Now I really wanted to know, I must know him.

"Please Jake, tell me."

"Tara, I'm serious, you don't want to know." He wouldn't look at me, he kept staring straight ahead.

I was getting mad now. "Jake! Just tell me for God's sake!"

"Devin! Okay it was Devin!"

The sound of his name sucked the air right out of me. I couldn't speak.

"I told you, you didn't want to know."

So that was it. That was the connection. That was the hatred between them. It wasn't jealousy over me it was the murder of his sister.

"I can't believe Devin would be involved in something so horrible."

"Well maybe now you'll knock him off that pedestal you're so quick to put him on."

"Hold on Jake, he was always nice to me. I didn't know to treat him any different so excuse me if I treated him as nice as he treated me."

With that Jake swerved the car over to the side of the road and slammed on the breaks. The sudden stopped forced the seatbelt to tighten, cutting into my chest.

Jake swung his head around to stare at me and instinctively I pushed away from him. "Treat him as nice as he treats you? Oh so treating you nice is slamming you back against the bathroom wall so he can have his way with you? Groping you and kissing you without your permission. That's being nice!" He got out of the car and slammed the door shut. He turned back around and yelled, "I'd hate to see what someone being mean to you is like!"

I closed my eyes trying to push down the heat rising in my chest, closing off my throat. I was so embarrassed and hurt. I had no idea that Jake even knew about that incident. He was standing out on the edge of the freeway, his hands locked behind his head. I just wanted to come up behind him and hug him. I was so sorry. Why was I defending Devin, what a pig.

I opened the car door and quietly walked up behind Jake. Oh my God was he crying? I forced this situation, I created this mess.

"I'm sorry." He just stood there. I wasn't really expecting him to come to me.

"I shouldn't have defended Devin regardless of what I knew or didn't know."

Jake sighed and dropped his arms to his side. It felt safe enough for me to take another step closer so that I was standing directly behind him. I could smell his sweet scent on the breeze and it made my stomach tingle. I loved him so much and I hurt so much for making him sad. Again my tears began to fall. I had to hug him but I was so afraid he would pull away from me.

Jake was a whole foot taller than me, I barely reached his shoulder. I placed my hands on his sides. When he didn't move I slid them forward around his belly. I felt a huge rush of relief when he didn't pull from me. Then I squeezed him close to me and pressed my face against his back and breathed him in. The heat of his body warmed my soul and I could feel it reverberate from my head to my toes. He brought his arms up and placed them over my hands. I swore from this moment forward that I would never, ever hurt my Jake again.

He turned around in my arms and he looked down at me and I could see his salt stained cheeks and red eyes. How could I have done that to him? I loved him, why did I make him cry. I hadn't realized that my face was covered in tears.

He held my face. "Why do I always seem to make you cry?"

"Me?" Then I felt my wet cheeks. "I guess I'm crying because I made you so sad. I'm sorry I hurt you."

"I love you Tara." He bent down and kissed me and I knew I had been forgiven.

We were back in the car and heading up into the Adirondack Mountains. I couldn't believe how beautiful it was. God certainly kissed this place. I rolled the window down to feel the cool wind, it was about 10 degrees cooler, and it was so nice to get out of the muggy heat. The trees loomed high above us and mixed in with the pines were huge maple and birch trees with leaves already turning a brilliant orange and red. However, the beauty could not erase the thoughts of Devin and Jake's sister from my mind. I had many questions for Jake but I didn't want to tempt fate by bringing it up again. I just couldn't understand how Jake could work or even be so near to Devin without wanting to kill him.

As if reading my mind Jake looked over at me and asked "What are you thinking about?"

"Nothing." I continued to admire the landscape so as not to give any indication that I was mulling over our last conversation.

"Really?"

"Mm-Mm."

"Tara, out with it." He rubbed my leg as if to tell me it was okay.

"Well…I can't quite comprehend why or how you could bear to be near Devin knowing what you know."

"I have known Devin since I was a teenager. Actually my parents know him quite well, we were really good friends. Then he started acting strange and doing some crazy stuff that I wasn't interested in and so we grew apart. I was into music and he was into girls and whatever. I hadn't seen him for quite awhile until that night. To be fair I don't think it was Devin that did anything to Rachel. He just didn't stop it, he was like their leader and they did what he said. He wasn't even the one who beat me up he had his lackeys do it. While I was in the hospital he visited me and threatened me again and said that he would be watching me to make sure I would never tell. He said that if he ever got in trouble he would know it was because of me. Now it's like a little game to him. I try to avoid him and he finds me, he taunts me, always trying to get me to break. Every girl I talk to he goes after them, every bar I play in, he makes it his new watering hole. I'm playing way out at the Kilt because I didn't think he'd want to hang out at a no where little pub when he's so accustomed to his uppity places but no he hangs out like a regular." Jake shrugged his shoulders and shook his head from side to side.

I swallowed hard, looking straight ahead, not believing he was being so forthcoming. It finally occurred to me that the reason why Devin paid me so much attention had nothing to do with my acting ability it was just a way to get to Jake. I should have listened to Jake in the beginning. I'm going to tell Devin when we get home that I'm not doing that stupid play.

"I'm sorry." It was all I could muster.

"It's not your fault. I'm sorry that you're messed up in all of this by association." He rubbed my cheek and smiled.

I continued to survey the landscape and noticed dark skies in my side mirror. I turned around to see a huge sheet of blackness behind us and my heart began to beat a little faster as the images of my most recent dream flashed before my eyes. Jake noticed my nervous behavior.

"It's just a little storm Tara, don't worry. We're going to pull over here soon and get some gas an' take a break okay?"

"Okay" I tried to avoid looking in my side mirror for fear I would see the red fiery eyes but that didn't keep me from occasionally looking behind us as if someone were following us.

Jake pulled into the next gas station he saw. I quickly made my way to the bathroom after giving him my bankcard to use for gas. When I finished I wandered around the store looking for something to snack on. I grabbed a diet dr. pepper and some chili cheese Fritos, and a reeses, pms food I guessed. Jake met me inside and he made himself a hotdog and grabbed a coke.

On the way back to the car it started to sprinkle. It was like twilight in the middle of the afternoon, the dark clouds snuffed out the sun's rays. Then the rain stopped and a strange calm descended upon us, there was no wind, and the color of everything had a weird green tint. I was starting to really freak out. I hadn't realized that I was just standing there at the door of the car looking off into space while Jake was calling my name. Finally Jake came over next to me and tapped me on the shoulder.

"Tara!"

Finally out of my trance.

"Yes." I looked up at him.

"What on earth is wrong with you? I called your name like 10 times."

"I don't know. I was just thinking about the tornado. I'm scared."

He almost started to laugh, "Tornado? Tara we don't get tornados here. Get in the car. I think you need some sleep."

That was the last thing I needed. We got in the car and were already speeding up the highway. Jake finished his hotdog before he even got in the car so he was snacking on my chips. I suddenly didn't feel very hungry anymore. The storm was catching up to us. The rain started again and was getting harder. I looked up ahead expecting to see the eagle guiding us to safety but there was no eagle.

Between mouthfuls of Frito's Jake asked "What's the matter Tara? It's just a thunderstorm."

"Yeah, I know. I just don't like thunder." I crossed my arms in front of me and ground my teeth together expecting the worse.

The rain caught up to us like a curtain being pulled across us. It was coming down so hard it seemed to be bouncing back up from the road. It was difficult to see and the wind was blowing leaves across the freeway. I could feel it push our little car and immediately regretted not getting the standard size. I squeezed my eyes shut for fear I would see the little girl in the back seat or the mutated goats head with fiery red eyes appear in the sky but they were more prevalent behind closed eyes. My eyes fluttered open and could feel the car slowing and pulling to the right.

"What are you doing? Where are we going?" The shrill in my voice made me sound like a crazy person.

"Relax Tara, I can barely see. I'm pulling over until the storm passes or at least until the rain slows." He was peering through the windshield looking up into the sky. To my right were huge pine trees, it was so dark I couldn't see past the tree line. We sat quietly in the parked car as the rain beat on the tin roof so hard I thought it would soon come right through. So far there was no ghost girl, no devil eyes, just a horrid storm and I was safe inside the car with my boyfriend. I started to relax. Jake put his seat back and closed his eyes. He wore his black knit hat today which pulled back his beautiful hair so I could see his lovely face. He looked so peaceful. Soon his breathing changed and I could tell he was sleeping. I tilted my head back and rested.

A huge crack of thunder woke us both. We bolted straight up. I looked at the clock and it said 1:30pm. We had slept for over an hour. It was misting out but the hard rain had past. The clouds were still thick and black but at least you could see. Jake turned the ignition and nothing. My eyes widened and I stared at him but he was focused on the keys. He tried to start the car again but it made no sound.

He grabbed the steering wheel and laid his head against it.

"Jake, what's wrong, why won't the car start?" My eyes darted around waiting for an answer.

"I didn't shut the headlights off when we pulled over. The battery's dead."

"The battery's dead? What are we going to do Jake, we're in the middle of nowhere?" My voice got higher and more panicked. I wasn't sure what I was afraid of but the thought of being stuck out here didn't make me feel all that comfortable.

"Tara, it will be fine. I'll just call the service station and have someone come give us a jump." Jake reached into his pocket to get his cell.

"Do you have service?" His eyes were squinting and looked over to me. I quickly reached into my purse and grabbed my cell, flipped it open and no bars.

"Nothing." I shook my head back and forth, this couldn't be happening.

"We passed some emergency call boxes I'm going to get out and walk to one. Give me the paper work on the rental, there should be some numbers for vehicle assistance."

I reached into the glove compartment and pulled out the rental agreement and handed it to him. "I'm coming with you."

"No. You stay here just in case someone stops to help."

Why weren't there more people on the road? Surely we could flag someone down. I didn't want to stay here by myself. He kissed me goodbye and began walking down the freeway. And there I sat alone in the car, just like in my dream. Dark clouds, stormy, I was just waiting for the hooded stranger to appear next to me.

The dark ominous forest, like a picture from prehistoric times, lay in wait outside my window. I climbed into the driver's seat to get as far away from it as possible. I sat, waiting, watching, but no cars.

"Tara" I looked into the rearview mirror and there she was sitting in the back seat, the little girl. I jumped and turned around but she wasn't gone. I looked again in the mirror and she peered up at me through her stringy blonde hair. "He's looking for you."

I screamed and fumbled with the car door handle, pushing until finally the door opened and I fell out onto the ground. I scrambled away from the car for fear that the hooded goat's head would be coming next as crazy as that sounded. I stood up and she appeared right before me. "He's coming for you." She looked horrible, pale skin, blue veins, dark circles under her eyes, her dress was dirty and torn.

Again I screamed "NO!" and I backed up from her and found myself standing along the haunted tree line. Out of thin air she appeared before me smiling and in her sing-song voice, "And he'll get you." She started laughing-a grating, sick sound.

I took off running into the trees as fast as I could to get away from her. This couldn't be happening-what happened to her, why was she tormenting me now? I ran faster and faster the tree branches whipping against my face and arms, leaving small stinging cuts. I could hear footsteps behind me which only made me press further but the further I ran the darker it became. I panicked-what if I couldn't find my way back-what about Jake?

There was a loud knocking sound. Where was it coming from? I kept running, harder, faster. The knocks came louder-*Knock, knock, knock*. I slowed my pace to look around and see if I could figure out what the sound was.

"Tara!" It was Jake's voice. He must be looking for me. I turned around and started to run back. Then I heard BANG! BANG! BANG! I screamed and covered my ears, it was so loud.

"Let us in!" "Let us in!" "Let us in!" the little girl sang and danced around me. I started to cry as I dropped to my knees on the moss covered forest floor. "Stop it! Why are you doing this? What's wrong with you?"

"Tara!" Again I could hear Jakes voice and I jumped up I started to run. Then a window shattered. Did someone break into the car? I could feel someone pulling on me and everything around me in the forest went blurry and when it cleared I was laying in Jakes arms on the ground with a few other strange faces peering down at me.

"Tara! Are you okay?", again Jakes voice fraught with fear.

I fluttered my eyes, confused.

"I was just in the forest, how did I get here so fast."

"No, you were unconscious in the car. We were banging on the car door and yelling your name, telling you to let us in but you weren't moving. We finally had to break the window."

I remember all those things but not quite in that same setting.

"So there really wasn't a little girl chasing after me and I wasn't running in the forest?"

Some other guy was listening in, "What?"

"Shhhh." Jake squeezed me tighter and bent down to whisper in my ear. "No Tara, you were just sitting in the car."

I still didn't understand.

"But how?" Jake read the confused look on my face and decided now was not the time to get in to details.

"We'll talk about it later. Let's get the car jumped."

I stood up and walked to the rear of the car. Jake was able to get some help and they were in the process of jumping our battery. I paced back and forth the recent events running through my head. It felt so real, I thought it was real, how could I be dreaming? I usually know when I'm dreaming. That still didn't explain the wickedness of the little girl. She seemed to taunt me and frankly she scared me. Jake's voice interrupted my thoughts, telling me it was time to go.

We cleaned the glass off the seat and thankfully the rain had stopped. I felt bad that they had to break the window. What was this going to cost us I wondered? We were soon on our way and with no way to cover the window the cool air blew freely inside and whipped my stray hairs in my face and I used my hand to hold them back. It was a beautiful site seeing the sun break through those gray clouds, like God was shining down upon us. The colors beamed across the sky and I saw my first full rainbow from one end to the other. "Look Jake a rainbow!"

He smiled at me, not looking at the rainbow. "Uh huh"

I kept checking my phone and still no service. I wanted to call my Uncle and let him know where we were and when to expect us. With all the delays our six hour trip was turning into more like eight. It shouldn't be too much further though, I could feel it. Just then an eagle flew across my beautiful rainbow as if it were greeting us.

Chapter 12: The Rez

As we descended out of the mountains and the beautiful tree tops my cell phone beeped that I had missed calls. Finally a signal, I quickly called my Uncle.

"Hi it's Tara."

"Tara, you almost here?"

"Yeah."

"Well meet me at the longhouse I have some business there okay?"

"Okay…See you soon Uncle."

"Onen"

"Onen"

I closed my phone and smiled over at Jake. I was so excited to be seeing my family and to hopefully get some answers.

"You speak Mohawk?" Jake looked straight ahead, his hands firmly on the wheel.

"Only a few words, they still teach it in school up here though."

We were on the outskirts of the rez, as everyone who lived here referred to it. "You need to make a left up here." I was desperate for a bathroom and to get out and walk around. We passed the big casino, it was huge. I hadn't seen it, only heard about it, since it was built about 10 years ago.

"We're meeting him at the longhouse. It's up here on the right."

We pulled up and all of a sudden I got cold feet. I was afraid to get out of the car for some reason.

"Tara, you okay?"

"I think so. I just need a minute."

Just then a little kid was at the car door and made me jump. I almost peed my pants. I stepped out of the car.

"You're Tara and you're Jake!" The little boy was dancing around kicking up dust.

His dancing had me giggling. "Well if you know us already, then who are you?"

"I watched you come. I'm Darian." He took off running inside, his little Mohawk haircut blowing in the wind.

Jake looked at me. "What a funny little boy?" I smiled back in agreement.

We walked inside and now I understood why there were so many cars parked outside. All at once everyone yelled "Surprise!"

Everyone was there, family from both sides of my parents and a ton of cousins I had never met before. I was overwhelmed and I could only imagine how Jake was taking all of this. I looked over at him to find the biggest smile on his face. All the little kids were running up to him and hugging onto his legs.

The hugs felt as though they numbered in the hundreds. All I could hear was "Remember me I'm your Aunt Boogie, I'm your Uncle Sammy, I'm your cousin Kyla, Bubbles, Bucky, Honeybee, Rocky," and the names went on and on. I felt a grip around my arm and I caught my breath but when I turned I let out a sigh of relief. There stood one of the biggest Indians of them all, my Uncle Gerald, the Chief of the Mohawk Tribe on the Canadian side. He caught me in his widely known huge bear hug.

"You're crushing me Uncle." He let me loose but still held me to look at me.

"You look like your mother." He was smiling his hazel eyes glistening with tears. Their father was Mohawk but their mother was white, hence the hazel eyes. I broke out in laughter as I glanced at his shirt. It read 'I'm F.B.I. Fucking Big Indian.'

I pointed at his shirt, "Isn't that the truth!" Everyone was big on the reservation. It seemed to be a sign of our generation. We were a people of hunters and gatherers, with centuries of feast or famine built into our genes. The constant availability of food was taking its toll on our people both through weight gain and the high prevalence of diabetes. Even I wasn't considered skinny by most standards but I was able to keep my weight under control by all the running I do and now all the walking I do from living in New York. I always hated how my friends seemed to be so skinny but I always had hips and my dad always teased me that I had a "bubble butt."

We also weren't known for our healthy eating; however our traditional foods weren't bad for you it was the adjustments to the recipes made over time and probably portion size that made up the difference. I could smell the delicacies of our heritage, fry bread, corn soup, hash, and the list went on. Our arrival was definitely widely known and planned for since the place was packed and there was enough food to feed the whole rez.

I grabbed onto Jake and introduced him to my Uncle.

"Uncle, this is Jake…" and I paused. I'd never used the term boyfriend before although I considered him my boyfriend I wasn't so sure he considered himself the same thing. Just then the little boy with the Mohawk from earlier came running up.

"It's her boyfriend!" And just like that he was gone.

My Uncle stuck out his hand and Jake's hand was lost in his bear like grasp. "I see, welcome Jake."

"Thank you sir, it's an honor to meet you, thank you for having me." Jake smiled and stretched out his hand after Uncle released it probably trying to get the feeling back into it.

Uncle gestured to the table of food. "Make sure you eat, there is plenty. Tara get him a plate of food. Jake you sit here." I stomped off to get a plate of food for Jake, realizing that even though the women of the tribe held a lot of decision making power we were still considered nurturers of the tribe. Jake's eyes flashed to me in protest.

"No, please, I can do it." He stepped forward but Uncle placed a hand on his chest to stop him.

"Sit here with me. Tara will get your food."

I didn't hear the rest of the exchange as I was weaving my way through the crowd of people and standing in line for food. It all looked so breathtakingly good. I hoped Jake liked it. I placed a bowl and plate on a tray along with silverware. I filled his bowl with corn soup. The main ingredients were hominy, ham hocks, pork, and kidney beans. I scooped some potato hash, chicken, sausage, clams, and topped it off with a couple pieces of fry bread. I picked up a beer on my way back to their table. Look at all this food, no wonder we were all fighting our weight.

I placed the tray down in front of Jake. "Here you go. I hope you like it."

Jake smiled back at me, "Thank you! I'm sure I will."

"Where's mine?" Uncle was serious too. His wife, my Aunt Clara, had passed away a few years ago, so there was no one to serve him. I was starving; the smell of all this delicious food was making my mouth water.

"I'll be back, Uncle." I turned to get back in line and I felt a tug on my arm.

"Wait, I'll go." It was Jake.

"What are you doing?" I was furious.

"Tara, it's not right. I know you are starving. Let me get the food and you eat mine."

I noticed everyone had sort of stopped what they were doing and looking at us including my uncle.

"Jake you are making a scene. It's disrespectful to refuse your food. Please sit down and eat at once and I will serve my Uncle."

Finally he could see the seriousness of the situation and he kissed me on the cheek and loudly said, "I just wanted to say thank you for brining me with you to meet your family and I can't wait to eat this lovely meal." With that he turned and everyone continued about their business.

Within ten minutes I was back at the table with Uncles food. His tray was similar to Jakes except he had two plates of food. When I arrived back at the table Uncle was listening intently to Jake talk about his music.

"Well I hope you brought your guitar with you. We're going to have a bomb fire tonight and you will have to play for us." Uncle loved music so I'm sure Jake was already winning his affection and permission.

I set the food down in front of Uncle and turned to see that Jake's plate was almost empty. "Did you like it?" I was excited that he seemed to enjoy the food.

"Yes it was outstanding."

"Tara, get him more."

"Oh no, this is fine. I'm done." Jake rubbed his belly. I was jealous. I tried not to be but I was so hungry, I thought for sure everyone could hear my stomach talking. At least I knew they wouldn't run out of food, there was so much.

"Well if no one needs anything else I'm going to go get myself something." I quickly left before anyone changed their mind. There wasn't a line anymore so I was able to breeze through it and of course my eyes were bigger than my stomach. My plate was heaping.

"You gonna eat all that?" A little voice said next to me.

I glanced down and it was the little boy from earlier.

"Probably not, I was just hungry. What's your name?" I started walking back to the table and he followed me.

"I'm Darian. You're my cousin. I thought I saw a little girl with you, where is she I want to play with her?"

I stopped. In the middle of the room, I stood there, tray in hand, the words he spoke slowly sinking in.

"What's the matter Tara? Do you know where she is?"

Jake looked over at me and I could see the concern on his face. I tried to snap out of my trance.

"No Darian, there was no girl with us."

I continued to walk to the table and I could feel that I was beginning to shake so I gripped my tray tighter so I wouldn't drop it. Darian continued to follow me.

"But I know I saw her. She had blonde hair and wore a pretty dress."

He was the one, the one they called the 'dream guesser', but he was making me angry now because he was relentless.

"Tara, you're lying to me, I saw her."

With that I whipped around on the little boy and screamed "There was no little girl Darian! She's not real!" I had reached the table by then and I slammed my tray of food down spilling my soup. Immediately I felt horrible for my outburst. Darian took off running and everyone was staring at me.

The blush crept up into my cheeks and I slowly sat down. Jake reached over to caress my arm but I pulled away. I didn't deserve to be consoled. I should have had more patience with Darian. Everyone seemed to continue eating as if nothing had happened but I felt awful and for being as hungry as I was I could barely eat. I came here to seek answers which I feared now I wouldn't get because of my outburst. He was the one I needed to speak with, to help me understand what was happening. To be honest I wasn't sure he would have the answers with or without my snapping at him. He was so young, something I hadn't expected. Maybe he wasn't the only one on the rez that had this ability; maybe there were more of us.

I picked at my fry bread as I mulled over these thoughts in my head. I was being an awful host to Jake who was enjoying his beer and getting acquainted with all my family. My Uncle wrapped his arm around his shoulders and took him to introduce him to everyone as I sat here and sulked. No one was happy to see me I thought to myself just the new white boy. As I sat there watching Jake and playing with my food someone sat down next to me.

"I didn't figure you would eat all that food."

It was Darian.

I smiled. I was so relieve that he came back.

"Hey little guy, I'm sorry for yelling at you. Will you forgive me?"

"Sure." He placed a feather on the table. "So you never saw me in your dreams?"

"No, can't say that I have. Whatcha got there?"

"Well sometimes I transform into an Eagle, it's an Eagle feather. Do you know they are illegal to have? Did you see an Eagle?" His voiced raced on making it difficult for me to keep up as I was still trying to process his first comment.

"Wait, what do you mean you transform into an eagle?" I shook my head trying to grasp the meaning.

"In my dreams I like to fly and soar high like an eagle." My eyes widened at the admission. "You did dream of me, didn't you?" His eyes lit up and his smile widened.

"I guess I did." But how did he find me?

"Since the Chief told me you were coming I've been looking out for you. That's how I knew your boyfriend was coming and I thought the little girl was coming too." He lowered his head, like he was sad.

"Well you don't seem hard up for company." I looked around at the dozens of kids running around.

"It's not that, she told me she had a secret for me."

"A secret?"

"That's what she said."

"And when did she tell you this?"

"On your ride down, that's why I thought she was with you."

A chill shot through my body. The only little girl that was with me was in the freakish nightmare that chased me in the woods. How could he be excited to see her? There had to be a mistake or some game he was playing with me. The more I thought about it the more confused I became. How was it that the little girl seemed to change from good to bad?

It was getting dark outside and the crowd was thinning. I had no idea where we were staying tonight but I assumed my Uncle would take us in. I finished my food or rather was done picking at my food. Darian cleared my tray for me. My Uncle finally made it back to the table with Jake in tow.

"You ready Tara? We have something planned down by the river."

"Sure"

I followed them out with Darian right on my heels. Jake, Darian and I followed my Uncle to his house in my car. I got out and could smell the fire burning and see the bright lights out back. The drums were beating out our traditional music.

"What's this?" I turned to look at Uncle.

"Oh just a little party and some dancing."

We walked back behind the house and there was a huge bomb fire. A group of young guys were at the helm of the drums. Beautifully costumed women and men were dancing around the fire, most of whom I was related to. Their clothes were beautiful, leather, beads, feathers, porcupine quills and the colors were mesmerizing.

Another big guy with long black hair was on his was up to us carrying a couple beers. He had a huge smile on his face. He handed me and Jake a beer.

"It's been a long time, you've grown." I was confused. Was I supposed to know who this was? I looked up to my Uncle and then back at the towering Indian before me. He wore no shirt just jean shorts, come to think of it most of the younger guys didn't wear shirts. He had a nice chest and 6-pack abs to show off but most were sporting signs of good home cooked meals or too much beer.

"You don't recognize me do you?"

I shook my head from side to side. I had only been here once and it was when I was like 10.

"I gave you a ride on the St. Regis river on my boat and you got sick and threw up. Remember?"

"Bucky?" The smile crept onto my face more from embarrassment. "Yeah!"

"Oh my God, you're so big and old!"

"I'm only 25. I guess I did grow a little taller. It's nice to see you." He gave me a huge bear hug and at that moment I heard Jake clear his throat.

"Oh this is Jake. Jake this is Bucky, one of the only people on the reservation I'm not related to."

"Nice to meet you Jake, they call me Buck now." Jake shook his hand and Bucky took his other hand and grasped his shoulder, a sign of welcome. Jake was tall but I think Bucky was even taller. As I was sizing them up Bucky reached down and grabbed me and threw me over his shoulder. I screamed and he just laughed.

"Time to welcome you back to the rez, the river wants to say Hello!"

"No! Put me down! Bucky! Stop it, put me down!"

He took what seemed like giant leaps towards the river and I thought for sure I was going in but Uncle interjected.

"Buck! Put her down."

Immediately he set me down as if a drill sergeant were giving an order. I took a deep breath and gave a big sigh of relief. I was afraid of that river after all the stories they used to tell me of eels swimming in there.

"Sorry Tara, didn't mean to scare you. Welcome back." He gave me a hug and a quick peck on the cheek and he was gone. Jake walked up behind me.

"Well that was an interesting display of manhood."

"He always was more brawn then brain." I turned around to catch Jake staring off at Bucky, the glow of the bomb fire make him look even more beautiful then he already was. "Are you okay?" I forced him to look down at me with my question.

"Yes, of course I am." He smiled then and his blue eyes just melted every bit of will to stand I had and I quickly flung my arms around his neck and clasped my hands together so I could use him to balance myself. I was so lucky. I breathed him in and he squeezed me tight.

He whispered in my ear. "Are you alright?"

"Of course I am, I've got you." I smiled up at him and he kissed me on my forehead. We headed to a seat hand in hand to enjoy the wonderful display of native music and dance. It was warm out and the mosquitoes were getting their fill. The smoke from the fire helped somewhat and the smell of citronella candles that filled the air probably didn't hurt much either. Jake left me to go inside the house for a minute. He came out with a blanket, a beer, and diet Pepsi for me, plus bug repellent. He spread the blanket out on the grass. We sat and enjoyed the wonderful music and dancing. I could kick myself for waiting so long to come visit my family up here. Jake was impressed and he made sure to mention it to me many times throughout the night.

It was getting late. Uncle brought out a tent for us saying it would be cooler outside rather than inside without any air-conditioning. It took us quite a few tries to get that tent together but there was no fighting and I thought that was a good sign. The sky was crystal clear and the stars were shining like diamonds against the black sky. I loved to lay and create pictures in the night.

"What are you doing?" Jake lay down next to me.

"See that cluster of stars? It looks like a kite and when you stare straight at it, it seems to disappear and then when I look to the side of it I can see it again."

"Yep. I see it."

"I always wondered if it was a cluster of planets instead of stars. I wish I could fly up in the sky. Darian told me something this afternoon that will sound weird."

Jake propped himself up on his elbow. "Really, what?"

"He said that he like's to transform into an eagle when he dreams and that he watched over us as we traveled here." I snuck a peek in his direction hoping to see his reaction but I could not get a fix on what he was thinking.

"That is weird. Is he the one you need information from?"

"It seems that way. But I need to talk to Uncle too."

"Yeah, Darian seems a little young. But then again you were young too."

"I guess so."

"Do me a favor, can we not talk about dreams just for tonight? I know that we came here to get you answers but it would be nice to just relax and just enjoy the evening."

"I suppose. But tomorrow I need to really work on finding out what's going on."

He slid his arm around my waist and pulled me close to him. For the first time I wasn't in the mood. Even though I couldn't talk about dreams they were still on my mind. Jake leaned in and began kissing me and all the questions I had and visions of creepy little girls, flying eagles, and murderous glowing red eyes vanished from my mind. I just let it all go and wrapped my arms around him and pulled him on top of me.

He pulled away from me, "Tara, we're out in the open here."

I didn't want to stop kissing him. I kissed his face, his neck, I pulled his shirt down and kissed his chest and then back up to his neck and his ear. I just let loose and wanted to keep going to let it all go and live in the mo-

167 Dream Catcher by Tricia Currier

ment and enjoy myself and revel in the fact that I had a hot boyfriend that wanted only me.

I was practically mauling him when he grabbed my hands and pinned them to the ground next to my head stopping me in my tracks. Not again. He's not going to pull Mr. Nice guy again is he? He slowly brought his lips down to mine.

"Slowly Tara, I'm not going anywhere." He kissed me softly on the lips and brushed them along my cheek to my ear and then traced my jaw line to my chin. He was hardly laying on me, using his arms to keep most of his weight up off of me. I arched my head back, the feeling of his kisses were too much for me to bear. He kissed me along my throat and down to my chest. He released my hands to undo my blouse and immediately I reached my arms up to encircle his neck.

"Stay, don't move." Jake's blue eyes were smoldering in the fire-light.

I dropped my arms back down to the side of my head. Jake was straddling me as he slowly unbuttoned my shirt and I could feel his finger-tips across my skin. I felt as though a thousand volts of electricity was racing through my body looking for an outlet. I was about to explode and here he was telling me not to move, to be still.

"You're beautiful Tara"

My eyes shot up to his and the heat exploded over my chest and rose over my throat and into my face. If it were brighter he would see that my face was scarlet. I wasn't used to the attention and praise.

"Jake please."

He smiled and the weakness overtook me. If he prolonged this any longer I didn't think I could go through with it. Just then he bent down and kissed my throat, his lips traveling down to my chest, my blouse fell open and I could feel the warm air on my exposed breast. I was glad it was dark and the glowing embers only added shadows to the night.

I caught my breath as Jakes lips found my breast. I couldn't tell him no because I didn't want to, I wanted him so bad. This was torture. My body craved him but now my brain was over-thinking, were we prepared, I knew I wasn't. I didn't have a condom, I wasn't on the pill. How many times has he done this, he's my first. What happened to I'll wait till marriage. All these thoughts were running through my head and it was like I was having an outer body experience. I didn't even realize that Jake was slipping my pants off and I looked to see that his shirt was already off. I was no longer enjoying myself because I was worrying.

He must have noticed the concern on my face because he stopped.

"Tara, what's the matter?"

"I'm sorry. I'm a little scared."

Jake got up and headed into the tent. I immediately covered myself up. Did I scare him away? Within seconds he was back with a sleeping bag. He unzipped it and covered me and then scooted in next to me gathering me up in his arms.

"I didn't mean to scare you."

"I really don't think it was you, it was me and all my thoughts."

"What sort of thoughts?" He held me to his bare chest and he smelled so divine, it was intoxicating.

"It's embarrassing."

"Please don't be embarrassed in front of me."

"Well the whole waiting until marriage popped into my head again. Then I wondered if we were prepared, well more like you because I'm not on the pill. Then I wondered how many times you've done this and with whom." I buried my head into his chest at that last admission hoping he didn't hear me but also hoping he did.

He tucked his finger under my chin bringing my head up to look at him.

"Tara, we don't have to do anything you don't want to do. I promise, whether we do or don't I'm not going anywhere, I'm yours. I haven't had many intimate relationships, not for awhile. And with Devin constantly hounding me he seems to make sure he gets the attention of all the girls. To be honest I was always more interested in my music then the girls that hung out at the bars of course that was until I was picking you up off the floor at the Kilt."

All this emotion was just more than I could handle and I started to cry like a big baby. I was pretty sure that time of the month was coming because all my nerves and emotions were riding high. I turned over, my back against him and he held me. I watched the embers burn and it wasn't long before I heard Jake's heavy breathing. He sleeps. Quiet, peaceful, slumber that I so longed for. I buttoned up my blouse and rolled onto my back to stare up into the sky. A star shot across the vast night sky and I made my wish. For the first time I felt at peace as if nothing were after me or trying to invade my dreams. My eyes stayed closed and soon I was drifting off to sleep.

"Tara, come on, follow me."

I opened my eyes and there stood Darian.

"What are you doing?" I was trying to keep my voice down so I wouldn't wake Jake.

"I want to show you something." He started to walk away from me.

"Aren't you supposed to be home sleeping in your bed? Won't your parents be worried?" I sat up and put on my jeans and shoes.

He stopped and turned to look at me, "I am home sleeping and so are you."

I walked to him and he stretched out his hand. I grabbed it and he started walking me down along the river bank. I turned to look at Jake behind me and saw both him and I sleeping soundly.

"Tara, what would you most like to do?"

"What do you mean?"

"In your dreams, what would you most like to do?"

"I've always wanted to fly." I couldn't hide the smile on my face at that revelation.

"Well why don't you? Why do you always stay human and do human things? It is a dream you know."

"But I can't even choose what my dream is going to be about much less what I'm going to do or be."

He continued to lead me along the river bank which I knew would end at a plateau and we would be staring out over the water where the St. Lawrence and the St. Regis rivers met.

"But that's where you're wrong Tara. Before I go to sleep I tell myself what I want and so when I fall into my dream I have more control over what I become. But even now you are conscious, you can choose to do whatever you want."

We reached the plateau and stopped.

"What now?"

"It's time to test your new knowledge."

"How?"

"Stop thinking human, stop limiting yourself to your human world."

"Darian, why do you sound so old, you're only 8."

"Not in my dream world." His sly little smile brightened his eyes and then he was gone, vanished into thin air.

I stood there, the warm night air still, only the sound of the water lapping at my feet. The light of the moon shown down around me, I could see the trees, the water but no Darian. What was I supposed to do? Test my knowledge, but how?

Just then a huge gust of wind blew from behind me forcing my hair into my face. I used my hands to try and plaster my hair down so I could see. I heard a fluttering of wings and then a huge bird buzzed past my head. I squatted down on the ground my scream piercing the night air.

"Shhh…Tara, it's just me, Darian." The bird flew past me again then straight up in the sky. Like a bolt of lightening the sleek bird dove back down towards the water.

"Darian?"

"Come on Tara! Think of something, it's your dream, you can be anything you want!" He came up from the water with a fish in his large talons.

I tried to think--what could I be? What else would be fun besides me? How about everything. Okay, what would be cool? I wanted to fly so I decided that I would just make myself fly. I jumped up with all my might and I could feel it, I was higher for a split second and then I fell back down. What was wrong, why couldn't I just fly if I wanted to?

Darian flew over and perched himself on a tree next to me.

"Tara, you're not taking this serious. If you want to control your dreams you really have to believe that you can do whatever you want."

Maybe he was right, maybe in my subconscious I knew it was impossible, that's why Darian chose a bird, an animal he knew could fly. I decided to try again. I closed my eyes and pictured myself flying. I thought maybe I should start with something smaller, easier, graceful, and colorful. I smiled at that last thought. I could feel myself lift off the ground. I was afraid to open my eyes but I knew I was doing it, I was flying I could feel it. I opened one eye and then the other. I could see the water below me and the sky above me. I was flying! Darian screamed my name interrupting my glorious moment.

"Tara! NO! Think of something else! HURRY!"

I couldn't understand why he was freaking out.

"Why Darian, you wanted me to control my dream so I'm controlling it, I'm flying just like I wanted." It was glorious. I didn't think I would ever want to wake up again after this.

"Change NOW! You're going to be eaten! Look below you!"

Confused, I looked down to find a huge fish jumping out of the water at me, trying to eat me. Thoughts were racing through my head, what should I do; what should I change in to; I thought a butterfly would be safe, easy, fun. The fish was launching up at me, his mouth open wide. Like an anchor I dropped into the middle of the lake with a huge splash. I lost the whole thing and just turned back into plain Tara. The ice cold water stung my skin and stole my breath. The thought of eels had me struggling through the pain as I tried to keep myself afloat. The water was so dark I couldn't see a thing. I screamed when something touched my leg and I tried to convince myself that it was just a fish. But then I felt something slimy wrap itself around my leg and with hard jerk it pulled me under. I feverishly kicked as hard as I could and pushed upward but it pulled me down further into the blackness like one of my dreams. I felt my chest tighten, my lungs were burning, and I could hold my breath no longer. Before I took a breath of the cold river water I remembered what Darian told me, this was my dream and I controlled what happened. I reminded myself that this was just a dream and forced myself awake and pulled myself out of the darkness.

My back heaved up off of the ground as I took in a huge breath of air. I had been drowning in my dream and I still felt as though I needed to catch my breath. I looked around and Jake was gone. I was all alone lying on the sleeping bag. I coughed again as if I were trying to force up water. My throat felt raw. I looked around again and then saw Jake, Bucky and Uncle running towards me. I sat up and could see the fear on their faces only just now realizing what might have occurred. Jake was the first to reach me.

"Tara, you're okay. Oh my God, I thought you were having a seizure or something."

"I…I, couldn't breath." It was all I could get out, my throat was burning, my eyes darting around embarrassed by all the excitement.

Bucky reached me next.

"I called the ambulance, they'll be here soon."

I looked up to Jake with pleading eyes, "I'm fine really. I just couldn't catch my breath." I sounded hoarse.

"Tara, again with the fine, you're kidding right? I tried to wake you, you were screaming. It sounded as though someone were choking the air out of you, you weren't breathing." The tears were welling up in his eyes. I just started at him in shock. He stood up and walked away.

I started to cry, I felt so bad for making him upset. Uncle reached me now.

"You okay?"

"Yes Uncle." He hugged me tight.

"Buck, get her some water and tell the ambulance not to come."

Bucky took off and did as instructed. Uncle let me loose but placed his hands on my shoulders.

"It will be okay Tara. You will get this under control. You have a very special gift and once you learn how to use it, it will be very valuable not only to you but for many others."

Uncle released me. My feet were like lead, I couldn't bring myself to go to Jake. I caught Uncle looking over my shoulder and fortunately I wouldn't have to, Jake walked up behind me. I felt Jakes hands on my shoulders and he gave me a light squeeze.

"So you're okay?" Uncle looked at me and then to Jake behind me.

"Yes, I'll be fine." I felt the squeeze on my shoulder when I said "fine." I would have to think of another word to describe my wellbeing or I would end up sending Jake over the edge.

Uncle walked back up to the house disappearing around the corner. I turned to look at Jake. It was getting lighter outside but I could still see the fireflies lighting up the bushes.

"Come on Tara. Let's get some rest." He took my hand and led me back down to the blanket. The early morning brought with it a cool crisp breeze. Goosebumps formed on my arms. I was really tired since I was busy most of the night almost being eaten by fish and swallowed by eels in my dreams. So much for being able to control my surroundings, I guess my first test was a complete failure. I curled up in Jake's arms where I felt safe and warm; this is where I wanted to stay forever not in my dream.

Chapter 13: Dream Guesser

I woke up the next morning to water dripping on my face. I opened my eyes to a fish starring me right in the eyes. I gasped and jumped up. I thought maybe I was still dreaming but it was just Darian squatting next to me holding a piece of our evening meal. Jake walked up from the bank.

"I told him you wouldn't think it was funny."

If he only knew I didn't think it was funny in more ways than one. I swatted the fish away, knocking it to the ground as Darian giggled.

"Hey I just washed him." He picked up the fish and wandered toward the house.

"Stupid fish" I mumbled under my breath.

Jake sat down next to me, "Well you're in a good mood this morning."

I tried to brush my hair up into a ponytail with my fingers; it was useless it was all over. "Well how would you like to wake up to fish water dripping on your face with a gaping mouth and eyes staring down at you?"

"Come on Tara he was just having a little fun."

Yeah, I bet, I thought to myself. I huffed and rummage through the tent to get my bag and started to walk towards the house to get a shower.

"Uh…Good morning to you too," I heard calling from behind me.

I was so wrapped up in my thoughts about my dream last night that I forgot about Jake. I stopped in the middle of the yard and I turned to him, held my hand up to my eyes to block the morning sun.

"Good morning."

I felt like such a jerk but if I ran to him he would know it was only because he had to remind me so I decided to just go take my shower and try to get out of this sour mood. I turned and continued through the yard up to the house.

I walked in and could smell bacon cooking. Uncle was in the kitchen cooking breakfast. I would have to say that eating was a big part of our culture and something everyone enjoyed doing. I was sure to put on a few pounds in the short amount of time I stayed here. I headed down the hall to the bathroom and nearly tripped over Darian as he came out of the bathroom.

"Darian, watch out!"

"Geez, why are you so grouchy?"

"Hey you try being nearly eaten by a fish and drown by eels and see how good you feel in the morning." I pinched my eyebrows together and shot a nasty look to his back as he walked down the hall.

"Hey it's not my fault you picked a stupid butterfly to change into."

I stormed into the bathroom and slammed the door closed. Little brat! He could have warned me. I turned on the water and stepped into the hot shower hoping to wash away this crummy mood of mine.

When I finished I came out to everyone eating breakfast in the kitchen. Uncle, Jake, Darian, Bucky, and a young lady I didn't know. The kitchen table was piled high with plates of bacon, sausage, pan fried potatoes, scrambled eggs and pancakes.

"You hungry Tara?" Uncle got up and patted the seat for me to sit.

"Um, I'll just have some coffee."

Everyone's heads turned to me like I said something wrong.

"What?"

Jake got up and cleared his plate and walked outside on the deck without saying a word to me.

I walked over to the coffee pot and poured myself a cup. I took a few sips as I leaned up against the counter. I noticed Bucky paying special attention to the pretty woman next to him.

"Aren't you going to introduce me Bucky?"

He whipped his head around and I could see the smile on her face from the view I had of her profile.

"Tara, this is Deidre, Deidre this is Tara."

She turned to look at me and she stood up. She was beautiful with her copper skin, almond shaped eyes and long black hair that was nearly down to her bum. I stuck out my hand and she took it delicately and shook it. Her smile lit up her face and nearly took my breath away. How Bucky got so lucky I'll have no idea. I just hope he knew how fortunate he was.

"So how long have you and Bucky been going out?"

Bucky spit out his food and started choking. Darian was laughing so hard he nearly fell off his chair. Deidre bowed her head and started to giggle.

"What? What's so funny?"

Uncle interrupted the laughter "This would be Bucky's sister, Deidre."

My face immediately turned red. "Oh. I didn't know he had a sister. How was I supposed to know?"

"Well I thought she would be helpful to you in the answers you seek as she seems to have similar abilities as you. I had Bucky invite her for breakfast."

I was really having a bad day. I seem to be sticking my foot in it wherever I turned today.

"Well I'm sorry for that assumption, Deidre. I appreciate you coming over. Um, if you don't mind I'm going to have a cup of coffee first and I'll get with you, will that be okay?"

"Sure that's not a problem at all. Just take your time." Even her voice sounded like a song. How she was related to that behemoth I'll never know.

I decided I was a little hungry and grabbed a pancake, no syrup, no butter and took it out with me onto the deck where Jake was still standing. I strolled up next to him and leaned against the wood railing. Why was I always feeling bad for something I did around him?

"It's really beautiful here Tara. The view is amazing."

I looked out over the trees and to the river. It was beautiful. I was happy to know he wasn't standing here fuming over me. I took a bite of my pancake and a sip of my coffee to wash it down. Jake pushed away from the railing and walked behind me. I decided to stay for awhile but he didn't go anywhere he just moved to put his arms around me and he rested his chin on my head.

"I don't mean to get angry Tara. I just don't like feeling like I have no control. I love you so much and all I want to do is protect you and keep you safe. When I see you struggle in your sleep and I can't do anything to help you I get so angry. I'm sorry if I take it out on you." I could not believe he was apologizing to me. If anything it should be me apologizing to him.

The door opened and Bucky stepped out. He was wearing a t-shirt and jean shorts with flip-flops. His long hair was pulled into a low ponytail braid.

"Hey I'm going to get the boat ready so I'll be about an hour and we'll head out, okay?"

I turned to look at Jake, "Where are we going?"

"Bucky thought it would be nice to take us around the river and show me some of the reservation from the water."

Immediately my stomach started to heave with thoughts of riding on a boat with Bucky at the helm. I glared at Bucky and not knowing what to say I said the first thing that came to my mind.

"It's nice to see that you own a shirt!" Feeling stupid I blasted past him and into the house. Stupid Bucky, I know he's going to try and make me throw up again.

Uncle caught me by the arm before I could head out the front door.

"Here take these, it will help."

He handed me two pills.

"What's this?"

"Dramamine, it will keep you from getting motion sickness."

I smiled.

"Thank you Uncle." I headed back to the kitchen and grabbed a diet pepsi and swallowed the pills. Then I headed to the tent to get ready for our little trip down the river.

It was going to be a really hot day and to be honest I was happy we would be out on the water. The wind and the spray from the water always felt nice. I was wondering what boat we were going to use and how we were all going to fit. As I recall all Bucky had when I was here last was a little tin boat with a motor.

Uncle called me. They were piling in the car to head to the marina. I had been sitting out on the back lawn by the wood dock. I was expecting Bucky to pull up here to meet us. Everyone was in the car by the time I got there, everyone but Bucky.

"So I guess Bucky must have upgraded his little boat then?"

Deidre turned to face me from the front seat.

"Well he sunk his old boat and he finally saved up enough to put a down payment on a new one. He's on the water all the time so he really went all out."

I arched my eyebrows, sounded like Mr. Bucky has done well for himself.

"Where's he working?"

"At the cigarette factory and he's also doing some odd jobs on the side."

The ride over didn't take long. We had to cross over the bridge into Canada. They have a special lane for residents of the Mohawk tribe and Jake just had to show his license. When we got out at the Marina I couldn't for the life of me figure out which boat was Bucky's. I mean they were all beautiful. How could he own one of these beautiful boats? Uncle led us along the board walk and he stopped next to a nice sized white boat with the word OKWAHO printed on the bow, which was Mohawk for Wolf that was Bucky's clan. That must be it.

Bucky popped out from somewhere on the boat. "Hey, we got lucky it's going to be beautiful today."

We all climbed aboard.

"Thanks for inviting us to come out Buck. This is great; I don't get an opportunity to go boating very much living in the city and all." Jake was grinning from ear to ear. It was if Bucky could do no wrong in his eyes. Actually I don't know what my problem was, he hadn't really done anything wrong since we've been here.

"Hey no problem, I'm happy to have the company, usually it's just myself when I go out." Bucky gave me a big smile. "This should handle the waves a little better, Tara." He patted one of the seats.

I smiled "Yeah."

We each took a seat along the back of the boat. There was plenty of room. I didn't know anything about boats but I could tell this must have cost him a pretty penny. Jake was checking out the storage and noticed the fishing poles.

"So you do much fishing?"

"Oh yeah, lots of trout in these waters."

"What kind of boat is this anyway?"

"It's a 2007 Bayliner. It's not really a fishing boat, it's more for cruising but I use it for both."

"Wow Buck, pretty impressive."

"Thanks."

Bucky pulled out of the Marina and we were headed out into the St. Lawrence River. Our reservation was bordered by both the St. Lawrence and the St. Regis. It was pretty awesome to see where the two rivers meet you can actually see a line because the St. Lawrence was bluer and the St. Regis is brown. I'm sure that Bucky would drift along that point to show Jake.

Once we were out in the open Bucky kicked it up a couple knots and we were skimming along the water. The ride was so smooth; I probably wouldn't have needed the Dramamine after all. I was beginning to feel sleepy from the medicine too, which I didn't like. The view was beautiful. Blue skies without a cloud in sight, green pines lined the water's edge. The wind was cool and blew my hair back out of my face. I wanted to sit out on front so I could see where we were going so I decided to ask if it was okay.

"Bucky, can I sit up on the bow?"

"Sure, just hold on, okay?"

I turned to look at Jake and he cocked his eyebrow at me but before he could protest I was up and moving toward the front of the boat then I crawled on my hands and knees out onto the bow. Bucky didn't slow it down either and it had my adrenaline pumping. I made it to the front and I sat crisscrossed holding tightly to the wire railing. I felt like I was flying. This was safer than a butterfly I thought to myself.

A big ship was coming towards us heading to the locks. Bucky moved over to pass him and we hit the wake from the ship. At the speed Bucky was going our boat jumped up high out of the water and smacked back down hard. My butt came up off the bow and I nearly flipped over the wire railing. The water sprayed across the boat which made the bow slippery causing me to slide between the metal posts and over the edge. I tried to hold on but I fell right into the water. Within a fraction of a second I went from feeling like I was flying to trying to swim.

Bucky was the first to notice I went missing. I heard the engine cut and someone screamed my name and then my head went under. I tried kicking and paddling my arms but it was no use I just kept sinking. The water was so cold and it was getting harder and harder to move my arms and legs. My lungs started to burn and I was at that point where I felt like I would need to suck in air. My body was tingling and I felt very weak. A vice squeezed around my stomach and the last bit of air was thrust out of me. My eyes opened and I saw the bubbles escape my mouth. 'This is it, I'm drowning, and I'm going to die.' The vice grip pulled and tugged at me until I saw blue sky and then it disappeared. I heard screaming but it was far away. When I opened my eyes again I had a sudden urge to cough and I threw up water.

I was exhausted. I opened my eyes and five sets of eyes were staring down at me. I looked around at all of them and then sat up. I wiped my mouth off and turned to look at Bucky.

"I can't believe you made me throw up again."

"I guess you should have been wearing a lifejacket." Bucky walked back towards the front of the boat and Jake jumped to his feet.

"You knew she couldn't swim and you let her up front without a lifejacket?"

"Hey don't go blaming me. She knows she can't swim either, she should have put one on." Bucky started the engine again.

Uncle cut in before a fight started, "Tara, are you okay? Do we need to take you to the hospital?"

"No, I'm fine." I looked at Jake. "I mean, I'll be okay, I feel okay."

Deidre had already wrapped me up in a towel and was trying to dry my hair with another one. Darian could care less and was playing with the fishing pole. Bucky just seemed pissed that I fell off his boat.

"See she's fine. Now can we get on with our tour here?"

I finally noticed that Bucky was wet from head to toe. He must have been the one that dove in after me. I can't believe I almost drowned, for real this time. Jake looked over at me and I could see the fear in his eyes. I mouthed the words 'I'm sorry' to him. He got up to move next to me and him and Deidre switched places. He wrapped his arms around me and he held me tight. He kissed my head and forehead. Bucky took off and we were on our way again. I guess it was my fault; I shouldn't have put myself in that position knowing that I can't swim but hindsight is 20/20. Who would have thought that could have happened, Jake that's who. Why was he always right?

"Bucky do you even have lifejackets on this boat?" I asked sarcastically.

He didn't answer me and I knew the answer was no. Bucky wasn't the lifejacket type, he was my lifejacket. And I'm pretty sure that's how he saw himself. As long as he was around nothing bad would happen to me. Well he didn't know me, Miss Accident Prone. Jake felt the same way towards me and I've proven again and again that simply being near me is an accident just waiting to happen.

As I expected Bucky pointed out the joining of the two rivers to Jake and then we were on our way up the St. Regis to Bucky's favorite fishing spot. Once there Bucky anchored us and then pulled out the poles. I had no interest in fishing. I was anxious to talk with Deidre. I got up to walk to the front of the bow again and Jake grabbed my arm.

"Where do you think you're going?"

Was he serious? The boat wasn't even moving.

"Jake, I'll be fine. I'm going up front to talk with Deidre." I snatched my arm away from him and took another step. Deidre walked past me and out to the bow. Uncle moved to the back to help Bucky with the poles trying to give us some space.

"Tara, I don't want you up there."

"Well you are not the boss of me." I went to walk away and he grabbed my arm again. I couldn't believe Jake was being so forceful.

"Come here please" and he pulled me with him downstairs to the cabin below.

"Jake, really, what's the matter with you?" This time I raised my voice.

"I can't protect you in your dreams; I just wish you would at least let me protect you when you are awake."

"I don't need you to protect me, the boat is not even moving!"

"Okay, okay! Don't get so angry with me." Jake stared off for a second and then back to me. "You scared me earlier. How come you didn't tell me you didn't know how to swim before we came out here?"

The whole situation made him anxious. He grabbed me up in his arms and hugged me.

"I'm not angry with you. I didn't tell you because I didn't want you to worry."

Jake pulled my head back away from his chest and looked at me with his sea blue eyes "I will always worry about you, I can't help myself."

"Please try."

With that he kissed me deeply. It was our first nice kiss of the day and I didn't realize how much I had been missing it. He had a way of making my body yearn for him with just the touch of his lips. I wrapped my arms up around his neck and slid my fingers through his hair and pulled him down hard against me. The boat started to rock back and forth. Another boater must have gone by. It caused us to stumble a little. He smiled at the slight interruption because we ended up seated on the long couch. He laid back and pulled me on top of him and I continued to take what was mine. He tasted so good. He pressed me against him sending a shiver through my body.

"Hey your pole and bait are ready." Bucky shouted down, interrupting my pleasure.

"Okay, be up in a minute." Jake called back up. He smiled at me.

"Duty calls."

"Nice timing," I grumbled. I stood up and Jake jumped up a little too excited to go fishing.

"Have fun."

He turned back and took me in my arms and kissed me. "You know I love you."

Now I felt better. I sauntered back upstairs and caught Bucky looking at me. He was standing there with two poles, shirtless. I rolled my eyes and he stuck his tongue out at me. He was like an older brother. I popped open the cooler for a soda and to my surprise there was diet Dr. Pepper, my favorite.

"Yeah, Diet Dr. Pepper!"

I looked over to Bucky.

"See I can be nice." He smiled at me and handed a pole to Jake. "Okay man you've got to earn your keep, this is dinner tonight."

Jake laughed but they were serious. Tonight we were grilling fish.

I headed up to the bow to sit and talk with Deidre, something I had been dying to do since this morning.

"Sorry to keep you waiting."

She was laid out on a towel, her copper skin glistening in the sunlight. Her long dark brown hair was fanned out above her head. She looked like a goddess, I felt a twinge of jealousy because she was so beautiful. She raised her hand to block the sun.

"That's okay, we've got time."

"Well not really, Jake and I are leaving in the morning." I sat down next to her and tried to run my fingers through my hair to brush it out. It was all knots from the wind and water. How did she get her hair so silky?

"Well what do you want to know?"

"Well everything? How long have you been able to control your dreams? Can you see the future? Have you been able to prevent anything from happening? What do the dreams mean? How is it that what happens in my dreams happens to me in real life?"

"Whoa, slow down…One thing at a time"

"I'm sorry. I've just had a lot of really weird stuff happen to me and I need some answers."

"The man you dream of is no man, he's a Demon."

You could have picked my jaw up off the ground.

"How do you know of the man I'm dreaming of?"

"He is a seeker, looking for pure spirits. He has found you and he wants you badly, he'll stop at nothing to have you."

"But why, what does he want with me?"

"You are to be his sacrifice to his master."

"I've heard this mentioned before in my dreams with other women. Is this what this group does, do they do some sort of human sacrifice?"

"I'm not sure what you mean about a group but the Demon, he wants to offer you to his master."

"Okay this is freaking me out. I don't understand. I have been dreaming about a bunch of girls getting murdered, actually a couple times I've been in the body of the murderer while he's doing it. Then within the week they find these girls dead with similar wounds. That's what I've been trying to figure out, how to stop this guy or group, not some Demon that wants to use me as a sacrifice." I was really starting to lose it now, this wasn't making any sense.

"Tara, I realize that you want to help these other girls but from my perspective I think the real person you need to help is yourself."

"Okay, say I need to help myself. How do I do that from my dreams because that's the only time I seem to be able to be in contact with him?"

"I wish I could give you more information Tara. Our gift is a learned ability." I raised my eyebrow at this, not understanding a word she was saying. "I mean you have the ability but you need to work at it. Keep doing what Darian showed you last night, changing into things of your choosing, switching your surroundings, making things appear, feeling certain things. For heaven's sake bring Jake into your dream. Just practice using your gift and explore it and when you are back home you will have to think on your feet and be ready when you meet that evil being again."

I turned to look into the sun. I closed my eyes and felt the warm rays against my face. So there was no secret weapon, no special trick, no rules, just practice. They could have told me this over the phone. Actually that wasn't very nice of me, it was pretty nice being up here and enjoying my family. I guess that's how it would be then, tonight I would just have to practice.

"So if you think you know who the guy in my dream is, then who is the little girl?"

"Be careful with her Tara, she is not always what she seems."

Tell me about it, the little wicked tyrant. But why, why was she not always as she seemed. There was so much more that I didn't understand.

"I still don't get why me? Of all the people in the world, why choose me? Why didn't he come after you?"

"I don't know Tara."

I peeked over the edge of the boat and could see fish swimming. The wind was picking up a little and my hair was falling in my face. I wanted to put it up but I was afraid to let go of the wire railing.

"Deidre, if people die in their dreams, do they die in real life?"

"I don't know, but people die in their sleep all the time and no one knows if they were dreaming when they died."

"Hmmm."

"Just be careful Tara."

We spent the day on the water enjoying the sun, swimming, well not me, and fishing. It was really cool to see Jake in a different environment. Of course he was just as handsome as ever, even more so, but of course I was biased. He took his shirt off too, revealing a nice set of abs and a muscular build. His chest hair was black but he didn't have too much. My favorite part was the bit that traveled down past his belly button to the top of his jeans. His skin was pale but getting red from the sun. I didn't think to pack any sunscreen because I didn't burn and I usually avoided the sun. I'm sure he was going to feel it tomorrow. Next to Bucky Jake looked thin and very pale. Bucky was at least 6 foot 5 and had bulging muscles. His skin was very dark, probably from hanging out on this boat all summer long. His hair was dark brown and was practically as long as Diedre's hair. He wore a pony tail braid over his shoulder. If I didn't see him as a brother type I would find him incredibly sexy and I was surprised he didn't have a girlfriend. He seemed to be sort of a loner so that might explain it.

I had all the answers I was going to get and we had enough fish to feed the whole clan so we headed back to the marina. Jake was sure to sit by me with his arm wrapped around me tightly all the way back. No riding on the bow this time. I couldn't help but wonder if the dream I had of falling in the water was actually a premonition even though it was somewhat planned out in my dream. I mean I was in control of my dream, I chose to turn myself into a butterfly but I didn't choose to turn back into myself and fall into the water. It didn't occur to me that maybe I should avoid the water for a few days after that dream. This was all so hard, I didn't know if I would be able to do it. Why would Deidre warn me of the little girl when it was the little girl that led me to safety and warned me of the man?

"Tara come on, we're here." I looked up and everyone was out of the boat carrying their stuff. Jake was standing there with his hand out waiting for me. I sat there lost in my thoughts and missed out on the enjoyable ride back.

"Thanks." I smiled, trying to shake all the thoughts from my head.

"So will that be okay?"

"What?"

"Tara, weren't you listening?"

"Listening to what?"

"Sometimes I think you are on a different planet. Buck offered to take me around the reservation and show me some places while you, Uncle and Deidre got ready for dinner. Will that be okay?"

We were walking quickly now trying to catch up to the rest of the group.

"Sure, sure that's fine. Whatever you want." Man I was lost in space. I heard nothing of that conversation. "Just don't be gone too long." I grabbed his hand. He squeezed it tight.

"I won't."

Chapter 14: Dream Catcher

Uncle cleaned the fish and Deidre and I cleaned up the kitchen while Darian gathered wood for the bomb fire that was sure to take place later tonight.

I wiped down the counters and Deidre washed dishes. I still had a lot on my mind and I wasn't ready to give up trying to find out more.

"Deidre, what type of dreams do you have?"

"What do you mean?"

"Well do you have many bad dreams?"

"Not many. I mostly have dreams about the health and well being of our tribe. I think because that's what the community wants to know. Sometimes I do dream of accidents and I usually warn people ahead of time depending on the dream. Does that answer your question?"

"Yeah. I'm just wondering why this is considered some unusual ability if it doesn't seem to come naturally and I have to practice at it."

"Well it's just like most talents the Creator gives us. The gift is given and it's what you do with that gift that makes the difference. You have to develop it and nurture it and learn to use it for the betterment of all. There are those out there that choose to use it for the wrong reasons." At this last statement she stopped what she was doing and stared at me.

"Well how can you use it the wrong way? I mean, they are just dreams. I mean sometimes I would warn someone of something and what I thought would happen didn't even happen so who's to say the person is bad if they don't say anything to warn someone if they dream something bad is going to happen."

"It's not just that Tara. You wondered why what happens to you in your dream happens to you in real life. Well sometimes people with this ability purposely go into other people's dreams to cause harm. The untrained person cannot stop them. It's a form of torture. Have you ever had the same dream over and over and over?" I had, many times. "Well it's probably not a coincidence. Someone is controlling your dreams, which means they are controlling you."

"But why did I dream that I was inside someone else?"

"You probably fell into someone else's dream or someone led you there to see something. I don't know Tara."

"Well sometimes I feel like my dreams are coming to life."

She looked at me quizzically so I continued.

"Well a couple times I would hear the same voices from my dreams, hear footsteps and nobody would be there."

"Someone must be reaching out to you or trying to scare you away."

"Well they are doing a good job of scaring me." I laughed nervously.

"Now you know that you have more power, you can be braver." She smile at me and walked outside to help Darian.

If she only knew how little that helped ease my fears. I was still frightened and would still be tonight when I went to sleep. Now I felt even more pressure, like I had the weight of the world on my shoulders to figure out these murders and the Creator picked me to lead the good guys to the bad guys. I was beginning to think that my plans to run off to New York were no accident that it was written, just like my gift, it was all planned. Jake interrupted my deep thoughts.

"I got you a surprise!" He kissed me on the cheek.

I smiled back at him, he was so irresistible. Bucky followed him in, his hair flowing down his back.

"I told him that it was an old wives tale but he insisted."

I opened the bag and pulled out a dream catcher. It was beautiful. The hoop was wrapped in mauve suede. It had purple and mauve beads and feathers.

"It's beautiful Jake really."

"The old lady in the shop said that the beads in the middle help the good dreams get through the web and the bad dreams get tangled up in the web and burn up in the morning sun." He was smiling. He came around behind me and hugged me and kissed me on the head. "So, no more bad dreams, okay."

'I wish it were that easy' I thought to myself. I turned to Bucky, "And I have heard from family members that they do improve their dreams." I said it in a sarcastic tone so he would be sure to know I didn't give a hoot what he thought.

Bucky grunted and walked out the sliding screen door to the deck. "So you like it?"

"I love it Jake, thank you." I'll probably need a dozen to catch the amount of bad dreams I've been having but this was a start.

I grabbed Jakes hand and led him outside. It was already getting dark and Darian had the fire going, the little pyro. Uncle was starting the grill for the fish. I couldn't believe it was already our last night. It went so quick.

"Hold on I'll be right back." Jake shook loose of my hand and ran towards the front of the house.

Okay. I headed to a lawn chair, sat down and looked out to the river. The sun was just going down and the orange glow danced on the water. Twilight was such a peaceful time. I could just see the sparkling lights of the fireflies sprinkling in the tall grass. I wished I could just stay here forever and not go back. Suddenly my dreams of being an actress and a singer just didn't matter as much anymore. Being safe, being with my family, being with Jake, this is what mattered most. Then a twinge of guilt snuck in and I thought how the girls that were murdered and the girls that may be murdered probably wished they could just be home safe with family and if I had the ability to help them, then I couldn't turn away from them. What did Deidre say about what someone does with their gift? I don't think I could live with myself knowing I could have stopped something terrible from happening and I didn't. Well I guess that means I'm going back to the city tomorrow. I turned to see who was coming up behind me and saw Jake carrying his guitar. I had forgotten he brought it and was so happy. I loved to hear Jake play.

Jake pulled up a chair next to me. He bent down and gave me a kiss and then sat and started to play. Everyone seemed to just stop what they were doing; to turn and stare at Jake and just listen to the beautiful music he created. He was simply amazing. I think even Bucky was impressed because I caught him sitting on the old log seat staring at Jake as he played. I had to say I was feeling pretty enamored by Jake but I always was I think. He finished playing and Uncle yelled to say that the fish was done.

Bucky was the first to comment on Jake's playing. "That was amazing Brother. You are some musician."

"Thanks Buck." Jake bowed his head and half smiled. He always seemed to be humbled by his music and had a hard time taking compliments. I just didn't understand it; it was if he didn't realize how good he really was, I didn't know how he couldn't.

We headed up to the deck for our last meal before heading home. It was like some big countdown I was dreading. I was not looking forward to going home. The meal was excellent and the company even better. Deidre and I cleaned up and brought out some dessert. Uncle decided to gather us all around the fire and tell us ghost stories. Problem was ghost stories on the Rez weren't really stories, they were experiences. When I was little my parents used to tell them and I was told to leave the room, that's how real and scary they were. I wasn't really sure I was in the mood for scary stories seeing how I've had my own scary experiences lately but I didn't want to be rude plus it was a chance to snuggle close to my Jake.

Instead of listening to the stories I was deep in thought on my own predicament at home, trying to piece together the puzzle. Who was this group of people, cloaked in darkness with their symbols and chanting, why do I keep dreaming of Sam and now recently Devin? And who was this little girl?

"That was really creepy." Jake looked down at me.

I smiled up at him. "Yeah."

The flames flickered and I was lost in the light and then those eyes, those red eyes glared out at me. I sucked in my breath and jumped back slightly.

Jake squeezed his arm around me. "You okay?"

"Um, yeah, just these stories are freakin' me out a bit." I took a deep breath and tried to calm my nerves. This was the first time since we've been here that I felt touched by the evil from my dreams but I think it was more from my doing and my imagination.

"Actually I think I've had enough. I'm going to go get ready for bed." I took off to go inside. I took the stairs up to the deck and went in through the back screen door. I wanted to wash up and brush my teeth. Bucky was coming out of the bathroom as I was heading down the hall, I hadn't noticed he had left.

"You coming back to the fire?" He stepped aside to let me pass.

"No. I'm going to bed. We need to take off early in the morning."

"Oh. Well it was nice seeing you again. Your Jake is pretty cool for a white boy."

"Thanks."

I wanted to give him a hug but I felt awkward. I mean we knew each other because of family but we didn't know each other. But I didn't have to deliberate too long because he closed the distance between us and grabbed me up in a huge bear hug. His arms were so strong. I felt so tiny in his embrace. He kept hold of me as he talked.

"If you ever need anything please call me, I'm always available and I'm not far away. I know I'm not family but you're just as important to me as if you were."

I smiled and blushed at his honesty.

He bent his head down towards me and I was afraid he was going to kiss me which he did but on my cheek. I could smell the beer on his breath. Oh well now this explains why he was being so overly sentimental. Bucky was always one to throw back a few or a few dozen.

"You can put me down now Bucky."

He whispered in my ear, "You're beautiful" and he kissed me again near my ear and breathed heavily causing a shiver through my body.

I kicked him in the shin and it was like kicking a wall. "Bucky put me down!"

"Yes Buck, why don't you put her down?"

Both of our heads snapped towards the voice and saw Jake standing at the end of the hallway. Bucky's grasp on me slowly released and my body slid down his rubbing against every ridge of muscle along his taunt body on the way down. I was mortified even though we hadn't done anything wrong.

"Sure man, I was just telling Tara here that if she needs anything she can always call me."

Jake raised his eyebrows at that, "I'm sure she will. Thanks for the offer Buck."

When Bucky finally unwrapped his hands from me I turned and walked into the bathroom, I didn't want to face Jake. I slammed the door shut and locked it. Immediately the knocking began.

"Tara, are you okay?"

I stood there, staring at myself in the bathroom mirror. The flush was still brilliant red on my cheeks.

"I'm fine."

"That usually means you're not fine. Let me in, please."

"No."

Bucky didn't mean anything by what he did. He was just being overly affectionate, like most people when they drank too much. I was familiar with it, I worked at a bar for goodness sakes. So why was I still blushing? Again, out of nowhere Jake acts like he has to save me. A few more seconds and I could have handled it myself but now I feel like he caught me doing something bad. I know that's probably not what he's thinking. I closed my eyes and took a deep breath. I was reading way more into this than necessary. I opened the door but Jake was gone, I waited too long. I closed the door and began getting ready for bed.

The scratch on the door was faint so I ignored it but then it grew louder. Pulling my toothbrush out of my mouth I leaned closer to the door and listened. Someone was scratching their nails down the door. I slowly reached for the handle to open the door but the door shook and rattled. My heart sped up and I almost choked on my toothpaste when I heard a huge thump like someone slammed up against the door. "Stupid Darian." I grabbed the door handle and swung the door open but no one was there. I stuck my head out into the hallway and looked both ways but the hallway was empty.

"Darian, you there?" I called out but there was no answer.

I closed the door and turned on the hot water in the sink. I brushed my hair and put it back into a hair tie to readying myself to wash my face. The hot water steamed up the mirror except for the pentagram symbol drawn in the center of the mirror. Again my heart began to pound and my palms began to sweat. How was this possible? Maybe it was there before and the steam revealed it but a witchcraft symbol in Uncle's house? Drips of water fell from the drawing it looked as though someone had just reached up and created the symbol. I took the hand towel and wiped the whole bathroom mirror clear and when I stepped back to examine the mirror the little girl was standing behind me. I screamed and swung around but of course she was gone. Maybe it was her, telling me I needed to get back home. My piercing scream alerted the cavalry and both Jake and Bucky came running.

"What happened?" Jake made it to me first.

"Are you okay?" Bucky nearly knocked Jake over as he came bounding into the bathroom.

"Tara who visited you?" Deidre seemed to know exactly what happened as she came prancing in like a fairy. Both guys turned around to look at her like she was crazy.

I wasn't about to discuss what I just saw and worry everyone more so I thought of something quick.

"I'm sorry to have alerted all of you, I saw a huge spider." They all just stared at me. "I don't like spiders." I tried to act as innocent as I could.

The guys took it at that and left but Deidre arched her eyebrows and gave me a little humph as she walked back down the hall. I don't think I quite had her fooled.

I quickly finished up. I didn't want to be left alone. I gathered my stuff and ran outside. The night was cooling off a little, I should sleep well tonight. Then the dread took over when I remembered that tonight I was to practice my dream making. Deidre told me that I needed to concentrate on what I wanted and where I wanted go before I slept. Jake along with everyone else was still hanging around the fire.

"Jake, I'm going to bed now." I gave him a quick squeeze from around his back and he reached up and patted me on the arm.

"Do you want me to come?" He turned to look up at me.

"No, that's okay. You stay and enjoy yourself. Come when you're ready."

I wasn't sure how long it was going to take for me to fall asleep and maybe it would be better to have them awake while I worked on controlling my dreams just in case things didn't go as planned. I decided to sleep inside the tent tonight because the breeze made it cool. I covered up and got comfy. I kept repeating 'I want to control my dream' over and over but all the concentrating was getting me no where. I could see the glow of the bomb fire through the tent. The flames of the fire cut through the shadows as if they were dancing across the fabric. I kept staring at the flames dance and dance as their clothes flowed out behind them like long robes. They twirled around all in time, their robes flowed high in the air. I couldn't see their faces; it was like a dark shadow. They danced together, happy, the music played as they twirled around together in each others arms. But then it was if they couldn't stop, someone was directing them to continue. I peered closer to see into their faces and I could see a black web creeping up their necks trying to overtake their faces. A fire burned along the walls lighting their stage bringing to light their features I so longed to see. Their lips were black, their eyes were black, they had black blush and it all stood out against pale white powder skin. Their clothes were black under their long black robes. Another group pushed onto the stage what looked like a prop but was actually the cement slab from my earlier dreams. They danced around it as I stood there staring at the mesmerizing display just now realizing that I was dreaming, that I was in a place not of my choosing. This wasn't how it was supposed to happen. I was expecting a fun dream, not this. They brought out a women and slammed her down on the cement slab. I stepped closer to examine her. It was Melissa. I bent down to release her, daring anyone to stop me, this was my dream. When I touched her she disappeared and I was standing in my Uncles back yard. I turned around and the bomb fire was still burning high. Everyone was still sitting around it enjoying the evening to include Jake. Why couldn't they see me? I called to Jake but nothing came out. My voice was gone. I wasn't doing a very good job of controlling my dreams tonight. I was beginning to think that maybe I didn't have the ability to control my dreams after all maybe it was all a fluke.

I continued to stand in the yard trying to get the attention of my family and friends when Deidre got up from her place across from Jake. She was even more stunning in my dream if that were possible. Her long black hair glistened in the firelight. I could barely take my eyes off of her. I looked over to Jake and saw that he was having a hard time taking his eyes off of her too. I swallowed but couldn't get past the lump in my throat but then remembered that this was probably my subconscious as I worried that Jake would think she was prettier than me the moment I found out she was Bucky's sister and not his girlfriend.

But then Deidre walked over and stood in front of Jake and sat on his lap. He seemed a little shy but she wrapped her arms around his neck and he held her on him. The rage burned hot inside of me and I stepped forward to confront the two of them, completely forgetting this was a dream but both feet were cemented to the ground. I could not take a step. I looked back up to the two of them sitting there enjoying the fire. She tilted her head to the side and whispered something in his ear. He smiled and my heart started pounding and I could feel the lump in my throat tightening. My stomach was doing flip flops. This was my dream. I refuse to let this happen.

Jake stood up with Deidre in his arms and he walked towards me. Finally I could give them both a piece of my mind but he walked right past me as if I were invisible. He laid Deidre on the blanket, our blanket, her beautiful hair spread out above her. I tried to turn around but still my feet were firmly planted and I couldn't move. I twisted around the other way just in time to see Jake lay down next to Deidre and kiss her and keep kissing her. His hand, which was wrapped around her side, began to move upward and I could take it no longer. I squeezed my eyes shut and with all my might I screamed his name hoping this time something would come out.

"JAKE!" I think I even felt the ground rumble or maybe it was just my rage.

When I opened my eyes they were gone. I twisted back around and the scene at the bomb fire was the same as before. Everyone was sitting enjoying the fire with Deidre sitting across from Jake as if nothing had happened. I stepped forward and the hold on me had been relinquished and I was free. I moved toward the fire and Deidre looked up to me. I gave her a murderous stare.

"I had to; it seemed like the only thing that would get you motivated to start working."

"But Jake!"

"Tara, you have a lot of work to do and you didn't believe in your ability so I needed to do something drastic. I'm sorry if I hurt you but please know that it wasn't Jake or any part of his mind. Okay?" She was pleading with me now and I did feel somewhat better knowing that Deidre seemed to have all the control and Jake was just a pawn in her demonstration.

"I guess I understand. It definitely helped." I rolled my eyes.

"Now use your imagination and try to be creative but don't put yourself in any danger."

All I really wanted to do was curl up in Jake's arms and have him wash away all my insecurities and tell me how much he loved me.

Jake stood up from his chair and walked towards me. He stood in front of me and held my hands, bent down and kissed me gently on the lips. His hair fell over his forehead and I reached up to brush it out of his eyes.

I smiled up at him. "Where should we go, what should we do? We have all night."

We had an evening full of us doing all my favorite things and I really packed it in. We started off laying under the stars talking, walking along a beach holding hands, getting our picture taken in front of the Eifel Tower, backpacking in the woods, attending Christmas Eve Mass with the Pope, scuba diving, dancing at clubs in New York and LA, and the list went on until finally I saw him down on one knee with a ring in one hand proposing to me. The tears began to flow and I yelled "Yes, Yes, Yes, I DO!"

"You do what? Tara what's wrong why are you crying?" Jake was holding me close to him. I realized that he just woke me from my magical dream. I rolled over and rubbed the sleep out of my eyes and looked up at him.

"Don't you remember any of your dreams tonight Jake?" I asked hopefully.

"I slept like a log, I don't think I dreamt of anything." He rolled over and I cuddled up behind him.

"Well I dreamt of us."

"Oh so you were crying, that's not good." He sounded half asleep already.

"They were tears of joy."

I didn't hear a response.

"Don't you want to know why?"

And then I heard him begin to snore.

"You asked to marry me" I said to myself because he was already sound to sleep.

I closed my eyes and wished I could go back to my perfect dream. I laid there and pictured Jake on one knee smiling up at me. The early morning sound of crickets chirping and the frogs croaking were interfering with my memory. The sounds kept taking me away from my picture of Jake to a grassy area. The sun had not come up yet and the mist lay heavy on the ground. Tiny lights circled in and around the blades of grass and up into the forest trees. It was dark but the flittering lights made a soft glow against the mist. A trail broke out before me and I could hear the faint sound of a piano playing one of Chopin's Nocturnes. I quietly walked along the path. The forest was magical, and sparkling with millions of little lights. One zoomed past me and I saw wings fluttering. They were small fairies. As I continued down the path the music became louder. Soon I could help myself no longer and I began to flit about dancing to the music, holding my arms out around my imaginary partner. I closed my eyes and danced and danced. When I opened them I was about 10 feet in the air.

"Ohh"

I looked down and my feet were sparkling, the fairies were carrying me. I spun around and I was dancing on air. I felt like a little girl lost in a wonderland. The dark ivy vines clung to the trees and the sun tried to break through, flowers and moss covered the forest floor and the beautiful piano music rang through the trees. I twirled around and the little lights swirled around me, my hair was wispy and hung long down my back. On one of my turns I bumped hard into what I thought was a tree but I felt arms wrap around me. I kept my eyes closed knowing it was Jake. Finally I brought him into my dream. I leaned back against his chest and the squeeze around me became tighter. Worry flooded my mind as the grip on me grew tighter.

"Jake not so hard."

"Don't you recognize me?"

I drew in my breath and the grip tightened. I tried to turn but his hand covered my eyes and pressed my head back against him.

"Shhhh…In due time." His hand moved up to my forehead so I could see, just not him. My beautiful magical forest was gone. I was as if a plague sucked the life out of every living thing, all the trees were black and dying, the morning light turned to darkness and only the moonlight shown down through the trees causing a blue tint to everything. We were standing on the ground now but the ground was soot and ash.

"Ahhh..do you hear that, it's one of my favorites."

I could hear it; it was "Moonlight Sonata" by Beethoven. Under normal circumstances I loved this song but now it only added to the dismal scene before me.

"It's time for you to come home to me; I've been waiting a long time for you."

Finally I felt the grip loosen and I turned in his arms but it was just a tree with branches wrapped around me. I was angry with myself. I needed to learn not to be intimidated by fear and not to be scared out of using my ability. I had the control all along to change this situation from the moment it turned into something I didn't want it to be and yet I chose to let my fear get the best of me. I realized then that I still had a long way to go but was worried that I didn't have the time I needed.

Chapter 15: Back Home

Everyone showed up at Uncle's house to see us off. It was a quick couple days but well worth the visit. We knew that we would have to come and visit again soon. I felt like I hugged a hundred people.

"Don't forget that I'm here if you need me." Deidre gave me a huge hug. I was so thankful for her help and advice.

Bucky swung me up in his arms, "Now don't go being a stranger and wait another 10 years to come see me."

"Well you can come see me too you know." He dropped me and shook Jake's hand.

"It was nice to meet you Jake."

"You too Buck."

I was happy that there seemed to be no weirdness after last night's run in.

Uncle gave me some cash, "Now don't try and give it back. You struggling artists need all the help you can get." He smiled widely and then gave me a big hug and kiss.

"I'll miss you, Tara."

"I'll miss you too Uncle."

We got in the car and started to drive away and I heard someone yelling my name.

"Stop Jake."

Jake stopped the car and I rolled down the window. It was Darian.

"Here, this is for you."

He handed me an eagle feather.

"You can think of me when you are away."

"Thanks Darian. I love it!" I gave him a kiss on the cheek and he ran off.

Jake drove and I sat back and enjoyed our trip back home.

The drive home was less eventful then the drive up north. Thank goodness for that seeing how we both had to work tonight. It never occurred to me to ask for our travel night off too. I don't know what I was thinking. Poor Jake was going to be exhausted. I offered to drive a couple times but he refused.

We dropped the car off and I swore to Jake that I would pay him back for the rental and the broken window. We had the insurance so we only had to pay the deductible but still I wasn't about to let Jake pay for that, Uncle's money would be gone before I knew it.

The cab dropped me off at my place and I told Jake I would meet him at work. I raced upstairs, not having much time, I wanted to take a shower and quickly call my parents to let them know of my trip. The door was locked but no bolt and no chains. I thought Melissa would be home by now. She had a job working at a coffee house during the summer. She might have headed to her boyfriends after work. I had a slight feeling of worry but it passed.

It was nice to be home back in my own place. I couldn't wait to sleep in my bed tonight after two nights on the ground. After my shower I checked out the fridge and everything from when I left was still in there, untouched. 'Melissa must have just stayed at her boyfriend's house.'

I grabbed a diet dr. pepper and headed out the door to work. The 20 minute walk had me sweating as if I hadn't taken a shower. I still was not used to the muggy days of August here in New York. Of course it didn't help that I had two shirts on, my uniform shirt and another shirt to cover up said uniform shirt. I couldn't stand the scanty tops that Patrick made us where now. There was no way I was about to walk to work in my uniform and so I could feel the sweat dripping down my back. I had my hair up in a hair clip and I wore cut off jean shorts and tennis shoes. I was kind of glad I didn't have a job I had to dress up for though.

As I got closer to work I saw Devin's car parked out front. I had a whole new attitude towards him. I knew that I shouldn't treat him different-ly but it was really going to be hard.

I walked into the bar but I didn't see him. Ed gave me a nod from behind the bar. I walked up to the bar and sat my stuff down.

"Can I get a water Ed, please."

"Hot, huh?"

"Muggy."

I chugged my water. 'Much better' I thought to myself. I grabbed my top shirt and pulled it up over my head and hands wrapped around my stomach. I flinched but I was still stuck in my shirt. The hands pulled me back and I fell against whoever was behind me.

"Welcome back. Thanks for coming home to me."

I ripped the shirt off my head at that last statement. It reminded me of my dream I had just this morning. I flung around and Devin stood there with his devilish smile and jade green eyes. The shirt pulled my hair clip out and my hair spilled down around me. He reached up to push it out of my face and I drew back away from him.

"Tara, what's the matter? Aren't you happy to see me?" He was so handsome and that made him dangerous I told myself.

"I have to get to work." I walked off and headed to the bath room and caught Jake staring at us from the other section of the bar. I didn't know he was already here. When I came out of the bathroom Jake was waiting.

"Tara, you can't treat him any differently. He can't know that I told you."

"Jake, it's not fair, we can't live in constant fear of him and what he may do."

Jake's face turned angry.

"Tara, I mean it. He will hurt you if it means getting at me and I don't know what I would do if anything were to happen to you. Things need to be the same as before I told you."

"Well I'm not going to that stupid party, I'm not going to be in that play and I'm not going to the Broadway play with him." I folded my arms across my chest and pouted like a little girl.

"Geez, I didn't realize you had that much planned with the guy." Jake rose up his eyebrows. He was trying to be funny but I was serious. He took my face in his hands and forced me to look into his eyes.

"Tara, please, just do what you already promised. If you need to make excuses to back out of a few things, then fine but do it nicely." He kissed me and I just wanted to take the night off and go back to my place. I wasn't ready for work.

I put on a smile and headed back out into the bar. Devin sat at the bar and drank and I tried to be polite when I read off my first drink order to Ed.

"So is that cast party this week?"

"You're talking to me now," he said without looking at me. He was going to make this hard.

"I wasn't not talking to you. I was just grumpy because I'm hot and tired."

He looked at me now and gave me a devilish grin.

"Yes, we're meeting this week and handing out practice schedules and performance schedules."

"Are you in the play too?"

He laughed out loud.

"Oh no. I help with the production and do some behind the scenes but I'm no actor."

"Oh. So I'll see you at practice though." I smiled, almost flirting with him.

He turned towards me now and pulled me closer to him. Uh oh, maybe I flirted more than I thought.

"You bet. I'll be there all the time. These new uniforms look really good, especially on you." He slid his hand down the curve of my waist and rested on my hip.

"Well I'm not a big fan." I scooted away from him and grabbed my drinks, quickly getting myself away from him. He was something else. I felt like he could make you do things you didn't want to do just by that stare of his.

I tried to call Melissa during one of my breaks to let her know that I was home but there was no answer on her cell phone. I tried calling the number she left for her boyfriend but also no answer. I was trying not to worry but it was getting impossible. My parents were happy to hear that I had a nice time. They had already heard the whole story by the time I called. Uncle was quick on the draw when it came to calling the folks. I was sitting in a booth while talking with my parents and I grabbed the newspaper. There was a follow up story to the young starlet found murdered in the trailer park in Jersey. I had forgotten that I had hidden the knife in my dream. I wondered if they had found it. I decided to call the anonymous tip line and let them know about the possible murder weapon.

I had just finished leaving a message with the police operator when Patrick walked into the main bar area. I jumped up and pretended like I was wiping off the table.

"Tara, come here."

I rolled my eyes and headed over to him.

"Hey, I'm going to need you to work some extra hours this week okay?"

I wanted to protest but then I thought this may be just what I needed to get out of my obligations with Devin.

"Oh, okay."

"I'll need you in here for our lunch hour each day for the rest of the week, so by 11am."

Oh my God, I could feel my feet hurting already.

"Sure" I tried to smile, really I did.

"Okay, well don't just stand there, get to work." He bolstered off to his office and I headed to the bar. It was getting crowded now and I needed to get busy. Devin caught my eye as I walked by.

"How are you going to make it to the cast party and practice if you have to work all week?"

I squinted at him. "Do you make a habit of listening to my conversations?" I grabbed some menus from behind the bar and stalked off. He was driving me crazy.

"If I didn't know better I would think you were purposefully trying to get out of going?" What would make him say that? I turned around and he was looking over towards Jake and my throat tightened. I decided to stay calm and play it off.

I smiled my sweetest smile and walked up to him and placed my hand on his neck turning his face towards me, "Devin, you know that's not true. I need this job. I'll do what I can to make it there. I promise."

He took my hand and he kissed it and I tried with all my might not to cringe. It was a fine line I was walking. I didn't want to over do it and have him get the wrong idea but yet I didn't need him thinking I had any issues with him. But I think I did my job by distracting him from his original focus. Of course now his focus was on me, which made me very uncomfortable.

I forced a smile and he seemed satisfied as he smoothed my hair with his hand. He bent down as if to kiss me and for the first time I realized how small I was in his presence and how muscled his body, arms and chest were. I felt my nerves charging, my heart hammered in my chest as if at any moment he could squeeze the life right out of me with just the strength of his hands. His hand was still touching the side of my head and his face bent toward the other side of my head and he whispered.

"I look forward to having you to myself this week." And with that he turned and walked back to the bar. I took a deep breath and dared myself to look in Jakes direction. Just as I suspected he was watching our encounter. I knew this fear was only in my mind and that Devin meant me no harm. It was just the thought that he was capable of such callous behavior that had the hair on the back of my neck standing on end.

Chapter 16: Incarcerated

They say a watched pot never boils well a watched work clock never seems to move but finally it was 2am. Jake walked me home but didn't stay. We were both too exhausted to be of any company to each other. I didn't feel confident enough to take the elevator by myself so even as tired as I was I took the five flights of stairs.

I reached the top and I could hear two men talking in the hallway. I peeked through the crack in the stairwell door and saw two police Detectives standing outside my door. The first thing that came to my mind was something happened to Melissa. I busted through the door and practically ran towards the Detectives.

"Did something happen to Melissa?"

"Excuse us Miss but do you live here?"

"Yes."

"I'm Detective Dallas and this is Detective Foster. Did you by chance make a call to the tip line regarding the recent murder of Michelle Taylor?"

"Who?"

"Did you make a call to our tip line today?"

"Yes, but I thought that was anonymous?"

"Well, yes, but we have some questions we'd like to as you. Can you come down to the station with us?"

"It's 2:30 in the morning. I need to check to see if my roommate is home, I haven't been able to get a hold of her."

"Yes, well we need you to come with us. No one answered the door."

"She's not there?" I was consumed with worry.

"Please Miss, come with us."

I followed them into the elevator, they slid the iron gate shut and the buzzing light flickered off and on. I hate this elevator. Once outside they directed me into the squad car. I didn't even notice that it was parked out front when Jake and I walked home. They had me sit in the back. I felt like a criminal. The car pulled away and I turned in the seat to look behind me and I thought I saw the little girl standing out front of my building waving. I wiped the window to clear the fog but there was no one there. I was so worried about Melissa.

It didn't take long and we were at the station. They started asking me basic questions such as name, address, phone, etc. but then they asked to get my finger prints.

"Why?"

"It's standard procedure. Please Miss."

So they took my finger prints too. Finally by 4:00am one of the two cops from earlier came into the room and sat down at the table next to me.

"Can I get you anything, water, coffee?"

"No."

"Well we appreciate you helping us out. We have a few questions. First how is it you know Miss Taylor?"

"I don't know her."

"You don't know her, you're sure?"

"Yes, I'm sure."

"So you've never been to her house before?"

"No, why would I if I don't even know her."

The cop took out a cigarette from a pack hidden in his coat and lit it.

"Do you want one?"

"No thank you."

"Tara, I'm confused. If you don't know Miss Taylor and you've never been to her house then how is it that we found the murder weapon exactly where you said it would be?"

"I"

He held up his hand to stop me.

"Wait. We also found your finger prints on the murder weapon and in the house. Now how do you explain that?"

I felt lightheaded. Could this be happening? I was there, I did touch the murder weapon, and I hid it, but how to explain that I did this all in a dream. I decided that now was as good a time as any to just come out with it and tell them how I think that I have some connection with this killer and

209 Dream Catcher by Tricia Currier

how I'm able to see the murders in my dreams and how I hope to use my ability to stop the murders or at least find out where their secret fortress was. I continued to explain how I was worried about Melissa now and that I think she's been missing for a few days and I thought that something bad was going to happen to her if it hadn't happened already. The Detective listened to me intently. When I finished he stood up and left the room. After about fifteen minutes he came back.

"Miss Mason, now you say when you have these dreams you are sometimes inside the body of the killer?"

"Yes"

"So you would actually kill the person?"

"Yes, well not really but it would feel like it when I was in their body but then I would wake up."

"Okay, well we're going to have to hold you for a little while until we can sort this out."

I was getting scared now. Sweat began to drip down my temple.

"What? Why? I didn't do anything wrong. I explained to you what happened. I'm really worried about Melissa and I think you need to look for her." A lump began to form in my throat and I felt like I wanted to cry.

"Detective Perry is going to take you to a holding cell. Please go with her."

A tall brunette walked in with cuffs in her hands and it wasn't looking good for me.

"What! No! I didn't do anything wrong. You don't need to cuff me. I'm not the bad guy."

I jumped up from my chair and the chair flung backwards and hit the wall. Two more Detectives joined us in the small room and now it was four against one. This had gone from bad to worse.

"Just calm down and everything will be okay." Detective Dallas raised his hands and lowered them.

"It's not okay! You're trying to lock me up!"

"Grab her Joe!"

A bigger Detective came at me and had me in seconds, my hands behind my back. I reared up and slammed my head back and heard a crack. The hold on me released.

"Shit, she broke my nose!"

"Go get the nurse we need a sedative!"

This time Detective Dallas grabbed me and slammed me down hard against the table. I could see the other Detective holding his nose blood spewing out all over. Serves him right I thought. Then I felt a pinch in my upper arm.

"That ought to get you to calm down a bit, you crazy bitch."

Immediately the fog entered my brain and I could barely keep my eyes open. Everyone looked like blurry shadow figures. Dark eyes, dark lips, then suddenly no faces, but hoods, capes, and blood. I had no will of my own, no strength, and no power. I felt the grip of darkness pull me down and I just floated. I tried to fly but hands were holding me and pulling me in different directions. I could see firelight but my eyes wouldn't stay open and then I hit something hard as if I finally landed. I could hear muffled voices and I strained to make out what they were staying.

"Yes that's her. Take her to the dungeon."

I couldn't put two and two together. The steely grips were about my arms and I was hoisted up off the ground. I strained to open my eyes but I couldn't, I couldn't even walk. They drug me for what seemed like an eternity. My feet plowing into the dirt behind me, my arms felt ripped from their sockets. I tried to will myself awake like Deidre and Darian taught me, I tried to take control but I had none. Was it because there was nothing to fight for, because there was nothing on the line? But there was, Melissa was out there alone, possibly in trouble and she needed me. I tried again to force myself out of my stupor. My eyes opened slightly, but a bright light burned them but I made out blurry shadows behind bars. I could hear them talking.

"Maybe there is a chance she's telling the truth? There was another set of fingerprints on that knife."

"You're telling me she moved the knife in her dream?"

"Well there have been people known to have a sixth sense that are more in tune with the dead. Maybe she's one of them?"

"Yeah and maybe she's just crazy."

I closed my eyes and immediately the pain was back and I was being drug again. My arms ached and just when I thought I could take it no longer they stopped and let go and I dropped to the ground.

"That's no way to treat our guest of honor."

Immediately I was picked up and held in someone's arms.

"What's wrong with her? Why is she like this?"

"They drugged her master."

"Hmm. Well I can't have her like this, we'll have to wait. Bring me out the other one. I'll have her first."

Whoever he was lay me down on the ground and I heard shuffling of feet and the screams. It was Melissa. Her scream was the strength I needed to push me out of my haze. My eyes shot open and glanced around. I felt more awake but my body was still not cooperating. I turned in time to see Melissa being drug in by two larger men. Now these two were not wearing the cloaks but rather the t-shirts and jeans and necklace that the people who followed me were wearing.

They brought Melissa up to the cement slab and the man in the red cloak slapped her across the face.

"Stop screaming!"

"Please, don't kill me. I promise I won't say anything. I'll do whatever you want."

"I already have what I want. You have nothing of value that will save your life tonight. You should feel honored. This is a special night and you are part of it."

His words were dripping with sarcasm. She wasn't buying it, she began screaming again and he slapped her so hard across the face blood smeared her cheek. I jumped up then, I had to stop this. I ran towards the man in the red cloak, grabbed hold of the cape, and pulled hard. He turned as the cape slid off. The jade green eyes peered into mine, the golden brown hair swept across his face revealing a devilish smile that could only be Devin. I drew in a breath. It couldn't be. I thought before it was just me bringing him into my dreams but this couldn't be a mistake, it was him.

"Surprised Tara?"

I couldn't speak; I just shook my head up and down. As much as I hated him for what he had done to Jake's sister I didn't want to believe that Devin could be responsible for all of these girls' deaths.

"And to think there was a time that you wanted me every bit as much as I want you now." I wanted to wipe that smug smile off of his face.

I lunged for him and tried to slug him but he grabbed my arms, pushed back until I hit up against the hard rock wall knocking the wind out of me. I expected some help from Melissa but when I looked over his shoulder she vanished.

"No one here to help you, oh what will little Tara do? You know you aren't strong enough to defeat me. I have plans for you and now is as good a time as any to start them."

He wrapped his hands around my neck and started to squeeze. I couldn't breath, he was choking me and then he closed the distance between us and started to kiss me.

"Or maybe I should take you for myself first."

He leaned back and smiled and squeezed tighter. The smile on his face made him look as though he was possessed; this wasn't the Devin I knew.

I needed to think of something fast or I would soon be dead. Maybe something small and colorful wouldn't be such a bad thing this time. Just Then his hands clasped together instead of around my neck.

"What the hell? Tara!"

He unclasped his hands and I was free. I flittered about until I could get my bearings and then I followed the scent of fresh air and the subtle light.

"Oh you think you're smart!"

He began swiping at me and trying to catch me but I rose up higher above him where he was no threat to me. I continued down the tunnel leaving him yelling at his guards behind me. I was too panicked to even think of the ramifications of what all this meant and how and why Devin was doing this. I reached the end of the tunnel and finally I could see. I changed back into my human form and I realized that I was in an abandoned section of a subway tunnel. I continued to follow the tunnels until it led to another platform up and out. I was on Essex Street and East Broadway. I repeated the street names over and over in my head so I wouldn't forget. I tried to will myself awake but I couldn't. I was trapped here. I needed to get out of here; they would be after me soon.

The city streets were empty, abandoned. Trash blew across the barren streets. Where were all the people? I began walking towards the direction of home. I didn't really know what else to do. I closed my eyes and tried to picture myself in a different area. I imagined myself back in my apartment with Melissa and Jake by my side. I opened my eyes and I was still standing on the sidewalk. I thought I heard voices up ahead and walked in that direction.

"You just don't get it! You may have killed her by giving her that sedative."

"I just don't understand how that can put her in any danger, if anything it's keeping her from hurting herself."

"It's not herself she needs to worry about. She told you about her dreams, well there are some pretty scary people after her. I've seen the outcome myself. She's woken with injuries from her dreams. Yeah, I know, it sounds crazy and I thought she was off her rocker when she told me too but then it happened. I saw it with my own eyes. It was if she was possessed and someone was hurting her from the inside and I could do nothing about it, I couldn't wake her."

"Well then what difference does the sedative make if you couldn't wake her before either?"

"She's learned to find the control she needs in her dreams to help wake herself up when she's in danger but now you've just taken that control away from her!"

I could see them talking as I peered through the dirty building window. I screamed to Jake but he couldn't hear me. Their voices became muffled and I couldn't quite make out what they were saying. I strained to hear but the sound of footsteps kept drowning out their conversation.

'Footsteps? People, oh thank God!'

I turned hoping to find help but my hope turned to despair when I saw Devin and three of his lackeys walking up the sidewalk towards me.

"I didn't think you'd gone far." His cocky grin was enough to make me hate him.

"Don't you take one more step closer to me." I threatened him with no real power behind my words. I put my hands up as if to stop them.

"You haven't got a clue have you Tara. You don't have any power over me. You belong to me and right now I need you for something very special." His smile was so sincere, how he could be so evil and look so handsome was beyond me.

"Why me Devin, why not choose someone else for your special occasion?"

"It has to be you, you were chosen by him, and you'll become very powerful once you join him. You'll see. You will be happy, I promise."

"Who is this person you speak of Devin?"

"He's my master." The way he said this brought chills up my spine.

"Huh, well he won't be mine." I turned to walk away. No one will be master over me.

I should have known it wouldn't be that easy, I screamed in pain as he yanked hard on my hair and I fell back against his chest.

"Don't you ever turn your back on me." He ground out the words between his teeth. "Don't make me hurt you again."

I reached up and grasped the hand that held my hair, trying to hold myself up to dampen the pain. "Oh so it's my fault, all this pain you are causing me." The tear slid down my cheek. I didn't want to give him the satisfaction of knowing how much he was hurting me.

He threw me down on the ground and immediately I scrambled to get my footing and I took off running. I quickly glanced behind me to see the three guys chasing me but Devin just stood there as if he knew not to waste his energy when the other three could easily do his dirty work. I tried to will myself to move faster. I could hear they were gaining ground. I turned into a dark alley and jumped over wooden crates. Rats went scurrying in different directions when I tripped over a garbage can. I screamed but jumped up and kept running. Something grabbed my arms and pulled me into another dark section. It startled me so much I would have screamed but for the hand wrapped tightly over my mouth.

"Shh…quiet, they'll hear you."

I recognized the voice. It was the little girl. I heard the footsteps running past. I let out a sigh of relief. Maybe I had lost them. She unmasked my face. I slid down the concrete wall and sat.

"Thank you."

"You're welcome."

"What's going on, I just don't understand why Devin is doing this?"

"His spirit is evil."

I sat back against the cold wall where we were hiding trying to make sense of all the madness.

"So it's really him that has been kidnapping and murdering the women in the city?"

She shook her head up and down.

"You once said that he's from many histories, do you mean he's been here before?"

"Yes, many times. Not Devin, but his spirit. You must stop him, only you can live freely in his world and out."

"I'm trying but I don't know how?"

"Keep using your dreams Tara. You were given a powerful gift. You must use it to stop him."

"But here you are living freely in his world, why can't you stop him?"

She placed her hand on the side of my head and pictures of her death were flashed before me. Her pretty little dress stained with blood, ripped apart, her heart cut out. I wanted to scream but the fear of them finding us won out.

"I understand. Why do you suppose he wants me?"

"Probably because you're one of only a few that can stop him."

I thought about that for awhile and it sort of made sense. I still didn't understand how Devin could let himself be taken over like this. He seemed so normal as if he didn't know anything about any of this. Maybe he was a better actor then he let on.

"Gotcha!" The grip around my arm was like a tourniquet. He drug me out into the dark alley. "I knew that I would find you." Devin's voice was unmistakable.

He picked me up and slammed me up against the wall.

"You'll never get away with this Devin. I know everything and I will tell them all. You're going to jail where you'll never be able to hurt anyone again."

"Tara, he'll never stop. He'll always find a way." His eyes changed, they looked sorrowful.

"What are you talking about, it's you Devin; you're the one, the one hurting all those women."

"It's not what you think Tara. I love you." He leaned in and kissed me with more passion then ever before. I didn't want to push him away, not this time, but I knew I couldn't trust him. With all my might I forced him away from me.

"Tara please, don't, I want to be with you."

I shoved him again and spat in his face. "You are nothing to me!" The color of his eyes changed and it was if Devin had left and the Demon had returned. His hands were about my neck and he had me pinned up against the wall. This is it, I thought. He's going to kill me this time. I closed my eyes, the loss of oxygen was making me dizzy. I pictured myself back in Jakes arms, loving me, where I belonged. Then I thought I could hear Jake's voice calling my name. It was working. If I was going to die, I wanted to be with the one I loved. I felt the grip loosen and Jake's voice grew louder. I felt hands on my shoulders, shaking me. I couldn't feel the tightness on my throat anymore and I risked a breath and I gasped. My eyes fluttered open and once again my blue-eyed guitar player was holding me. I reached up to feel my neck and could feel nothing squeezing me. I gasped for air again.

"That's it Tara, breathe baby! Breathe!" Tears began to flow from Jake's blue eyes.

I looked around and saw the bars and then the police Detectives.

"Is he gone?" I kept looking around thinking maybe I was still dreaming.

"Is who gone?" He furrowed his brow, concerned by my question.

"Devin."

"Devin's not here."

"Am I awake?"

"Yes, you're awake. What happened?"

"We have to find Melissa. I think I know where she is." I sat up and could see full on the shocked looks on the police Detective's faces. I could only imagine what this night must have been like.

"Whoa, let's take it easy for a minute. I think you may need to rest and let's have you checked out by the Doctor before you go running off anywhere." Detective Dallas chimed in trying to be helpful when really all he was doing was delaying the rescue effort for Melissa.

"You mean she's free to go Detective?" For the first time Jake took his eyes off me to address Detective Dallas.

"Well after what I've seen and what you've told me it seems the pieces add up as crazy as it all sounds." He looked down and shook his head back and forth.

I jumped to my feet, grabbing Jake's arm in the process.

"Hurry we have to find her."

Detective Dallas grabbed my arm. "Now slow down. Like I said you need to be checked out first."

I snapped at him, "Look I'm fine okay. If we don't go looking for her now it may be too late!"

He sighed deeply but didn't release me. "You stay here and have the nurse take a look at those injuries, in the meantime tell me where you think she is and we'll check it out."

It seemed like a reasonable deal. I decided not to put up a fight and explained to them both the vision I had seen in my dream along with the street signs. It would only be a matter of time before they found Melissa, unharmed I hoped.

Chapter 17: Abandoned Subway Station

As I expected, my injuries were only superficial. I was officially released from jail with no pending charges. I was free to go. It was mid-morning and I was worn out. I half expected the Detectives to be back by now. Detective Dallas said he would call me when they had news. Jake and I shared a cab back to my apartment. Immediately I checked the answering machine for messages but nothing.

"Jake, the little girl was in my dream again. She helped me hide from." Then I realized that I hadn't told him that it was Devin I was seeing in my dreams committing all these murders or being witness to them.

"From who Tara?"

I dropped my head into my hands. Did it necessarily mean it was Devin? Why else would I keep seeing him?

"Tara, what's wrong?" His eyes were steely blue and relentless.

"Umm the murderer, it's…" The phone rang and I dove for it hoping for news of Melissa and thanking God for the interruption.

"Hello? Yes, this is her. Yes. You didn't? Are you sure you looked in…Right. Okay. Well thank you."

"What happened, what did they say?"

"They said they found the street signs but that it was just an old subway platform with not tunnels built to it yet." I sat back down on the couch.

"So they didn't find Melissa."

"No. It just doesn't make any sense. I mean I saw it clear as day, the sign said Essex and Broadway. In my dream there were tunnels that led up to that platform."

"Well you heard them Tara, they said it was just a platform, nothing else." He hugged me tight.

"I know. I just felt really strongly that they would find her there." He sat back.

"Well you better get some rest. We've both got work tonight. I'm gonna head home." He kissed me on the cheek.

"Okay. I suppose I better get a little rest."

"I'll meet you at the Kilt tonight then?"

"Yeah."

Jake headed home and left me to my thoughts. I still couldn't believe that my directions led the police to nothing. I needed to see for myself and decided I better check this abandoned platform out but first, a shower.

I was anxious to investigate the vacant platform and knew that this was the perfect time to do it since Jake thought I was resting and he would never let me go it alone. I just had to make sure there was nothing there.

I took the train to the subway station and then the subway to Essex street on the BMT Nassau Street Line. There wasn't a stop for Broadway. I got out and walked around, it was so crowded. I sat on a bench just waiting, for what I don't know. Maybe the Detectives were right, there was nothing more to my dream and Broadway and Essex really didn't mean anything. I continued to sit and watch the people as the trains pulled up and left. I noticed there was one track that never seemed to have any trains. I walked over to the transit worker to find out why.

"Excuse me. I was wondering if you could tell me where that track leads to?" I pointed to the north side of the platform.

"Uhh, that's an abandoned track, it doesn't go anywhere."

"So you don't use it?"

"Nope, not since the early 80's."

"Where did it used to go?"

"To Broadway-Lafayette, but like I said it's out of service."

My curiosity was piqued now. I walked over to the track and looked down the long dark tunnel. I looked at the time, 3p.m. I had enough time to take a quick look. I looked around and no one was paying me any mind. I knew there was no way those Detectives checked this tunnel out, they couldn't have.

As I stepped off the ledge someone's hand on my shoulder pulled me back onto the platform scaring me half to death. They couldn't think I was trying to commit suicide, there was no train coming.

"What did you do that for?" I yelled as I swung around expecting to see the transit worker and instead Detective Dallas stood before me.

"I had a feeling you wouldn't leave well enough alone."

"Oh well, I just wanted to check it out for myself."

"Well you want me to walk down with you?"

I was surprised with his reaction; I thought for sure he was going to be angry with me.

"Besides, you're going to need a flashlight." He smiled sweetly.

"Thanks. You don't know what this means to me. I'm so worried about her. I just know that she's here somewhere."

He jumped down onto the track and then hoisted me down next to him. I felt a lot braver now that he was with me.

"Hey! What are you doing, you're not supposed to be down there." It was the crusty old transit worker.

Detective Dallas turned to reassure the old guy. "It's okay. I'm on official business."

Immediately the transit worker stepped back and relinquished his fight. I continued on, stepping over the uneven ground trying to hurry without breaking my neck. Every step I took I felt closer to Melissa. The lights were glowing on the walls but soon they went out and Detective Dallas took out his flashlight.

"So how far are you going to walk?"

"I don't know. In my dream it was quite a long way before I reached the room."

We continued on stumbling through the darkness. I thought I could see light up ahead and hoped that our journey was soon coming to an end.

"I think I see some light up there. Maybe you should cut out your flashlight just in case they are there."

Detective Dallas clicked off his light. It took me a moment for my eyes to adjust. I could just make out his silhouette. The light grew brighter and my surroundings began to look familiar. Detective Dallas reached out and grabbed my arm. When I looked down I hesitated slightly as the image I saw flashed back to one of my earlier dreams of the white bony hand gripping me tightly as I stumbled along the tunnel.

Detective Dallas felt my hesitation and stopped, releasing my hand. "What's the matter?"

I continued to walk up ahead, "Nothing. You sure that you checked this out and found nothing?"

"Well, yeah Detective Foster and I scouted the whole place out and didn't see a thing, not even a trace that someone had been in the area."

"Where is he now?"

"Who, Detective Foster? He's back at the precinct. They are looking into a few other leads. I had a feeling you would try and make a go of this alone and so I thought I better come help you out."

"Well that was really kind of you."

The hairs on the back of my neck stood on end. He told me there wasn't any tunnel leading to the platform, maybe it was a miscommunication. We continued to walk through the dark tunnel which became brighter with each step. Finally we reached the end and the huge archway led us into a large circular room. It was slightly different from my dreams. This room had large Corinthian columns that circled the large room with a rounded ceiling. I looked up and half expected to see paintings by Michelangelo. The floor looked like granite but it was so dusty and dirty it was hard to tell. In my dreams there were fire torches that lit the room and here they were just lanterns. Next to each lantern was an arched doorway that was covered by brick, doorways to nowhere. I began to call for Melissa but my voice just echoed in the large room.

"I guess she's not here."

I didn't want to believe what I was saying. I looked around but it was just a big dusty old empty room. There was no cement slab, no pentagrams, no mutated goat heads. Maybe it was all just a dream. But this place is real, I saw it. It may not look exactly the same but it's the same place I saw in my dream. Maybe they left and found a new place. I turned to head back out the way we came.

"Where are you going?"

I stopped to look at Detective Dallas. "Well she's not here; we might as well get back. I have a shift to work that I'm going to be late for." I turned back around and started out again.

"Wait."

"For what?" I turned to look at him and saw the glow of red in his eyes and my heart stopped. It only took me a second to come to my senses and I took off running towards the tunnel entry. I ran as fast and hard as I could. I stumbled a few times cutting my hands and knees on the sharp rocks. I couldn't hear him behind me, maybe I was just imagining things and now I was making a complete fool of myself. I stopped running and looked back. The light shining through the archway was just a glimmer. I was so blinded by fear I didn't even hear him call after me. He did call after me, didn't he? I took a few more steps and started to worry that I had made a huge mistake. The light from the flashlight burned my eyes and I put my hands up to shield them.

"I told you to wait." I could see Detective Dallas standing in front of me pointing the flashlight at me.

"But how…"

My words were interrupted by a tight grip on both my arms. I was yanked backward and knocked off my feet. I screamed but the sound was muffled as something was tied round my head and over my mouth.

"Hurry, they're expecting her."

I screamed again and tried to talk to Detective Dallas through the binding over my mouth. I wasn't getting through to him and now I was being drug through the tunnel just like in my dreams. My arms felt like they were being ripped from their sockets. How was I to get out of this mess? But I had to go through this to get to Melissa; they would lead me right to her. I still struggled as much as I could but the grip on my arms just got tighter, which hurt worse. I knew what lay before me and I did what I could to prevent it from happening. The tunnel became lighter and I tried to look upward to see who was holding me but a sack was forced over my head.

"Pick her up and make her walk."

I was dropped to the ground and the sharp rocks stabbed at me all over.

"You clumsy fools! I would like to deliver her unharmed. Pick her up."

I was yanked up and onto my feet. I tried to see through the burlap sack they had on my head but I could only make out the lights. They pulled on my arms and led me further into the room. I heard cement blocks scraping across the floor and suddenly the lights were gone and we were walking again. We must have gone through some sort of door but I didn't remember seeing any doors. I heard the clanging of bars and keys and the creaking noise when it was opened. I was given a big shove and I fell onto damp ground. I quickly pulled off the burlap sack as the clanging of the metal gate shut behind me. It was Detective Dallas standing on the other side.

"You sit tight and I'll be back."

"Detective Dallas, please. Don't leave me here. Why are you doing this? Please don't leave me here, let me go!" I pleaded with him but his face was stone cold.

"Like I said, I'll be back." And then he was gone. I was sitting alone in a dark cell. The floor was hard clay and the walls were rough cement blocks, it was more like a dungeon then a cell, a dungeon, just like in my dream. I needed to get out of here. Too many things were falling into place and I knew what would be coming next. I half expected to see the little girl. I started screaming hoping that someone, anyone would hear me, or maybe if someone else was being held captive they would answer back. But my screams went unanswered. There was no sound. I felt completely alone. I just couldn't piece it together, how was Detective Dallas involved, of course it made sense to have someone working with you that was above the law and it did seem a little odd that he let me leave so quickly this morning. Maybe it was all just a setup. How could I be so naïve?

A good amount of time had passed and still no one came back to my cell. I had no idea what time it was but I knew that I was late for my shift and Jake would be wondering where I was. I hoped that he would put two and two together and remember the Essex and Broadway coordinates that I repeated several times to the Detectives. Hopefully it would only be a matter of time before he would come looking for me and I would be rescued. What was I thinking, no one was going to find me in this dark hole. No wonder so many of the girls were declared as missing, who would find them under the city? Probably only a select few were actually found and of course they were found murdered, who knows how many on the missing persons list were just plain dead, never to be found again.

I needed to snap out of this negative way of thinking if I expected to live through this. Oh, if my father only knew what I've been through, I can hear the 'I told you so' already.

I looked around my cell for anything of use. I felt around the walls and scraped my hands on the jagged sticks. I thought maybe I could use them to pick the lock on the cell door and began trying to dig it out of the clay and brick wall. On closer inspection I realized that they weren't bricks holding up my wall it was bones. I jumped back when what appeared to be a hand was reaching out to me from the wall. Then I inspected all the walls and they were the same, bones from their victims. I thought I was going to be sick to my stomach. How long had they been using this place? I sat in the middle of my cell afraid to touch the walls, not wanting to look at them. I buried my head in my knees and began to cry. It was hopeless.

A piercing scream interrupted my desperation.

"Melissa!"

I jumped to my feet and I began screaming her name. I knew she was here. I tried to shake the iron bars but they wouldn't budge. Her screams were deafening and I wished my imagination would just stop working overtime. I stood there with my head hung low, the tears running down my cheeks. I didn't hear the footsteps of my visitor.

"Don't be so sad, no one lives forever."

I looked up and Detective Dallas was standing there. He placed his hands over mine on the bars and I jerked mine away and stepped back into my cell. He unlocked my cell door and stepped inside closing the door behind him. My heart began to race. I took another step back. I look into his face and saw that his eyes were smoldering. I caught my breath immediately fearing what might happen next. I took another step back but hit the wall, I jumped forward freaking out over touching the bones in the wall and he was instantly in front of me. He placed his hands on my shoulders.

"Relax, its okay."

I shrugged away from him. "Get your hands off of me!"

"Come here now, don't be like that." He moved towards me and cornered me. He placed his hands on the wall on each side of me trapping me.

"Please don't."

"I'm not going to do anything that you don't already want to do."

"What did you do to Melissa?"

"Nothing. That wasn't her."

"I know it was her! I could..."

He bent down and forced his mouth on mine pressing me back against the bone wall. Disgust heaved up into my throat. I tried to push him away but now his hands were holding me and he used his body to press me into place. He forced his tongue in my mouth and I bit down hard.

"Aahh! You Bitch!!" And he slapped me hard across the face. He reached down and grabbed both of my legs and wrapped them around his hips and slammed me so hard against the wall it knocked the breath out of me.

"You like that?" I couldn't fight. I was still trying to catch my breath. He kissed me again and I gasped trying to get my breath back. He reached behind me and grabbed my hair forcing my face up to him.

"Now kiss me like you mean it!" He forced his tongue into my mouth again and once again I bit down on it this time as hard as I could until I tasted blood. Before he could hit me again I heard someone else.

"If Devin catches you he'll kill you."

Detective Dallas whipped his head around and dropped me at the same time. I peered around him toward the cell door and saw Edzilla. I knew he had a part in all of this.

"Well what he doesn't know won't hurt him now will it!" It seemed Detective Dallas didn't like being told what to do. He grabbed my t-shirt and ripped it off revealing just my bra.

"It's your life man." And then Ed was gone.

Detective Dallas turned to yell towards Ed. "Hey there's no sense letting a perfectly good piece of ass go to waste!"

He turned his gaze back to me.

"Come here little sweetie pie give me a little taste." He lunged for me and I ran from him and straight to the cell door which he left unlocked. I flew out of the cell and slammed the door shut behind me.

Chapter 18: My Match

I took off running in the direction I heard the scream. It was dark and I could barely see a thing. I could hear voices so I tried to be quiet. I came upon a wooden door where I thought I could hear Devin's voice.

"Just relax. It's very important. Your survival depends upon it."

Then I didn't hear anything else. I waited at the door for any sound of Melissa. Then I heard groaning and gasping. My imagination was going to get the better of me if I didn't open the door. What if I didn't go in and she ends up dead? The groaning got louder and it sounded like someone was in pain. I decided to open the door. I was relieved to find Melissa but the scene before me was not what I was expecting. I immediately closed the door. I stood alone in the dark corridor not knowing what to do.

The door opened and Devin was standing before me his jade green eyes searching my face for what I was thinking.

"Tara, don't be afraid."

"Can you please explain to me what I just saw in there?"

"Melissa was matched with a partner"

"So her survival depends upon it?"

"Exactly, after this union if she is with child her life will be spared."

I couldn't believe how mater of fact he was speaking. I couldn't take it anymore. This was crazy. I had to find a way out of here and some authority that would believe me and take them down. I knew that Melissa was safe and they wouldn't do anything to her until they knew if she was pregnant so I had time to find help. I started to walk away, back home, back to reality. The grip on my arm invaded my thoughts and I spun around.

"Where do you think you're going Tara?" Devin looked at me with all seriousness.

"Devin, you are all insane. I'm leaving."

"No, you're not. You are my match."

His words gored me like a bull's horns.

Not noticing my horrid reaction he pulled me close to him and held me as if I were his long lost lover. Instantly I pulled away from him.

"I can't let you go Tara. My master wants you dead but I'm trying to convince him otherwise, if you leave, if you report us, I will have to sacrifice you."

"Devin, do you hear yourself? What is the matter with you? You, your followers, your master, you're all evil. You are bad people and you all deserve to go to hell!"

I took off running now down the long corridor and all I could hear was his laughter echoing behind me. I really wished I was dreaming but I knew that I wasn't. I looked behind me but the darkness overtook the corridor and I could see him no longer. I turned back around and ran smack into Detective Dallas and bounced back onto the ground.

"So did you find what you were looking for?"

I scrambled to my feet and tried to race around him but he caught me by my hair and pulled me back towards him.

"I wasn't finished with you."

"Let me go!"

He held me with his arm across my midsection with his hand grasping my breast and the other hand tangled in my hair. He brushed his lips across my neck scraping me with his stubble.

"You're all mine." All the frustration of the night pent up inside of me I released in a huge scream.

Unexpectedly the corridor filled with firelight, torches lining the walls lit with fire. Detective Dallas' grasp on me released and he reached up to his throat.

"Are you okay?" I couldn't escape my empathetic nature. f

He didn't respond to my question but I got the feeling he wasn't okay. His eyes started to bulge and his face was turning blue.

I heard footsteps walking towards us and I looked down the corridor.

"That's where you are wrong Detective Dallas, she's not yours at all."

It was Devin. Detective Dallas fell down to the ground gasping for air now. "This will teach you not to touch what's not yours." He said this while looking straight at me.

"I'm not yours," I said defiantly.

The Detective rose up to his feet now rubbing his neck. "Yes master."

"Take her to the main room and prepare her for the reception."

"Yes master."

I wasn't about to go along with this so I took off running and suddenly felt a great force holding me tightly, squeezing the air out of me. I stopped in my tracks and now I felt like I was on fire, the pain was immense. I mustn't scream I didn't want to give him the satisfaction.

Devin walked up next to me. "I can make the pain go away Tara. Just promise me you will do as you're told. It can go so much more smoothly if you just give in and love me as I love you."

I glared at him but kept pushing against the force even though the pain was more then I thought I could bear.

"Stop fighting me and I will stop the pain." He traced my face with his finger as he waited for me to give in. I never, ever wanted to give in to him but I couldn't stand the pain any longer. My flesh must be ready to melt off my bones by now. As soon as my thoughts asked him to make it stop, the burning stopped. I looked down expecting to see blackened skin but my arms looked normal, not a mark on them. I looked up at him with surprise on my face.

"Now go darling, there is a lot for them to ready you for."

The detective took me by the arm and led me to another room. This room was a lot nicer then my cell from earlier but it still looked as though time had forgotten it. It was a beautiful bedroom, with a four-poster bed made from cherry wood. The bedding was antique white lace. The wallpaper was yellowed with age with a paisley pattern. He sat me down at a vanity table with a marble table top. I peered into three large mirrors and heard the door close and lock. I turned to look at the bed again and saw that a beautiful lace dress was laid out on it, it looked like a wedding dress. I whipped my head back around to the mirror and saw another women sitting there. Suddenly it was like I was looking in on a scene from an earlier time.

"Sweetie get my veil."

"Here you go mama." The little girl from my dreams bounded up with a gossamer veil in her arms.

"If all goes as planned we'll be taken care of. You won't have to worry about anything for the rest of your life."

She held the little girl's face in her hands and gave her a big kiss.

I knew it didn't end well because I saw the outcome already but why was I being shown this now?

The next scene I was shown was the women in her beautiful lace dress covered in blood, laying in the middle of the pentagram drawn on the floor of the great room, fire burning around her. The little girl was balled up next to her crying. I guess I was getting a vision of what was to come. Well I wasn't about to put on that dress and I needed to find a way out of here quick.

I ran to the door and just as I suspected the door was locked and it wasn't budging. I heard voices outside and ran back towards the bed. The door opened and Devin walked in.

"How come you aren't dressed?"

"I'm not wearing that."

"Yes you are."

"Why should I so you can kill me?"

Devin walked to me and rubbed his hand down my arm and then brought his hand up under my chin tilting my face up towards his.

"Why would I want that?"

"Well that's what you've been doing to all these girls, what makes me any different?"

"Because you are my match, we're meant to be together, forever. Now quit being silly and put on the dress."

He turned to leave.

"No!"

He stopped and took a deep breath. He turned around and what I saw now was not Devin. His eyes were glowing red.

"You will wear the dress and you will change now."

"No, I will not!"

"Fine, have it your way. Ed bring him in here."

I looked to the door anxiously and in walked Jake with his arms tied tightly behind him and Ed right behind him. I started to run towards him but Devin put out his hand and stopped me.

"Jake!" My tears began to fall over how happy I was to see him.

"Now Tara, you either put on that dress or Ed here starts having a little fun with what's his name."

"Don't do it Tara, I'll be fine."

"Put something over his mouth please, I don't want to hear anymore screaming today." Devin didn't even turn to look at Jake he just kept looking at me. "Well, I'm waiting Tara."

I still didn't move and so Devin nodded his head and Ed took out a knife and before I could say a word gave Jake and nice sized cut down his arm. Jake tried to hide the pain but it was unbearable for me to watch and I knew I would have to wear the dress.

"Okay! Okay! Stop!"

Devin nodded again and Ed stopped. Ed grabbed Jakes new cut and twisted his hand over it causing Jake to yell out. I looked at Ed and pleaded with him with my eyes but he averted my gaze. Jake must have come looking for me when I didn't show up for work, problem was I'm sure he came alone.

Devin picked up the dress and handed it to me and I snatched it from him.

"Darling don't be so cross with me. Soon we will be matched and you'll have all you ever dreamed of."

Dreamed of, that's it. The only way I can get myself out of here is if I dream myself out. The little girl told me that I had the power to defeat him in my dreams, now I just needed to find a way to stall my upcoming nuptials.

"Well I still need some time to freshen up a bit so if you don't mind I would like a little privacy." I tried to beguile him, tilting my head down and looking up at him through my long lashes. It worked.

"Anything for you my love." And he bent down and kissed me tenderly on the lips. "Soon you will be all mine." I opened my eyes to see Jake squeezing his eyes shut. It hurt so bad to kiss another in front of him but it had to be done. The nerves were making knots in my stomach and I was afraid that I would be unable to sleep under duress.

"You wouldn't happen to have some wine would you? I'm thirsty and a little hungry." Again I tried to act sweet.

"Sure. No problem." He turned and stopped. "Get him out of here!"

My heart ached for Jake. I just wanted him here with me but I couldn't act sentimental towards him now. Jake looked over to me and with Devin's back to me I mouthed the words 'I love you'. Jake looked defeated. He closed his eyes and put his head back. Devin swung back around and glared at me as if I he had caught me doing something wrong.

"He can't give you what I can!" He pushed me on the bed and I could see the red glow in his eyes. He was on top of me before I could scramble away. He tried to kiss me but I moved my head away in time to see Ed force Jake out of the room. Devin reached his hand under my thigh and slid it up to the crook in my leg and wrapped it around his hip placing himself firmly between my legs. His body was hard as stone, my own personal body armor, I couldn't move. I struggled to escape him but he grabbed my hands and held them above my head. The fierceness in his eyes scared me.

"Don't hate me Tara, I've been searching many ages for you." He bent down to kiss me and I wanted so bad to just turn away from him but I knew I couldn't risk angering him. He kissed me with such passion that I almost forgot where I was and what was happening. He released my hands and instinctively they curled up in his hair. With my eyes closed it was if I was with Jake and it made it all alright.

"I knew if you just gave me a chance you could love me too." Devin's voice broke the trance I was in and when my eyes opened to see his glowing red eyes my body stiffened. He could feel my hesitation and he quickly began kissing me again with more force and passion all the while pressing his groin between my legs making me want him. His tongue flicked down my neck and reached my chest where he kissed the outline of my bra sending quivers through my body. I needed to get out of his grasp before it was too late.

"Devin, um, we have to stop, we can't, not before the matching ceremony, right?"

His eyes opened and he stopped in his tracks. My breathing slowed and I was able to break free from the hold he had over me. "You're right; the master would be very displeased with me if I took you from him."

He got up to leave.

"What do you mean from him? I thought I was your match."

He turned to look at me, and the anguish in his face caught me by surprise.

"We must wait until the matching ceremony. Get ready Tara, I'll be back."

"Um, you were going to bring me something to drink?"

"Yes, I'll have it delivered to your room" He stalked out of the room.

Chapter 19: Sweet Dreams

I paced back and forth waiting for the wine. I knew there was no way I would be able to sleep without it. On my 10th walk back and forth there was a knock at my door. I stopped in the middle of the room and the door opened. It was Ed with my bottle of wine and a glass. The cork had already been removed. He stealthily walked in and set the bottle and glass down on the vanity. As he walked away I had to ask him why.

"Ed, please, why is Devin doing this? Why are you doing this?"

He looked at me with his inkwell eyes, no emotion on his face. "It's what the master desires and I have no control once his mind is made up, I just do his bidding."

My eyes filled with tears. I just couldn't understand how he could let someone or something rule over his judgment.

"Even if he wanted to kill me, slice me up into pieces that would be okay with you?"

I thought I could see a hint of emotion but then the callousness came back. "I have to go." And then he was gone.

I didn't bother with the glass and just took a huge swig straight from the bottle. I didn't have long to calm my nerves and try to sleep, this was the only way I was going to make it out of here, the only way I would be able to save myself, Melissa, and now Jake.

After three more swigs of wine the bottle was almost empty. I lay on the bed staring up at the ceiling trying to get comfortable. I closed my eyes to let the sleep take over but all I could feel were my tingling nerve ends. Any other time I couldn't keep myself awake and now I couldn't sleep to save my life, literally.

I wasn't lying there for very long and someone was knocking at my door. I was never going to get to sleep if I kept getting interrupted. I looked up as the door opened and in walked Detective Dallas. I sat up in the bed and he walked in dressed in all black with a black cloak draped about him.

"It's time."

"But, but I'm not ready, I can't. I'm not dressed yet." I stammered, trying to stall, I needed more time.

"What do you mean? You look lovely." His eyes traveled down my body and I could feel the heat rise up to my cheeks.

Of course he would think I looked lovely in just my bra and jeans. I looked down and saw the beautiful lace gown flowing from my body as if it were made just for me. Perplexed, I studied the gown as if it weren't real. I didn't remember putting the dress on. Did I get dressed before I lay down? I didn't remember. The wine must have gone straight to my head.

Detective Dallas' booming voice broke me out of my stupor.

"What's the hold up? Come on!" He took three strides towards the bed and grabbed me by the wrist and yanked me up. This man was really getting on my last nerve. I struggled to pull my wrist away from him but he gripped tighter. "Quit making a fuss, they are all waiting for you."

I tripped as we walked down the tunnel and I was grateful he was holding onto me or I would have gone face first onto the rocky floor. Apparently I was fitted with high heels too.

We walked along the dark corridor and I could smell something burning. It was a horrible smell. There was a glow up ahead that I could only assume was fire. I could hear a low hum of voices but I couldn't make out the topic of conversation. The tunnel we were walking down widened as we approached the orange glow and soon I could see the large archway and Corinthian columns that I had first seen when I came in here looking for Melissa. However, now everything was beautiful and polished. The floor glistened and reflected the lit torches.

I walked into the room and Detective Dallas' hand tightened around my wrist. All I could see was a sea of black cloaks. I tried to swallow my fears but the huge lump in my throat wouldn't le me. The black mob surrounded a massive bomb fire in the middle of the room, a fire built on this beautiful marble floor. The smell was overpowering, so bad I started to cough and I almost gagged but I couldn't take my eyes off the fire. Where did they find so much wood in the city to build such a large fire?

My thoughts were interrupted by a piercing scream. I looked across the room to find a young lady being drug through one of the many archways. She was twisting and squirming and now pleading.

"Please, NO! Let's try again, I promise I will conceive! Please NO!"

She continued to scream and I couldn't help but walk towards her but was stopped by a hand on my shoulder. I looked up to see Detective Dallas giving me a look of disapproval. I didn't care, I needed to help her. I broke away from his grasp and started running towards the girl. Ed stepped in front of me and wrapped his arms around me.

"No Tara. What will be will be."

"Ed you can't be serious. Please help me, help us!" I pointed to the girl still struggling in her captor's arms. He pulled me tighter to him and I couldn't move. The screaming stopped but I could hear gurgling noises. I angled my head around his shoulder and saw the blood dripping from her neck.

"NO!" Ed's grip tightened around my waist.

I looked up at him and his eyes were cold, unfeeling.

From up above I heard some one say, "Pitch her in." And then a murmur echoed through the room. Flames shot up as they flung her body onto the roaring bomb fire.

The gravity of the situation finally sunk in. "The smell, you're burning bodies? Oh my God! Oh my God!" The lump in my throat blocked my voice now. Ed walked behind me, still with a grip on me but mainly to hold me up. I could see the young lady as she burned and on closer inspection I could now see the charred remains of past victims. I wanted to vomit. The smell was stinging my nose.

I pulled away from Ed's grasp but with nowhere to run and was soon surrounded by cloaked strangers. I was being herded like a sheep, away from the fire to the front of the room. I looked in the direction I was being pushed and there stood Devin in his red satin cloak. Behind him was the pentagram with the goat head and gleaming red eyes. So many times I've dreamt of this place and now finally here I am, ill prepared, not ready to die but unable to think of a way out of this.

He grabbed my hand and pulled me close to him. He smiled and kissed me on the cheek. I felt like I was in a dream world, this was so unbelievable.

He looked me over, "You look lovely."

I didn't have the strength or feel the need to thank him. His compliments meant nothing to me.

"Bring him in." He waved his hand to summon his guest. I glanced in the direction he was looking and saw Jake stumble along the back wall. Instinctively I sucked in my breath and then regretted the reaction. Devin looked down at me and I could feel anger rolling off his body. I didn't want to look up at him; I couldn't take my eyes off of Jake. They were pushing him in, his hands behind his back. Any thought of him saving me was out of the question. They brought Jake to the front of the room, close to me. I could see that he wasn't treated very well. His face was bruised and bleeding. I wanted to reach out to him but knew that would be a death sentence. The traitor tears came, spilling down my cheeks. I wanted this to all be over, and be back in his arms safe.

"I remember a time when you were ready to give yourself to me, Tara. It wasn't so long ago." I hid my head and looked away from Jake. I had hoped he would never know of this betrayal. "And now you cry for him? Who do you love Tara, me or Jake?"

I knew this was a trick question. If I told him Jake then lord knows what he would do. If I told him that I loved him then I would hurt Jake's feelings. But surely Jake would know I was only saying it to appease him and that I didn't really mean it.

"I'm waiting Tara, who do you love?"

My eyes darted to Jake and he nodded his head upward as if giving me the okay.

"You Devin, I love you."

"Great! Now that we have that settled, you will have no need for him anymore." And he swiped his hand in the air as if dismissing him.

The blade slid across his throat so quickly that I hardly had time to react. The blood spewed out and actually splattered my white dress. Jake slumped over and the blood pooled around him.

"JAKE!! Oh my God! NO! Not my Jake" I dropped down to my knees and crawled to him, my hand landing in a pool of Jake's blood. I pulled him up in my lap, his eyes were closed. He was bleeding to death and there was nothing I could do to save him. The last words he heard were that I loved another.

"Oh come now Tara, I couldn't have you pining for another when you're supposed to love me."

I looked up at Devin and saw pure evil, his eyes glowing red. I couldn't deal with him now. I just wanted to die and be with Jake. I cried so hard and finally Devin pulled me away from him. His cloaked minions picked Jake up and threw him in the fire along with half of my soul. I screamed and cried and Devin just squeezed me tightly, holding me back from following the love of my life into the fire.

"I hate you Devin and I will never, ever love you!" I flung myself on the floor and buried my face in my arms and cried. He didn't try and pull me up this time he allowed me to cry it out.

When I felt like I could cry no longer I lifted my head and saw the pillow from the room. Then I heard a knock and sat up. I was sitting on my bed still in my bra and jeans. The knock sounded again.

"Are you ready?" I heard through the door.

I looked toward the door and glanced at the bed and saw the antique white lace dress laid out on the bed, untouched, no blood stains.

Confused, I mumbled, "Just about." It had had all been just a dream. The relief flooded over me, I was so grateful to know that Jake was still alive. I had been dreaming but it had all felt so real. Was it all a premonition, did I have another chance? But before I woke up dressed, wearing high heels and there are no new shoes here this time.

"Open the door, I have something for you."

I got up and opened the door and Ed stood there.

"Devin wanted me to give you these." And he held out a pair of high heel shoes.

I yanked the shoes from him, "Thanks," and closed the door.

Well maybe it all was a premonition. "Jake." I had to find a way to change this course I was on.

Chapter 20: Matching Ceremony

I changed clothes, the dress fit perfectly. I put on the heels and fixed my hair. I couldn't believe I was going to all this trouble. I just couldn't understand why I didn't know I was dreaming. I wasted my only opportunity to take Devin down in my dream, to call for help, to get us all out of here safely. But at least now I knew what was coming, maybe I would have the upper hand. Maybe it didn't have to be, I had a chance to change it.

The knock at the door made me jump. The door opened and it was Detective Dallas, I should have known.

"It's time."

Everything was the same except he wasn't wearing a black cloak; he was still in his uniform, which meant he was still carrying his gun. He held out his hand and I reached for it, knowing that I would need it for balance more than anything. We made our way down the dark rocky corridor with the orange glow at the end. I had hoped the bon fire was just a symbol for something else and wouldn't be what I had seen in the dream.

We stepped into the foyer and the smell of burnt skin was overpowering. I tried to hold back my urge to vomit and my need to run, as fast as I could, out of this horrible place. Just as before there was what seemed like a 100 people wearing black cloaks surrounding the fire. I scouted the area looking for anyone of use. I caught sight of Ed. Our eyes locked and he just stood there staring at me as if he knew what were coming. His deep black eyes were void of emotion but I had to try. I mouth the words "help me".

My eyes shot to the archway as the scream blared through the great room. It was all still on course. If I didn't act soon this young lady was going to find her fate in that fire.

"Please, NO! Let's try again, I promise I will conceive! Please NO!"

I tried to step forward and Detective Dallas grabbed my arm and pulled me back. I needed to break this course or Jake would end up dead too. I looked up to see that Detective Dallas couldn't keep his eyes off of the death sentence about to be carried out before us. Everyone's back was to us. I knew I only had seconds before she would be screaming in agony.

I looked at the couple, if that's what you could call them, and he was yanking on her arm dragging her to the fire while she pulled as hard as she could. I peeked at Detective Dallas' gun and saw that I had two steps, unbutton the leather strap and pull out the gun. I looked up at him again and he was smiling as he watched the action before him.

Quickly and stealthily, I flicked the strap open and grabbed the gun. Before he knew what was happening I was two steps behind him.

"Hey! What are you doing?" I could see the fear in his eyes as I finally had the upper hand.

The struggled on the opposite side of the room came to sudden stop and the room fell quiet.

"Let her go!" I pointed the gun straight out in front of me, grasping it tightly and trying not to let them see that I was terrified inside.

"Let who go? Her?" He pointed to the tear-stricken girl.

"Yes!"

"She's nothing to you. You would be wise to let that go as planned."

"You're not going to burn her to death, now let her go."

"Tara, what makes you think we'd do that. We would put her out of her misery first."

Her match came up to me, with her in tow, unafraid of the gun. I was worried that I had used the wrong tactic.

"You can have her if you want; she's of no use to me." He turned around and slit her throat and she fell to the ground clutching her throat.

I dropped the gun, more in shock from what I was unable to prevent then from the mere fact they just weren't afraid of dying. Nobody cowered, nobody backed away from me. The anger in me boiled over and I ran straight towards the murderer's back and gave him a huge shove. This girl's life would be avenged and it would be him that burned in hell.

The flames lapped around his body quickly but he came running out of the fire as quickly as he went in. The others swarmed around him trying to put out the flames but their cloaks caught fire and they had to give up on him to save themselves. I had never felt so much satisfaction over someone else's misery in all my life. I hadn't realized that I had started to back away from the gory scene before me but I only got two steps before I backed into the chest of one of my captors. I turned to see Ed staring down at me. I closed my eyes and I just wanted to cry.

"Why? Why Ed? Why are you guys doing this?"

I opened my eyes and for the first time I thought I could see a hint of concern in his eyes. I wouldn't have the chance to play upon that weakness as a loud voice roared through the great room vibrating the walls.

"What is going on?" Devin stood up on a platform, near his much admired symbol, dressed in a red satin cloak.

To my surprise Ed responded. "It is her doing my Master; she has caused all this disarray."

I turned fast to glare at Ed but he wasn't looking at me. It was then that I could feel Devin's arms around me pulling me closer to him even though he was still at least 25 feet away. I tried to resist but it seemed the harder I dug my feet in the tighter the squeeze around me.

"This was quite the distraction Tara but not enough to keep you from me. We were meant to be together, forever and our army will be strong because of it."

I kept trying to break this course but it just kept finding a way to get back on track. By now I was within inches of Devin.

"Oh Tara, you look lovely." He bent down and kissed me, brushing my cheek with his hand.

He raised both of his hands in the air and yelled "Let the matching ceremony begin!"

My legs began to shake and I thought they were going to give out from under me. The only thing that kept me upright was the fact that Jake was not in the picture.

Devin grabbed my hand and led me to the platform.

"Before everyone, we will be matched and we will begin the making of our Army!"

I almost fainted. My legs became weak but it was his force that kept me standing. I looked up into his eyes and didn't see the red glow. Maybe this was my chance to talk some sense into him.

"Devin, please, you don't have to do this. Why are you doing this? Please let me go." I plead with him and the tears flowed, this time I was happy the tears came, hoping they would soften his heart.

"Oh Tara, this is the only way that you and I can be together." Then he paused and looked out into the sea of black cloaks. "But first I must rid us of any distractions."

I looked out and didn't see anything.

"Bring him in!"

"Oh my God, no Devin!"

And just as in my dream they led Jake out hands tied together looking beat up and bloody.

"Jake! What have they done?" My reaction was worse this time then it was in my dream.

"Why do you love someone that can not give you the power that I can?"

"I don't want power Devin. I am not evil. I want love."

"And what makes you think I don't want love?"

"That's a stupid question."

I was so angry but Devin was angrier and he slapped me hard across the face.

"Don't ever talk to me like that again or in that tone, do you understand me?"

I held my hand to my face and I could feel the burn and knew that it was beet red. Jake's eyes were wide with concern but I just shook my head back and forth to warn him off. Now the only thing left was the trick question which now I knew was no trick, either answer would kill Jake.

"Who do you love Tara, me or Jake?"

I didn't know what to do to make this stop. I had the upper hand I thought. I knew what was to happen but I still couldn't stop it.

"Does it matter Devin? You'll kill Jake anyway." I looked out and saw Ed staring at me.

"Of course it matters Tara. One answer will save his life and the other will end it."

I looked back at Devin and the red glow still had not reappeared. I guess Devin really was this evil.

"Well Tara, what's your answer, who do you love me or Jake?"

I looked at Jake and I could see the tears welling up in his eyes. I wanted to cry. He gave me the head nod to tell me it was okay to sacrifice his life. I shook my head no. I couldn't do it. I looked back out into crowd and again my eyes caught hold of Ed. This time his mouth was moving and stared harder and realized he was trying to tell me something. I was trying to read his lips. It down, let go, what? I couldn't figure it out. I glanced back at Devin and his eyes were boring holes into my face.

"Tara you have five seconds! Now answer me!" I could hear the rage in Devin's voice and searched again for Ed. He was very animated with his mouth this time and I could swear he said 'Get Down' but it didn't make any sense. I looked over toward the dark corridor and then it all made perfect sense. I lunged forward, wrapping my arms around Jake taking him down with me and before we hit the ground I heard the gunshots ring out.

My eyes were still squeezed shut when the shooting and scuffling stopped. I had a vice-like grip on Jake and I wasn't about to let go anytime soon. I was afraid to open my eyes to find that this was all just a dream too and I would have to start all over again from the beginning. I didn't think I couldn't handle it another time.

"Tara, open your eyes, its okay, everything is going to be okay." I had to open them now, it was Jake's voice and he wouldn't lie to me.

I peeked and saw that I was still lying flat out on top of Jake. He lifted his head to peer down at me with a big smile. "You okay?"

"Yep, you?"

"Yeah."

"Tara! Are you okay?"

"Bucky?" I jumped up and looked across the room. Bucky, Deidre and Darian were all running towards us.

"What are you doing here?"

Deidre gave me a big hug. "Well I've been having some pretty disturbing dreams about you and Jake and I convinced my big bro here to take a drive down to make sure everything was okay. Then tonight I saw everything and I was able to find Detective Foster and the rest is history."

"I bet that took some convincing."

"Not much, you already laid the groundwork for that. He didn't think I was completely off my rocker. When I told him that Detective Dallas had said that they both checked the location you told them about he knew something was up because they had never looked into your story. He said that Detective Dallas told him to just drop it, that it was a dead end."

"Wow. He sure had me convinced. Oh my God! Melissa?"

Bucky cut in this time. "They found her. She's fine but they took her to the hospital just in case."

I turned to look around and saw that most of the members were being arrested and only a few were actually shot to death, mainly Devin. He lay there bloody holes through his chest. I couldn't believe he was gone, that the reign of terror over this city was over. I couldn't help myself. I was drawn to his body. I peered down into his open eyes and just as Jake grabbed my arm to pull me away I thought I saw flicker of glowing red.

"Did you see that?"

"See what?"

"His eyes."

"Tara, he's dead. Come on, let them take him." Even in death his eyes were still mesmerizing.

The emergency technicians checked Jake and I out on the spot and figured we were okay to go. We both gave statements to the police with a promise to give more detail at a later time. I was so exhausted both mentally and physically that I didn't think I could stand much longer. We got a police escort home. I really wanted to go see Melissa but it would have to wait. I didn't want Jake to leave my side and so he came home with me along with my cousins. It was 3 in the morning and by the time I took a shower and got some food in all of our bellies it was 5 a.m.

I don't think I laid in the bed for more then 10 minutes before I fell asleep. I felt Jake's arms wrapped around me and then I was out. I didn't think I would dream much as I was too tired to dream but my mind had other plans. I had more then a dream, I had a nightmare. The night's events flashed before me, only it showed me the outcome of my dream with the burning girl and Jake's murder. I tried to wake myself but I just couldn't. I could hear a voice but it wasn't Devin and it wasn't Jake.

"You really think I would leave you that easily? You're my match and I'll be back."

Then the dream switched to Melissa in the hospital holding a beautiful baby swaddled in a white cotton blanket. She held it out for me to hold and delicately I took the baby into my arms. I looked into the eyes and they were a beautiful blue, he was the most gorgeous baby I had ever seen. Melissa was so happy and radiant. I was so happy for her. I looked back at the baby and the eyes began to glow red.

I jerked up out of bed and screamed.

"Tara, are you okay!"

"Just a dream. It's going to take awhile I suppose."

I heard the door shut. I got up and walked into the living room. It was Melissa.

"Melissa! You're home."

She half-heartedly smiled at me.

"You're okay right?"

"Yeah, I'm fine."

"You sure?"

She sat down on the couch and I sat down next to her. I tried to be quiet as my cousins were sleeping just a foot away on the floor.

"Yeah. I'm just tired."

I gave her hug.

"Tara, I'm pregnant."

"Oh my, wow!"

"I know. I was shocked too. Tara, there's no way it could have been from last night?"

"Oh Melissa, of course not, they wouldn't be able to tell that soon. This is obviously Jeremy's baby. I wouldn't worry."

"You're right. I know you're right."

We sat there and held each other as we both had been through such a huge ordeal. I could never mention my dream to Melissa, she could never know. This will all turn out to be just fine. I hope.

71143405R00149

Made in the USA
Middletown, DE
29 September 2019